COME AS YOU ARE

LAUREN BLAKELY

COPYRIGHT

ALSO BY LAUREN BLAKELY

Big Rock Series

Big Rock

Mister O

Well Hung

Full Package

Joy Ride

Hard Wood

One Love Series dual-POV Standalones

The Sexy One

The Only One

The Hot One

Standalones

The Knocked Up Plan

Most Valuable Playboy

Stud Finder

The V Card

Most Likely to Score

Wanderlust

Come As You Are

Part-Time Lover (June 2018)

The Sinful Nights Series

Sweet Sinful Nights

Sinful Desire

Sinful Longing

Sinful Love

The Fighting Fire Series

Burn For Me (Smith and Jamie)

Melt for Him (Megan and Becker)

Consumed By You (Travis and Cara)

The Jewel Series

A two-book sexy contemporary romance series

The Sapphire Affair

The Sapphire Heist

ABOUT COME AS YOU ARE

I couldn't have scripted a more perfect night.

For one fantastic evening, at a masquerade party in the heart of Manhattan, I'm not the millionaire everyone wants a piece of. Fine—multimillionaire. But who's counting all those commas? Not me, and not the most intriguing woman I've ever met, who happens to like dancing, witty banter, and hot, passionate up-against-the-wall sex as much as I do.

There's no need for names or business cards. And that's why I'm eager to get to know her more, since my mystery woman seems to like me for me, rather than for my huge...bank account.

Everything's coming up aces. Until the next day when

things get a little complicated. (Newsflash — a lot complicated.)

***

He's charming, brilliant, an incredible lover, and right now I want to stab fate in the eyeballs.

I've had one goal I've been working toward, and lo and behold, my mystery man is the very person who stands between me and my dream job. A job I desperately need since my hard-knock life has nothing in common with his star-kissed one.

But it's time to put that fairytale night behind me, and focus on learning what makes him tick. Too bad it turns out his quirks are my quirks, and his love affair with New York matches mine.

And as we spend our days together, I discover something else that feels like a cruel twist of fate — **I'm falling for this naughty prince charming, and that's not an ending I can write to our story.**

For Candi—for everything, and for the stories.

COME AS YOU ARE

1

Flynn

I'm used to whispers.

Little voices rustling around me. Asking, wondering.

That guy looks familiar.

Is he . . .?

Is that . . .?

Yes, I *am* that guy.

Sometimes they figure it out. Sometimes they don't. If they do, a pitch comes next.

Today, the locker room attendant at my gym mutters under his breath—*I think that's . . .*—then studies me like a philosopher studies the meaning of existence.

Good thing I'm mostly dressed.

As the short, stocky guy collects towels from the floor and tosses them into a hamper, he stares at me then pretends not to. He looks down then glances up again, and I swear I can see the pieces sliding into place as I slip the final button through its hole in my white dress shirt.

No, he's not about to hit on me. He's about to hit me up.

I sling my messenger bag across my chest, snick the locker closed, and run a hand through my still-damp hair. Grabbing my towel from the bench, I carry it over to him and toss it in the hamper. Lifting my chin, I nod at the dude and thank him for all he does in keeping the locker room at this high-end racquetball club sparkling clean.

He tilts his head, wags a finger, and turns his whispers into words. "Excuse me, but aren't you Flynn Parker?"

Called it.

Bonus points that he identified me as me, and not as my identical twin. This guy has a good radar.

"Yes, I am."

A smile lights his face, and he practically vibrates with excitement. "I'm Dale, and I need to tell you about an app I developed. I think you'd dig it."

If I had a beer for the number of pitches my ears have heard . . . well, I'd be able to stock all the pubs in Manhattan forever. I'd be a beer supplier, rather than a high-tech CEO.

"Give me your best thirty-second pitch," I say, as I fix on a smile. Here's the thing—in my field, you never know when you're going to be pitched something worth listening to. Hell, if the guy has an app that warms your slippers before you come home, I might be interested.

Or maybe I'd just throw on a pair of socks instead.

Dale rubs his hands together. "Get this. It's called How'm I Doing? And," he says, shaking his head like his app is blowing his own mind, "it rates your sexual performance."

I blink. Adjust my eyeglasses. Did he really just say that? "Excuse me?"

"You turn it on when you get it on, and based on your speed and your rate of thrust and the noises of your partner, it scores you. Like, are you a five? Are you an eight? Are you a—wait for it—a ten?"

Shockingly, I'm familiar with how a scale of one to ten works. "Does it do . . . anything else?"

Dale furrows his brow. "Besides give you a grade on how well you take care of business? What else should it do? That's hella cool. Imagine all the ways it could integrate with online dating sites."

Imagine all the ways no one would ever want to, one, use it, and two, learn the answers. Plus, if you need to use it, I'm guessing your score is on the low end.

But my role isn't to fund him. It's to give some feedback on the fly. Considering how much I enjoy a clean locker room that doesn't smell like the inside of a sock, the least I can do is provide a useful tip. The number of great ideas that have launched from the detritus of bad ones is enough for me to say to him, "Keep working on it, Dale. Keep refining it. And don't be afraid to pivot, either, and take it in another direction."

Preferably an entirely new one.

He scratches his head. "A new direction. Let me think about that. Maybe it can make recommendations. Positions to try. Tips on speed and such."

Yeah, I'm going to leave him with that thought knocking around his skull. "Good luck, Dale."

"Thanks, Flynn."

I leave and walk the ten blocks to my office, saying hello to Claude the doorman once I'm in the lobby.

The mustached man with the blue cap and matching tie greets me. "Good morning, Mr. Parker. Did I ever tell you about my cousin Charlie, the amazing miniature golfer?"

"I don't believe you did," I say, wondering if this is where Claude shares a family yarn about the time his cousin landed a hole-in-one in that impossible windmill obstacle. If so, I'd like to know how to pull off that shot.

"He started a GoFundMe campaign so he can become a pro," he says. "If you can contribute to his fundraising campaign, we can get him some new five irons, an elite coach, and some state-of-the-art golf balls. Would you consider it, Mr. Parker?"

If he'd said his ten-year-old niece's softball team wanted a sponsor to pay for a field, or that his nephew's middle school science class desperately needed to finance a trip to the planetarium, I'd say yes in a heartbeat. I'm not opposed to sharing my wealth.

I am, however, adamantly against bankrolling vanity projects. "While I wish your cousin the best of luck, I prefer to support non-profits that have specific charitable goals rather than individual goals."

Claude chuckles. "If you saw my cousin you'd see he's something of a charity case." From his post behind the black marble counter, he slaps his thigh and guffaws at his own joke. "Thanks for listening, though."

I give him a tip of the proverbial hat and head into the elevator. As the doors start to close, I breathe a sigh of relief. At last, I'm free from this morning's pitch-a-thon.

"Hold the door."

An arm thrusts forward, sending the doors swishing open again. A frazzled man in a rumpled suit wheels a suitcase behind him, the telltale sign of a salesman. Surely he has a great set of steak knives that also make julienned fries to sell me.

The guy looks me over and furrows his brow as the elevator chugs upward. "Hey, you look familiar. Are you who I think you are?"

"Han Solo, circa 1977?"

He snaps his meaty fingers. "I got it! You're the guy in the personal injury ads that run on the local cable access channel."

Thank fuck.

I laugh, shaking my head. "No, but I get that all the time. Great guess."

I make my getaway on the next floor, escaping safely into the confines of my office for the morning, and I don't emerge until afternoon rolls around and it's time to high-tail it to a hotel in midtown for a technology conference. When I get there, I head to the backstage of the ballroom for my keynote address on leadership.

A cute redhead dressed in black rushes over to me. "Hi, Flynn. Let me make sure your handy-dandy mic is on," she says, fiddling with the small clip-on device that'll send my voice slinging across the room. Up close, I can see she has a spray of freckles across her nose and a sparrow tattoo on her neck. "Once I give the signal, don't say anything inappropriate."

I mime zipping my lips.

"Also, we're tight on time so there won't be any Q and A," she says, and I could kiss her. No Q and A means no one can ask me about ShopForAnything and how the great white shark appeared in my calm tropical business waters a few weeks ago, jaws wide open, determined to eat my company for breakfast, lunch, dinner, and a midnight snack. It's the press's question du jour, fascinating to every member of the business media.

"Too bad," I say, like I'm bummed. Hey, maybe I *can* pass for an actor.

She raises her index finger and nods. "Now, your mic is hot," she whispers.

And I don't whisper back, *So are you*, even though she is, because, hello, that's rude. Hitting on a cute chick at a conference is, one, uncool, two, douchey, and three, not my style. Besides, striking up conversations with women who know who I am is about as satisfying as watching a parade on a cold day.

Come to think of it, I don't care for parades in warm weather either.

But the backstage woman is great, so I flash her a smile, and mouth *thanks* as the emcee introduces me.

"And now, it is with great pleasure and pride that I welcome Flynn Parker for our closing keynote address. His business reputation is unparalleled, having founded one of the most successful tech start-ups of all time and sold it for multimillions, earning him a reputation as a true internet superstar and visionary. He's now become a key player in an exciting new technology sector. Please join me in welcoming him to the stage."

Because I've given more keynotes than I can count, I stride onto the stage without breaking a sweat, and thirty minutes later, the audience claps and cheers.

"How'd I do?" I ask the girl with the sparrow tattoo once I'm offstage.

She shushes me and reaches for the mic. "You were still mic'd."

I shrug. "Could have been worse. I could have said, 'Free pizza tomorrow at the lobby of my office.'"

She wags a finger at me, whispering, "There's no more appealing combination of words in the English language than 'free' and 'pizza.'" She peers around the front of the stage. "Good luck making it through the crowd. Looks like they're already lined up waiting for you to exit. Want an escort?"

I wave off the offer. "Nah, I'm good."

If I stopped listening to ideas, I'd lose my edge. Edge is everything in business. It separates the visionaries from the has-beens. It'll separate me from ShopForAnything if I play my cards right. That's why I listen to every one of the pitches volleyed my way.

Once the crowd thins, I head out of the ballroom, making my way through the hotel's lower floor.

"Hi, Flynn." The bold, outgoing voice sounds like it belongs to a TV anchor, or maybe a politician.

I turn to see a brunette in a navy pantsuit walking by my side. Her dark hair is slicked back in a clip, and I'm going to bet my money on local TV reporter.

"I'm Nova Wilkins. I'm in market research," she says, and I lose the bet with myself. "I have to say your speech was very inspiring, especially your top five keys to a successful partnership. I've been a huge fan of yours for such a long time."

Fan?

Even though I've started a successful company and sold it for bank, I do know that I'm not short-stop for the New York Yankees or headlining a movie. I would never say I have fans, but I'm impressed Nova homed in on one of my "Top Five" lists. "Pleased to meet you, Nova. Glad to hear you liked that part of the speech. Have a favorite from among those?"

Her lashes flutter, and she brings a hand to her breasts as if she's trying to use a time-honored trick to render me helpless, akin to Wonder Woman's lasso of truth. Maybe she's in superhero market research.

"I do," Nova continues in her perfectly modulated tone. "I loved what you said about how both partners need to come to the table with clarity on what they each bring to a deal. With that in mind, I was hoping you had a second to listen to a pitch of mine?"

I stop walking and give her my full attention. "What have you got?"

"I'd like to propose I become your wife."

I snap my head back. Must have heard her wrong. "Excuse me?"

She nods, her expression business-like. "I have my top five reasons why I'm not an ordinary trophy wife. First, I have a master's degree; second, I'm studying Japanese, which was your minor in college. Third, I'm a judo master. And the fourth reason why I should become your wife— we have similar taste. I also like watching *The Mindy Project* and *Silicon Valley*, and I know those are your favorite shows," she says, and damn, she does her research. "And the fifth reason—I'm a fine cook, especially when it comes to Italian, and that's your favorite cuisine."

"It is." She's *really* researched me, as if I'd posted a request for a proposal online.

"I do hope you'll consider my application to become your wife, Flynn." She says it all with a straight face as if a clear and concise proposal is what it takes to get down the aisle.

The floor is mine, though, and I give her an equally clear and concise response. "While I'm immensely impressed with your research and attention to detail, especially the very clever way of presenting it as a top five list, I'm not in the market for a wife."

She knits her brow, a flash of worry in her eyes as I pick up the pace again, walking toward the lobby. "I understand. Though, I hope you'll reconsider because I have many other skills you might find useful. Shall I share my top five things I'm willing to do to please you in the bedroom?"

And that is one hell of a 180-degree turn in tactics.

Before I can answer with an even firmer no, a boxy security guard stalks over, drops a hand to Nova's shoulder, and barks at her, "I told you, you're not welcome here. I don't know how you slipped in, but I'm going to escort you out once more. You must actually pay to attend the conference."

She wails, changing her approach yet again. "Flynn, don't let them take me away. I want to marry you. I'll let you spank me. I'll let you bite me. Pull my hair. Call me names. You can dress me up like a doll. See? That's five things. Just marry me. I'll give you all the free pizza you want."

Oops. Guess that mic was still hot.

I give her a goodbye wave as I deadpan, "That's okay. I can afford pizza."

"I'll be in the lobby at your office to propose to you again. I love you madly. I have ever since you were on the cover of *Business Insight*'s 'Hottest Tech Nerds Under Thirty' edition."

"That was a good photo," I say drily, thinking of the shot from two years ago when I was twenty-seven. "So that's understandable."

The security guard yanks the woman's hands behind her back. "Time to go, miss. No pizza where you're going." He turns to me. "I'm so sorry about this, Mr. Parker."

"Hey, no worries. It's all in a day."

As he drags her away, she twists around to face me and shouts, "*Pepperoni.* You can eat pepperoni off my stomach."

"Tempting, but I've never cared for pepperoni." I give the latest gold digger a "good riddance" wave. Props to her —she used a different angle before throwing herself at me.

Once I exit the hotel on Sixth Avenue, I pop in some earbuds. Time to use the shield of the modern New Yorker, since it's clearly another day, another marriage proposal.

Maybe I sound calloused. Maybe I am.

I have nothing against marriage, nothing against women, and nothing against love. In fact, I wouldn't mind settling down one day. But I don't know how I'll ever find the right one. As soon as someone knows who I am, all I am is a bank account.

Yeah, yeah, woe is me. Grab the violin and sing a lament. I deserve zero sympathy for my mega first-world problem. Poor little rich boy can't find love.

I don't expect anyone to feel sorry for me. I'm one of the luckiest bastards around, but being ridiculously successful sure does make dating hard. I honestly can't remember the last time a woman was interested in me— just me, and not my wallet.

Today's impromptu proposal might be the epitome of my biggest dating challenge because I wasn't just hit on. I wasn't merely pitched. I was dug.

Gold dug.

And I'm tired of it.

2

Sabrina

Today I will get rid of the albatross.

I will extradite it from my life and make some moolah to boot.

I gaze up at the sign on the glass door for the consignment shop in the West Village. This shop has the highest ratings on Yelp for its offers on never-been-used items. The sign *Once More* is etched in calligraphy on the glass.

I square my shoulders, run a hand over my braid, and turn to my best friend, Courtney. I give her a crisp nod. "Today's the day."

She pumps a fist and utters a quiet but victorious *yes*.

"Try not to get too excited," I tease.

"I can't help myself. I've been waiting for this moment for, oh, the last eight months and three days."

"Some things take time," I acknowledge, as a soft summer breeze blows by. I run a hand over my leopard-print skirt, which hits several inches above the knee. Like a leopard, I'm tough, and I'm fierce. That's what I tell myself, at least. Surely leopards give themselves pep talks too. "But when you're ready you're ready."

She squeezes my arm. "And you're ready. You're so ready."

I fashion my hand into a fist. "We'll seal it with a vow." I cringe at my last word, then I shake it off. A vow between friends is different. "No matter what, today is the last day we see that dress."

Courtney squeaks, knocking her fist with mine. "Nothing you say could make me happier. Well, you dating again could."

I scoff. "One step at a time."

"I know, but the prospect of it makes me want to jump up and down and set you up with all the hot, sexy single men I know."

I arch a brow. "The men you know are hot?"

Laughing, she waggles her hand like a seesaw. "That's debatable. Maybe only a few are hot."

"Let's deal with the dress first."

I reach for the door handle and pretend I'm heading into an interview, dealing with a CEO who's been trying to stonewall me or with a biz-dev guy who doesn't want to give up the goods for an article.

When I open the door, bells chime.

They sound like wedding bells.

Damn it.

With a hand on my back, Courtney gently but ever-so-firmly pushes me over the threshold. Not exactly the threshold I thought I'd be crossing eight months ago.

A cute teenager with ringlet curls and combat boots rushes over to us. "Hi, there! Can I help you?"

I look her square in the eye, saying words out loud that were once far too painful. "I'm Sabrina. I have a wedding dress I never wore. I dropped off the unused dress this morning and was told that Sasha would appraise and have a price for me this afternoon."

The teen offers a sympathetic smile. "It's all for the best," she says, and I wonder how often she says that and if she means it. I wonder what questions she asks the other once-upon-a-time brides who never were.

I wonder if they're anything like the questions this dress has asked me every day for the last eight months and three days.

Would you like to turn me into drapes?

Would you prefer to slash me with a knife?

Would you like to sell me to the highest bidder on eBay?

"It's completely for the best," Courtney cuts in. "And I'm sure Sasha can find it a good home."

"Sasha knows everything about dresses." The teenager flashes a big smile. "Let me go find her. Feel free to look around. I should be back in a couple minutes. Also, love your boots," she says to me, and I look down and realize we're wearing the same style.

Boots, short patterned skirts I made myself, and solid tops. My uniform when I'm not working.

I wear my uniform most of the time these days.

We wander to a shelf full of vintage pots and pans in army green and lemon yellow. They're fifties kitschy and not my style on account of the fact that I have a hate-hate relationship with the kitchen. The oven detests me as much as I despise cooking. I swear, sometimes I think the stove plots my death since it overreacts every time I try to cook rice. What other explanation is there for the way the pot bubbles over?

I run my finger over the handle of a pot. "*Unused,*" I say, and the word tastes vile. "That's the worst kind of adjective to assign to a wedding dress. Especially one like mine. No wonder I couldn't sell it at the other two shops we tried."

Courtney gives me a skeptical stare. "You tried shops that don't carry wedding dresses."

"Be that as it may, I don't know if anyone wants a wedding dress that was never worn."

"Of course someone does, and that's why we're here. This store specializes in reselling dresses, among other things. And just think, your dress will soon go to some other bride who'll give it a good home," Courtney says, ever the optimist.

The dress is the last vestige of my almost nuptials.

I'd returned all the plates and mixers, as well as the Keurigs (Ray registered for three coffee makers? Was he going to set up an underground Keurig ring?) and the two pasta makers (show me *anyone* besides a cook on the Food Network who even knows how to operate one of those contraptions). I sold the ring recently, and thank God my ex-fiancé had a mildly decent salary, because that little stone will help pay some bills for the next few months.

Which is a good thing, since I lost my job last week.

Yeah, that only sucked a little bit.

But it wasn't my fault.

I take some solace in the fact that the newspaper where I'd worked for the last six years cut half its reporting staff, so it wasn't personal.

Courtney wanders past the pots to a collection of vintage glasses, the kind with old-fashioned sayings sold at roadside hotels out on Route 66.

"You really think I should sell the dress?" I ask. "I'm

not that bad off for money." I force a positive attitude not just into my tone but into my entire musculoskeletal system, as well as the circulatory one too. "Maybe I could turn it into a cute little retro dress?"

She stares at me, one hand poised over an old-fashioned glass that says *Sleepy bear lives here*. The daggers in her blue eyes tell me a retro dress is an unacceptable answer. "No. You're not going to wear it again as a cute little dress. That's bad juju."

I arch a skeptical brow. "Wait. You're a venture capitalist and you believe in juju? Do you believe in voodoo too?"

She scoffs. "Please. No. Just juju. And we are going to turn your juju around. Also, once you get rid of the dress, you can date again," she says, bright and cheery, like she's dangling gummy bears before a child in the woods. *Follow the trail of candy now. Come a little closer. They're so very tasty.* "You could even consider answering some of the knocks or pings or pokes you get online."

I shudder. "No way. I met Ray online. Not going there again."

"Be that as it may, I bet a date or two would take your mind off the whole work situation. Let's kill two birds with one stone. Come to the masquerade gala my firm is sponsoring. It's a charity fundraiser and a great way to get you out in the world of the living again."

"It's not as if I've been sulking. Work did keep me busy," I say, because I didn't go full hermit when Ray ditched me at the altar. More like full office, burying myself in story after story, in investigative piece after feature piece after news article. I took it all on, hungry for every single distraction.

Now I have none.

"Let's find you more work." Courtney waggles her blond brows and says my new favorite word. "You can *network*."

My ears prick. "Network? Don't get me excited."

"It turns you on, doesn't it?"

I laugh. "Yes, the prospect of paying my bills is quite arousing."

She presses her hands together in a plea. "Come with me to the party. A ton of tech publications will be there."

Before I can answer, the sound of heels clicking across the floor with purpose greets my ears. A voice shrilly shouts, "No."

My spine straightens.

"You."

A chill runs over my skin.

"Go."

I spin around to find a woman with jet-black hair, a gypsy shirt, and bangles up one arm. "You with your French braid and the barrettes in your hair."

I point at myself—*who, me?*—but there's no one else she could be referring to.

"You brought that cursed dress into my store this morning," she says, her voice wobbling, as she covers most of her mouth with her hand. My dress is draped over her other arm. She must be Sasha.

"Are you okay?" I ask, because . . . she reeks of Crazy with a capital, bolded, and underlined *C*.

Sasha raises her other arm, the one with my dress in its garment bag draped over it, and brandishes a jagged pink fingernail. "Today alone, I broke a nail." She turns her wrist in my direction. It's covered in Band-Aids. "And my cactus tried to kill me."

"You have a homicidal plant?"

Note to self: murderous plants might be an interesting feature story for a consumer magazine. A warning sort of piece. Wait, that's more *Dateline*.

Sasha drops her hand from her mouth, baring her teeth.

I flinch.

Her front tooth is chipped. She points to it. "This," she hisses. "This is your dress's fault. I cracked a tooth."

"On the dress?"

"On a walnut," she says righteously. "But I eat walnuts every day and today a nut attacks my tooth. How else do you explain that? Coincidence? I think not. Your dress swirls with negative energy."

No kidding. I swirl with negative energy. I'm surprised the store hasn't swallowed us into a sinkhole.

Still, I'm not letting my dress take the fall for a broken chopper. "I don't think it's the fault of the dress," I say, trying to reason with her.

Sasha thrusts her arm at me, pointing to the door. "Take it back, and don't come here again. I can't sell it to another bride. I couldn't live with myself if something horrid happened because of that evil dress. Imagine some unlucky woman struck dead by lightning on her wedding night! And in her groom's arms."

I give Sasha a look. "Okay, let's not be so dramatic. When was the last time a bride was hit by lightning on her wedding day? Just say you don't want the dress. I get it."

I grab the dress from her, and she recoils as if it's burned her.

"You need a dress exorcism," she says. "You need a ghost hunter to cleanse your dress of evil spirits."

I wave her off. "I'm sure you have a cousin who'll perform such a service for $159.99."

Sasha shrugs. "I do. I come from a long line of ghost hunters."

"Okay, I'm going. I'll get my evil dress out of your store," I say, turning my tone spooky before we get the hell out of Once More, land of the Looney Tunes shop owner.

Out on the sidewalk, fumes of frustration roll off me. "Can you believe that? Can you freaking believe that?"

Courtney frowns. "I'm sorry, sweets. I had no idea she was one of those *dresses are cursed* people."

"Is that a thing now? To believe dresses are cursed? Maybe I'm cursed. No wedding, no job—maybe I'll go home and find a crazy rabbit has tunneled through my place and my cousin is kicking me out of the last rent-controlled apartment in all of Manhattan." I heave a sigh of irritation so gigantic it stretches to Brooklyn. "I can't believe I can't sell this freaking dress."

"We can find another shop."

I shake my head. "Nope. I made a promise to be done with this dress. If this dress is cursed, I'm not going to bring that kind of bad luck on another bride."

"What are you going to do with it?"

The wheels turn so quickly in my head, they're a blur.

But the answer is clear. So clear I can't believe I didn't see it sooner.

I don't need to sell this dress. I need to *sacrifice* it.

A wicked grin forms on my face as I stand on Christopher Street in the Village, New Yorkers rushing past me and barking into phones, hailing cabs, and ordering Ubers.

"You want me to go to your costume party?"

"Of course I do," she says, excitement etched in her eyes.

"I'll be there."

When I reach my apartment, I grab my scissors because I have the perfect idea for a costume.

3

Flynn

"Would you like me to start your morning coffee, Flynn?"

"Yes, Kate." Grinning wickedly at the query from the melodic female voice, I lean back in the leather armchair and stretch my legs on the ottoman in front of me as the nearby coffee machine whirs to life. "Please run the dishwasher too."

Kate replies, "Of course. I will get that started on the energy-saving mode right away. Just the way you like it."

I laugh, pointing at the white disc on the chrome coffee table. "I love how you know what I like, Kate."

"Would you also like me to turn on the heat in the shower?"

Damn, this woman is an absolute genius. I do enjoy a toasty shower. Shaking my head in admiration, I answer her, "Yes, and please turn off the lights when I leave this morning. That's all I need right now."

"As you wish."

Spinning in my chair, I turn to my two colleagues—Carson and Jennica, my right- and left-hand people. Carson's dark eyes are lit up with excitement. As one of my top executives, he's been working tirelessly on the final touches for the voice recognition in our smart-home system. "Carson, all I've ever wanted since I was a kid is to live inside *The Jetsons*, and it's happening at last."

"I'll work on launching you into space next. But for now, I'm glad this works so well," Carson says, gesturing to the showcase for our system, dubbed Haven.

I give Kate, the voice I like to converse with, one final command, telling her to cancel the shower, since I don't actually plan to shower here in our demo home. But man, am I ever glad the system is firing on all cylinders.

Haven rocks. If I'm popping into a wine shop on the way home, I can check on the dog cam and see if Fido, Fritz, and Mitzi are lounging in their dog beds or eating yet another roll of toilet paper. From the subway, with the press of a button, I can flick on the thermostat to warm the place—I can even start the washing machine. If I want to talk to the lamps or the blinds, I can do that too.

Jennica flips her red hair off her shoulders and chimes in. "How about giving me the hot British voice when you're showing me all the whizz-bang features? Do I have to listen to Kate? Or can I please have Henry, Tom, or Daniel?"

I hold out my hands in a question. "What is it with British guys?"

Jennica leans forward, her blue eyes bugging out. "Hello? Have you heard them talk? It's like listening to sexy British butter." She brings her index finger to the tip of her tongue then touches the air, making a sizzling sound.

Jennica and I have worked together for ten years. I knew her in college, and she was by my side when I had my first company, and now she's here again with Haven. She's an unstoppable force and like an older sister to me. A second older sister, since I have one already.

"Butter?" Carson shoots her a quizzical gaze.

"Butter good. Butter yummy," Jennica says. "And I want Kate to be a hot guy with a sexy British butter voice. Switch her to Daniel for me, please."

Carson shrugs and tips his goateed chin at me. "We can't compete."

"Hey, speak for yourself. I have a deep baritone that's like sexy American butter."

Jennica cracks up. "Flynn, you should use that voice to go as a bad boy to the masquerade ball." She snaps her fingers. "Wait. I have a better idea. Why don't you go as a bad boy piece of code? Just get a leather jacket, some boots, and write some crap code on a T-shirt. Speaking of, I'm going as a Polaroid."

I pretend I'm deeply annoyed. "Why'd you tell me? Now I can't guess what you are when I see you."

"If you couldn't tell I'm a Polaroid, then I'd be doing it wrong. Steve is going to be a Snapchat filter," she adds, mentioning her husband.

"I already have a costume. Plus, I find bad code so morally offensive, I'm not sure I'd choose that. But my costume does rock," I say, proud of what I picked out.

"Tell us." Jennica grins.

"I'm going as ID theft," Carson blurts, and I spin and stare at him.

Dread drops into my stomach. "What did you say?"

Carson nods excitedly. "I have one hundred name tags,

and I'm going to slap them all over me with different people's names."

And there goes my idea.

"That's a great plan," I say with a forced smile.

"What about you?" he asks innocently, since he doesn't know he picked my idea.

"Guess you'll all just have to wait and see." I rub my palms together, moving on. "Now, let's review the final tweaks in Haven."

"No one can come close to Haven." Carson walks us through the updates he's made to the automation system that's rolling out next week. "Haven is far better than anything else on the market. And it's absolutely better than ShopForAnything," he says, meeting my gaze. There's a touch of nerves in his eyes, and I get it—I feel them sometimes too. Our newest competitor is merciless, and I have to guard our company from its pending ambush.

I can't fail because I have hundreds of employees depending on me to succeed, people counting on me for paychecks, for jobs, to make sure the company doesn't become ShopForAnything's cornflakes.

I won't let us fail. I'm well aware that while I might be fine and dandy in the nest-egg-for-generations department, I have people who rely on me for their daily bread. What motivates me every day at work isn't making more money to pad my coffers. It's building something new and taking care of the people who make it possible.

"And you're ready to roll out the marketing plans on a wide scale?" I ask Jennica.

"We are going to market this like Christie's marketed the holy hell out of that lost da Vinci. That was genius. Advertising, PR, videos—the works. And, go figure, but for some reason"—she points at me and rolls her eyes —"people seem to like you, so we're going to market the hell out of *you*. The secret weapon of the boy-next-door genius."

I laugh it off. The attention is still weird to me. "Recap the plans for me."

She spreads her hands like a movie director making a pitch on Sunset Boulevard. "You have the morning shows booked where you'll demonstrate all the cool aspects of Haven, and we also have magazine features lined up that'll reach some high-end consumers." She twists her index and middle finger together. "And I have *Up Next* interested in a potential in-depth feature on you, and how you made the change from your first business to this one. I'll know soon if it's a go."

The mention of the prestigious magazine makes me sit a little straighter. That publication is the holy grail when it comes to feature profiles. "That would be quite a coup."

"Your assistant has all the others in your calendar, and she'll be sure to tell you what color shirt to wear when you're on TV," she says with a wink.

I give her a thumbs-up. "Good. Because fashion is hard for me," I say, deadpan, since clothing is no laughing matter, which may explain why my wardrobe consists of jeans, pullovers, and the occasional business button-down that my sister picked out for me. Without her help, I'd be lost.

I head to my office, and I'm tackling some of the items on my to-do list when my assistant, Whitney, pops in. "Hi. I have all the name tags for your costume for the masquerade party tomorrow night. Do you want me to google popular names and mix them up with weird and bizarre ones?"

I drag a hand through my thick brown hair. "Nope."

"You're going to do it yourself?" she squeaks. Whitney's voice is naturally high-pitched—she almost always sounds surprised. This time, though, it seems legit.

"Why don't you give the name tags to Carson? I need a whole new costume. Any ideas?"

She taps her lip then blurts out, "A headless horseman. You'd totally be in disguise."

I cringe at the image as Whitney nods enthusiastically, delighted horror in her eyes. "That would be a fantastic costume. You could be totally hidden under a creepy cloak. It would be so scary and gross."

"Thanks, but I think I'm going to pass on the bloody stump for a head."

But I do need a kick-ass costume. Something that makes people think. That reminds them that I'm at the top of the game. Something as clever as ID theft.

As I review a set of proposals from hot young start-ups, the new costume idea descends into my brain, fully formed and entirely entertaining.

Surely, everyone will get it.

* * *

After work, I do a little shopping for the costume then head to the racquetball club to take my mind off work for a bit.

My sister, Olivia, joins me, her brown hair pulled back in a ponytail, her game face on. "Get ready for me to crush you and crush you quickly, because I have plans tonight."

"Got a hot date?"

She looks at me. "Yes, with my six-month-old. It's

called breastfeeding, and she's going to be hungry in about an hour."

"Glad to hear you still know how to party. How is my perfect niece?"

She points her racket at me. "Zoe is awesome, even though her uncle is being a pain in the ass for saying I have no life."

"Teasing." I grab a ball and bounce it. "Although, clearly you have no life if you're hanging out with a guy like me." I lower my goggles, lift the ball, and smash it toward the wall.

"I'm not teasing when I say I'm going to kick your pain-in-the-butt ass." As the ball rockets to her, she slams it back.

We proceed to pummel the hell out of the ball for the next thirty minutes. Olivia works in the same field as me —she's an ethical hacker, and like me, she's also highly competitive. She also hates when I win, so she makes sure I don't, finishing our match with a victory at the last second.

She smacks my shoulder. "Take that. Your older sister still has it, even while she's nursing."

Panting, I grab a water bottle and down a gulp. "Damn, you and your boobs are the toughest. Also, can we pretend I totally did not acknowledge your boobs right now?"

She thrusts out her chest. "You can't deny what nature gave me and what my baby made even bigger."

I cringe and cover my eyes. "Make it stop. Put on a bag."

When I open my eyes, she says, "Speaking of hot dates, what's your excuse for hanging out with me when you could be, I dunno, out with a sexy single woman? Assuming any sexy single woman would want you."

"Thank you, as always, for your support."

"It's endless."

I grab a towel and wipe my brow, answering her seriously now, "Same old story. Two days ago, I was propositioned after a keynote speech."

Her eyes widen. "For sex?"

"No, for marriage. That's what made it even crazier," I say and share the details of Nova's pitch to become Mrs. Flynn Parker.

"Damn," she says, whistling, "it must suck to be you."

She raises her racquet like a violin and plays a lament.

"Tell me about it. It was as sad as a sad song."

"Seriously, though, can you even imagine what it's like for athletes and really rich and famous people?"

"I can't. I honestly don't see how you could ever trust that someone was truly into you. Especially given what happened with Annie last year." I shudder at the memory of my ex.

"She was a tough one to spot as a bad seed, I'll give you that. But what about Dylan? He found someone who's truly into him, and if memory serves, he's as rich as sin, too, since he netted half of the sale of the company you two ding-dongs founded."

"True," I concede, since my twin, Dylan, tried using a matchmaker and wound up falling for her. She also happened to be immune to rich guys, so I think that helped smooth the path to trust. "But even so, I need to focus on Haven. Make sure we launch the marketing campaign flawlessly, especially with ShopForAnything breathing down my neck."

"I suppose whenever you do date again, we could just paint your face like a clown so no one recognizes you."

"Oh, yeah. Bozo scored with the ladies, didn't he?"

"Who doesn't want a big red nose and floppy shoes on her man?"

"Bozo was a real Casanova."

"Or," she says, snapping her fingers, "we could give you a new look entirely. Find one of those aesthetic centers and give you a face-lift."

I grab the door to the court, and we leave to head down the hall toward our respective locker rooms.

"It's either that or you're going to have to become a monk."

I laugh as I reach the entryway to the men's locker room. "Yeah, that's at the top of my list of life goals."

But as I turn into the locker room, grateful Dale's not here to talk up what's next in sexual performance grading, something Olivia said sits up in my brain and insists on being heard.

No, I don't plan on getting a face-lift.

The idea has some merit though.

4

Sabrina

I zoom in on the prize. The box sits high on the shelf, atop an old Candyland, a beaten-up game of Twister, and a 1980s Trivial Pursuit. Not just the '80s flashback version. The actual 80s version from shortly after the game came out when US history questions stopped at President Carter.

I reach for the Monopoly box and yank it off the shelf. It imitates a Jenga tower and tumbles down.

"Ouch." The cardboard smacks my face, and Marvin Gardens and its brethren scatter as the game spills onto the floor of the Salvation Army, where I'm now standing in the midst of an iron, a race car, a thimble, and dozens of pink and green bills.

Crudola.

Maybe *I* am cursed. Maybe Sasha was right.

Making sure I don't flash anyone as I bend to the

linoleum floor in my once-a-kimono-now-a-cool-red-dragon-skirt, I gather up the spilled pieces.

A woman with wild and curly brown hair and kind eyes joins me. "Let me help you."

"It's no big deal. I'll just pick it up, and then I'll take it."

"Are you sure you want it?" Her voice is gentle, full of concern over a game that looks like it's seen many lives. "It's missing a lot of pieces. We were going to toss it because the last time someone wanted to buy it, he said there was no Boardwalk and then left in a huff."

I smile. "Boardwalk is the dream, isn't it?"

She smiles back. "I'd like to live on Boardwalk."

"You're telling me," I say as I grab some stray bills. "But I don't plan to play the game. I need it for the money."

The woman arches an eyebrow and gives me a curious look. She lowers her voice and talks to me like I'm in third grade. "You know the money isn't real, right?"

"I do know that," I say, laughing.

She takes a beat and screws up the corner of her lips. "Why don't you just take the game for free?" she says in a conspiratorial whisper, sliding the box toward me.

"Are you sure?"

She winks. "It'd help me out to get it off the shelf. Plus, I have a Mega Monopoly that needs a good home if you want another one."

Mega Monopoly has the biggest bills. That makes it even more perfect. "You're an angel."

"Happy to help . . . you."

I swear she nearly added *someone in need*, and I bristle. Do I look that needy? I'm not starving. *Yet.*

But hey, I'll chalk this up as a victory since I don't need to shell out three bucks for an old game. Take that, universe. My dress can't be cursed, because how else can you explain why I'm now thanking the saleswoman and leaving the Salvation Army with not one but two free Monopoly boxes in the canvas bag on my shoulder?

As I head home, I wave to the woman who runs the dry cleaner near me, and she smiles back. Passing the florist on the corner, I ask how business is, and he tells me it's coming up roses. When I turn the corner at the bodega, I nod at the guy who's rearranging the sandwiches on display in the window. He smiles and mouths, *Roast beef today?* He winks. I shoot him a dirty look and mouth back, *Never roast beef.*

I've lived in New York City my entire life. I grew up in Queens and commuted to Manhattan for college, attending NYU on a patchwork quilt of cobbled-together scholarships. I can't imagine living in any other city. This place, despite all its issues and price tags, is my home.

I want to stay here, but I don't know how long I can last, even given my unusual living situation. I'm damn grateful for my crazy cousin, Daisy, who's generous and well-off enough to let me live in her rent-controlled apartment while she gallivants around Europe.

Her place makes it possible for me to pay other bills. Bills my mother won't pay since she's too busy wasting her own money. Bills like the ones needed for my little brother to go to divinity school. Kevin is brilliant and determined, and he wants to do good in the world and become a pastor. I've taken care of him since we were younger, reading him Percy Jackson and Harry Potter in grade school, tucking him in at night when he was in middle school, helping him with math in high school, and making sure he got into college, since Mom did such a crap job of everything, especially mothering. That's why I petitioned to and became his legal guardian when my mom left. He's more than my brother. He's mine to look out for, and I want Kevin to succeed more than anything. I understand where his drive for ethics, and right and wrong, and compassion comes from.

I send him a quick text.

Sabrina: Is your nose in Spinoza and stuff? :)

Kevin: No, it's in classical theories of religion. Geez. Can't you remember my schedule? Also, I'm in the library right now, studying.

Sabrina: Prove it. Send me a picture.

Five seconds later, a close-up of his big blue eyes and floppy blond hair in front of shelves of tomes pops onto my screen.

Kevin: You should have been a lawyer. Always asking for proof. It's impressive.

Sabrina: It's called being skeptical, even of my favorite person.

I add a zebra for no other reason than I like emoticons of animals.

I bound up the steps that lead into my building in the East Village as my phone rings. I gasp quietly at the caller ID. It's the main line for *Up Next*, the most prestigious magazine in the country. I submitted my best articles there the second I was canned.

I answer with the speed of light. "This is Sabrina Granger."

A deep male voice barks at me. "Bob Galloway here."

I gulp. *The* Bob Galloway? He's the top editor at the magazine. "Hello, Mr. Galloway."

"I'm calling because I read your clips and we might have a story for you."

I nearly break into a tap dance, and I don't even know how to tap-dance. "You do?"

"I wanted to see what your availability is in the coming week. We're looking for someone who knows business and knows how to write a goddamn feature. Seems damn impossible these days for those skills to reside in the same person, but you appear to be able to both write and make sense of a P and L sheet."

"Yes, I'm absolutely available," I say, loving that he already knows what I'm good at.

"Great. Let me finalize some details. I'll be back in touch later tonight. If you don't answer, I'll assign it to someone else."

Damn. He works round the clock, and he's tough as nails. Works for me.

"My phone is literally glued to my hand." I cringe at my incorrect usage and quickly correct. "Well, not literally, of course. But I'll be a quick draw."

He manages a small laugh. "Good to hear. But keep the other hand ready to write with."

"Yes, sir."

I release a huge, happy breath when he hangs up. Maybe my luck is truly changing. All I have to do is hold on to this phone at the party like my life depends on it.

Because it does.

* * *

An hour later, I finish my costume. I try it on, turn in front of the mirror, and slide on my mask.

It's perfect. It's sexy and smart, and I've always wanted to wear a mask like this.

Confession—I love masquerade parties.

Addendum—I haven't been to many masquerade parties.

In my mind, I've attended countless soirees and balls. I've dressed in elegant gowns, worn satin gloves up to my elbows, and descended grand staircases wearing a butterfly mask or a black satin one with silver and red feathers rising high on the side.

I run my finger along the gold outline of my mask, remembering my fascination with these stories when I was younger. As a girl, I was obsessed with historical romances. I found the tattered old books on my mother's shelves, and I didn't know she'd stolen them from the library. Innocent then, I gobbled up her contraband tales, devouring forbidden stories of the most rakish rakes, of the most roguish rogues, of the most devilish dukes who attended such masquerade fetes in hope of seducing the women they'd always had their eyes on.

Naturally, the hero could only seduce her if they were both in disguise, for she was a commoner and he was a titled man who could only be with a lady.

Or something like that.

I give a coy curtsy in the mirror then a shy little smile, pretending I'm the star of the story. All that mattered to me in those tales was that both hero and heroine were in disguise—half masks, eye masks, even full-face masks that could be pushed up at the critical kissing scene. I'd watch their seduction play out on the page. Mistaken identity, playacting, lords in disguise—all of it was so delicious.

Some scenes were chaste, and some were not. A waltz with an unknown lass, a stolen kiss in the hallway, a secret moment—every room was a potential location for a tryst at a masquerade ball, especially the library. If they went to the library, you knew it was going to be oh-so-good.

I flutter my hand over my chest, as the heroine would do.

No matter how far they went, they'd always leave on their masks. Names hardly mattered when you could zero in on his lush, knowing lips.

The mouths of the men in masquerade were made for sin. For making a woman weak in the knees—drunk on a kiss.

I fell for the hero's charms too. As the heroine swooned, I'd swoon. As the charming duke with raven hair kissed her throat then licked a path to her heaving bosom, my skin flushed hot too. I'd flip dog-eared page after dog-eared page, consumed by the tale, picturing the plunging necklines on the women and the tight breeches on the men that, naturally, barely concealed their manhood.

How I longed to be at such parties.

I turn away from the mirror, heading to my jewelry box on the bureau. I don't attend many such parties in real life though. Most of the masquerades I've gone to over the years have been the standard Halloween variety. The masks the men wore were of gorillas, zombies, or President Nixons.

Suffice it to say, none of those made me swoon.

I suppose the closest I came to a true masquerade party was in college when the drama boy I dated senior year invited me to one, and costumes and masks were plentiful and traded freely. So were kisses between the girls and boys, the girls and girls, and the boys and boys.

When I found him kissing one of the other drama boys, I ditched my Venetian mask and headed straight for the wine coolers.

I suppose I've never had great luck with men, or masquerade parties.

But perhaps that will change tonight.

I slide a third gold hoop into my right ear. Three tiny earrings on the right, one on the left. I weave a tight braid down my hair on the right side, since my mask rises high on the left.

Makeup comes next, and as I learned from those tales, one should never skimp on makeup. I slide a glittery gold shadow over my eyelids, then finish off the mascara.

When I'm done, I spread my arms wide, staring at my reflection in the full-length mirror on the back of my bathroom door. Yes, my wedding dress has given its life to the cause. Nothing is left of it but shreds.

Fitting.

I leave and head uptown on the subway.

On the train, barely anyone gives me a second look. God, I love this city. I could be dressed like this for work, for fun, or for giggles, and no one would question it or even bat an eye.

I exit and emerge above ground in one of the most

picturesque parts of Manhattan: the Upper East Side, or, as I like to call it, What Movies Want Us to Believe. This is what the rest of the country must think Manhattan is like, based on the sheer number of rom-coms shot here—blocks lined with four-story brownstones and canopied with trees. Wealthy women walking small dogs and beautiful couples kissing on the glittering stoops of those homes, since movie kisses always take place by a lovely glittering stoop.

I don't know any stoops that glitter. But in the movies, they do.

I turn the corner, looking for the boutique hotel, 10 East Club. It's a landmarked building, with the feel of old New York, when the city toasted itself in the Gilded Age.

When I reach it I lift my gaze, drinking in the gorgeous red brick, the white window panes, and the window boxes, teeming with flowers. The doorman in his cranberry-red uniform holds open the brass door for me. This is New York at its finest. Rich, moneyed, old New York.

But inside, it's going to be flooded with all the new money the internet has brought to the country's financial capital.

Ready or not, here I come.

I drop the mask, gold and white, so it covers the top half of my face down to my nose.

Time to network.

* * *

Champagne flows freely. Silver and gold lights are draped along doorways and over crown moldings, twinkling like fireflies in the softly lit space. Chandeliers sparkle on the ceiling. Music thumps loudly, and waiters circulate, offering appetizers.

But that's where the similarities to the tattered paperbacks I used to read end.

The costumes aren't lavish ball gowns and coats and tails. Instead, I spot a young woman at the photo booth wearing an Instagram sign slung around her neck and a feathered mask awkwardly hugging the lenses of her eyeglasses. Next to her, a skinny guy has donned virtual reality goggles as his masquerade mask. I watch from the bar, peering at the scene with Courtney as we refill our champagne flutes.

"We've raised nearly twelve thousand dollars already," she whispers to me from beneath the hat of a Pokémon Go Trainer. The cost of admission tonight goes to an organization that promotes math and science learning to children from lower-income homes.

"That's amazing. I'm proud of you," I say as she waves at a man with a white sheet over his head. He's no ghost—his costume is marked with *404 error—webpage not found*.

She turns back to me, eyeing me from head to toe. "And I'm proud of you. I knew you were crafty," she says, gesturing to my ensemble, "but this is a whole new level."

I curtsy, no small feat in my short white dress—it's not the wedding dress though. It's a new one I picked up on sale. The remains of my wedding dress adorn my arms. "Why, thank you. If I don't nab a job at a publication, I'll consider making costumes from discarded bridal wear."

"You'll get a reporting job like *that*," she says with a snap of her fingers. "You talked to Henry, right?"

I nod since he's one of the tech bloggers she wanted me to meet. "And Caroline as well," I say, naming the woman who works as a producer at a cable business network. I chatted with her briefly about doing some on-camera reports. "She said I'd have to ditch the three earrings if they were to consider me."

"You'd obviously ditch the earrings."

"Obviously. And also, obviously," I say, giving her my most deferential nod, "you were right that it made sense for me to attend."

She smiles brightly. "Of course I'm right. Now, before you try to skip out of here early, you need to talk to Evil Kermit. He runs a podcast network that just started. His real name is also Kermit."

I give her a look. "He's named Kermit and he dressed as Evil Kermit?"

She crosses her heart. "Swear. We funded the tech his network runs on. He's the front man for it. And he gets a kick out of his name."

"Evidently," I say, keeping my eyes peeled for a guy in green.

She scurries off, and I weave through the crowds, passing a woman dressed like Candy Crush, and a couple of guys wearing animal masks and ears, so they're Snapchat filters. Like a surveyor, I scan the crowd as music plays, a mix of rap and hipster, and I'm pretty sure it would be some sort of sin to play Ed Sheeran or Taylor Swift here. God forbid the taste be anything but ironic.

When I spot a man in green, he's removed his Kermit face mask, and he looks exactly like Seth Rogen, a little round in the middle with a thick beard and glasses. I head over and introduce myself. "I hear you're the man to meet," I say, then tell him I spent six years at the paper, covering the internet business and writing industry features.

He scoffs. "I know your work. We don't exactly do your type of journalism," he says gruffly.

I straighten my spine. "What is my type of journalism?"

"Long, detailed, thoughtful, analytical . . ."

I don't know if that was a compliment or a back-handed-AF compliment. I play it calm as I reply, "Long or short, the goal is always to be fair, to get it right, and to go the extra mile when asking questions."

He rolls his eyes, and now I know he wasn't complimenting me at all.

"Why would you think that's not a good approach?" I ask.

He leans in close. "Because you're sucking up to me at a party, that's why."

"I'm not sucking up to you at all," I say defensively. I'd really like to give him a piece of my mind.

"Then why don't you tell me what you could really bring to the table? Tell me why I'd want you on my network, and don't give me a canned answer."

I've faced off against CEOs, corporate executives, and douchebag billionaires who flaunt their McLarens like the car is a ticket for a woman to drop to her knees. This life-size puppet doesn't scare me. "No, Kermit, I meant it. I wasn't sucking up to you. I believe in being relentless and being fair. That's why I do what I do. I'm not giving you a canned answer because I'm not sufficiently interested in sucking up to lie. Either you like my style, or you don't."

His eyes narrow. "I believe in taking risks. Being scrappy. Going for broke. That's what I do, and that's who I want to work with." Before I can answer, his eyes drift across the room, and he speaks again. "I need to talk to someone. I'll catch you another time."

Kermit, who is aptly costumed tonight, turns away, his cloak trailing behind him.

As he exits, I'm unable to make heads or tails of that interaction, though it's safe to say there won't be any work coming my way from Kermit the Douche.

I head to the nearby bar, so I don't look like I was ditched by a frog. I spot a button on the floor, like the kind you'd use to make eyes on a sock puppet. It's bright red, with the word *start* on it in black marker. Grabbing it, I tuck it into my clutch in case I come across someone missing a button.

As I wait at the bar for the bartender to pour my champagne, I watch the crowd. Some people are dancing, most are mingling, and even though my phone hasn't rung, it's still a good night.

I'll drink this champagne then get out of here. I could probably make some headway on a new minidress I want to make from some emerald-green velvet I snagged at a thrift shop. Hell, if I play my cards right, I can catch a subway in ten minutes, spend some time with my Singer, and brainstorm story ideas to pitch to Henry and Caroline.

Sounds like a good end to a decent night.

The bartender hands me the champagne. I thank him, take a quick sip, and have just set it down to leave, since I shouldn't sew while buzzed, when I hear a voice.

"You're no ordinary angel. You're a next-generation angel."

I turn around and see a man dressed all in black, with lips that are made for sin.

5

Flynn

I'm batting zero. My night has gone like this:

A woman asks, "Are you a code ninja?"

I scowl and shake my head.

The next guess comes from an employee. "You're an awesome Dark Web."

"I'm not the dark web," I tell him.

A woman wearing a pink mustache cocks a smile and says, "You must be an SEO ninja."

Seriously, I am *not* a ninja at all. Maybe the all-black get-up is throwing them off, but I'm definitely not a ninja. Don't they get why I can't be a ninja?

"Nope," I say, with the dejected sigh of someone whose costume is understood by no one. It's quite sad to fail at dressing up. But I've earned my F in this class tonight.

As the woman dressed as Lyft walks away, I notice an angel chatting with Evil Kermit.

And I can't look away from her.

Those legs.

That waist.

That body.

The little bit I can see of her face tells me I can't complain about the shape of her jawline or those lips like a pink bow. But honestly, it's the costume that has me most intrigued. Because it says she has a brain that works well.

That's what I find most attractive in a woman.

When she's done with Kermit, she heads for the bar, and shortly after, I walk over to her.

"You're no ordinary angel. You're a next-generation angel," I say, since a clever costume deserves something much better than a pickup line.

Her lips quirk up. "I am?"

"And let me state, for the record, the costumes here are damn good. But yours is the best one I've seen tonight." I take a beat. "Angel investor. That's brilliant."

She wears a white dress, a halo over her head, and has the coolest wings I've ever seen, because that's where she stops being a regular angel.

She juts out her hip and gives me a smile. "Would you like to see my wingspan?" Her invitation sounds vaguely dirty but also adorably cute.

"I would love to see your wingspan," I say, meaning it from the bottom of my heart, and maybe from other parts too.

She steps away from the bar and spreads her arms wide. They flutter with ribbons of white fabric, something satiny or shiny, shimmering faintly. The strips of material that hang from her arms are covered in Monopoly money. Ones, fives, tens, and hundreds.

I reach for a strand. "May I?"

"By all means, touch my money."

I laugh as I run a finger over a yellow ten-dollar bill. The money is pinned to the fabric, covering her wings. It's the perfect sexy costume, with a twist and a wink and nod to our world, where angel investors often set new start-ups in motion with their first cash infusion.

But the insider joke doesn't stop at her wings. The concept extends all the way to her gold halo. The best part? She's wrapped bigger bills around it—a handful of thousand-dollar bills.

"I see you don't just have a halo. You have a halo effect," I say, referring to the marketing term as I signal to the bartender for a glass of champagne.

"Why stop at one bit of wordplay when I can have two?" she says, with a clever grin I'm pretty sure I want to kiss off her face.

"Where did you find a one-thousand-dollar Monopoly bill? I thought the game only went to five-hundred-dollar denomination."

"It does. Unless you have Mega Monopoly," she answers.

I mime an explosion by my temples. "Mind blown."

She gestures to her ensemble. "I made the whole thing myself."

"Clever and handy. I'm defenseless before your charms."

She laughs. "Good to know, since I make all my clothes. Will that render you completely helpless?"

"That's a likely possibility. As long as you aren't about to pitch me an app for how to make your clothes."

She laughs and shakes her head. Her hair is light brown, almost a caramel color, and it's braided down one side. From behind her gold mask, her hazel eyes twinkle at me.

"No. My app would say *go buy scissors, a sewing machine, and a pattern.*" She raises her flute to her lips, and I watch her drink, wondering briefly how the champagne tastes on her lips. She sets down the glass. A faint imprint of pink from her lip gloss decorates the rim. "Can you even imagine if someone tried to make an app for how to do that? There can't actually be an app for everything."

"But people try. Next thing you know, someone will make an app with a sign that says *taxi* on your phone screen, and you hold it up to hail one."

"I think someone did make that. Also, I didn't fund it," she says, laughing, as the bartender slides me a champagne.

"I didn't either."

She runs one hand along a wing full of money. "I only fund the best and brightest ideas with my Monopoly money." Her voice turns slightly more serious. "Do you get pitched on apps a lot?"

I take a drink of the bubbly. "I get pitched on everything all the time."

She nods. "That must be par for the course, being a VC and all."

I part my lips to speak, to tell her I'm not a VC. But I flash back to the racquetball game, to the face-lift suggestion from my sister. If this angel thinks I'm a VC, that means my face-lift is working. My costume is doing what I want it to do—it's making it possible for me to be me. To have a conversation as Flynn Parker the guy, not as Flynn Parker the multimillionaire.

She doesn't know who I am. And I don't correct her. "It can be."

She nods thoughtfully then roams her gaze over my black attire. She taps her bottom lip. "Hmm. Let's see what we have here tonight because I don't think you're a ninja."

I punch the air. "Keep going."

She studies me more closely. "You're something mysterious. You're trying to fly under the radar. Am I getting warmer?"

More like hot. "Yes."

Her brow knits. "You want to go unnoticed, at least for the moment."

I tense, hoping she's not putting two and two together as to my identity. Absently, I raise my hand to my glasses, wondering if they give me away. But then I remember. I'm wearing my contacts tonight, something I rarely do.

She snaps her fingers. "I know! You're a stealth start-up," she says, using the term for a new company that's keeping quiet.

I raise my arms in victory, a thrill racing through me. "Everyone else has guessed code ninja or SEO ninja, but you're the first person all night to get it right. I am, indeed, a stealth start-up."

Admittedly, donning black pants, a black shirt, and a black eye-mask might have made it challenging to guess. But then again, the angel figured it out, and all without the missing start-up button.

"Your lips gave you away."

She recognized me from my lips? I furrow my brow behind my mask. "What do you mean?"

"Your mouth," she says, raising her fingers dangerously near to my lips. "I could tell you weren't a ninja because your lips aren't covered. Ninjas cover their mouths." I relax again since she was referring to my clothes. "Only their eyes show. But you've covered most of your eyes, and you're showing *only* your mouth and your chin. That's how I knew you had to be something other than a ninja."

"I could kiss you for that," I blurt out. I take a step back and hold up a hand. "I'm sorry. That was probably terribly inappropriate."

A smile slowly spreads across her lips. "No, it wasn't inappropriate. It wasn't inappropriate at all," she says. Something in the way she takes her time with each word tells me she wouldn't mind being kissed. That gives me one mission and one mission only: keep talking to this angel.

But before I can ask her a question, she reaches into her purse, grabbing at something. She holds out her hand. It's in a fist. "Is this your start-up button?"

She opens her hand to reveal a red button.

Laughing, I take it from her hand, and slip it into my pocket. "You found my start-up button. Maybe that's why no one knew what I was. Or maybe you're just a genius."

"I prefer to think genius."

"I'd offer to buy the genius a drink to keep the conversation going, but the drinks here are free . . ." I let my voice trail off, inviting her to pick up the thread if she wants to.

She smiles coyly. "I wonder if you could come up with another way to keep talking to me."

And she wants to, so now it's my turn. The music shifts from hipster rap to something slower, smoother. One of those songs I never know the name of but you hear on trendy TV shows before a hot couple kisses. I nod my forehead toward the speaker. "I planned that," I say as I hold out a hand.

She laughs. "No, you didn't."

"But you have to admit it's good luck, like the button. Care to dance?"

Her lips twitch in a sexy smile. "Yes, I *care* to dance."

I take her hand and lead her to where the chandeliers cast patterns of light across the hardwood floors. The dance floor is surprisingly crowded, but I don't notice who's here since I'm not actually looking at anyone but the hazel-eyed angel. I twirl her once, and when I tug her closer, her eyes sparkle.

"You know how to dance," she says, a note of surprise in her voice.

"I'm not just a clever costume-maker and a producer of the finest knock-knock jokes."

She leans her head back and laughs, exposing a gorgeous throat that I want to kiss. Yes, this is instant attraction. But then, that's exactly how some attraction can be. And, perhaps, how it *should* be.

"One, your costume skills need work," she says, giving me a pointed look as we move in time to the music. "Perhaps you should enlist the help of a crafty costumer for your next ball, at least to sew on the buttons so they don't fall off. Two, tell me a fine knock-knock joke."

"One, I will take that as a yes to enlisting your help next time I go to a masquerade ball. Also, side note, are there more? Are masquerades like a thing around town?"

"I hope they are, and if so, we'll have to find them."

We. More. Next time.

We haven't even had a first time, and we're already talking seconds. This is new for me too, but I like how instant this attraction is for her as well. "And two," I add. "Knock, knock."

She gives a coy smile. "Who's there?"

"To."

"To who?"

"To whom," I say, like a grammar policeman.

She laughs. "Have I mentioned how much correct grammar turns me on?"

I wiggle my eyebrows and yank her closer, so we're inches apart. "No, but have I told you I never let my modifiers dangle?"

"And do you also know how to *conjugate* properly?" she asks in a purr.

"Even better. I can conjugate improperly too."

She raises a hand and fans herself. "Now you're getting me truly turned on."

She likes me, she's flirting with me, and she has no idea who I am. Yes, this mask was a brilliant idea in my list of brilliant ideas. The music picks up speed, and I twirl her around once more.

"Seriously, how did you learn to dance?" she asks again. "And don't say YouTube."

"Because that's where everyone learns everything these days?"

She nods. "Or Instagram. That's where I learned you can slice cake incredibly well using dental floss."

"Why not just use a knife?"

She shrugs. "I suppose it's for those times in your life when you desperately need to slice a cake and don't have a knife handy."

"Hmm. So, if I'm traveling and I need to slice a cake in my hotel room, I'd use the floss rather than call room service for a knife?"

She nods. "Clearly. What else would you do? Also, you have such pretty teeth. I would imagine you have lots of"—she slows, takes her time, and nibbles on the corner of her lips—"*floss*."

My breath hitches. "How is it that you're able to say 'dental floss' and make it sound naughty?"

"I suppose it's one of my many talents. So tell me, Non-Ninja, where did you learn to dance?"

"Don't laugh."

"I'll probably laugh."

"YouTube."

She laughs sweetly. "Seriously?"

I nod. "I figured I needed a life skill beyond math, numbers, and computers. I learned how to dance online."

She curls her hands over my shoulders. "You're a nerd." The words come out as if she just said I was a rock star or a pro quarterback. She says it with affection and, honestly, a whole lot of desire.

"Shocking, isn't it, that I'm a nerd?"

"A hot nerd, to be precise," she adds.

I bring her closer. "So are you."

"You're a very hot, witty nerd."

I'm damn close to kissing her on this dance floor. But I'd rather get her away from everyone else. I lean in to whisper, "Same to you, you incredibly sexy hot nerd I want to kiss."

She lets out a murmur, and when I pull back to meet her eyes again, I ask, "Have you seen the library here?"

"There's a library?" Her pitch rises.

"Yes. Why don't we check out the books and you can tell me more about your Monopoly strategy and the taxi apps you didn't fund?"

"Why, yes, your grace. I'd love to."

I laugh. "I'm not a duke."

"Can we pretend you are?"

"Of course, Angel. I can be whoever you want."

As long as it's not me.

* * *

The door crawls shut.

Inch by inch.

A slow-mo door.

I have no patience for its theatrics. I kick it shut, eager for the next part of the evening to begin.

Her laughter sounds across the library and echoes off its dark wood shelves bursting with books. A leather couch takes center stage, flanked by a mahogany table.

"Are you in a rush to read something?" she asks coyly.

Her voice turns me on. It's like bourbon and honey. A little throaty and husky, but with sweet undertones. Funny, how when you can't see someone's face—at least, not all of it—your other senses heighten. Your ears work harder, homing in on the voice, or you zoom in on the eyes. Hers are warm hazel with flecks of bronze and green.

"Why, yes, I was looking for a particular book." I stroll to the bookshelf along one wall, running my fingers across the spines, from old hardcovers like *Tess of the d'Urbervilles* to modern thrillers from the likes of Clive Cussler to non-fiction reads on the habits of highly effective people. "I thought if you wanted to go to the library you'd want to read. Naturally."

"Of course. Read me a story. A bedtime story." She leans against the wall next to a writing desk with a green lamp on it, the kind that has one of those chains you pull down to turn it on. She goes with the moment, and this night seems like role-play with her. I half want to understand who she is. But in a way, I'd rather experience everything she seems to want to give. Her body. Her mouth. Her mind. Whoever she is here in the library is as real as whoever she is behind the mask. My mission is to make sure she gets everything she wants.

I grab the nearest book and crack it open. It's a James Patterson. "Once upon a time, there was a woman at a party who wanted to be kissed," I say, walking to her, the pages open.

The angel raises her hands to her hair and sweeps off the headband that holds her halo. She tosses it to the desk. "That sounds like a very scintillating tale."

6

Sabrina

The night is glitter. It's fireworks. It's an unexpected victory in a game I didn't intend to play. I'm almost at the finish line, about to win Boardwalk.

Tonight doesn't belong to my failed wedding, to my cursed dress, to the thief who raised me. It sure as hell doesn't belong to my lost job.

This night is mine, and I'm going to take my winnings, this delicious morsel of pure pleasure the universe is serving on a silver platter. Tomorrow, I have to return to my regular life where I'm scraping by, fighting for every damn thing I need and want. Hell, I might turn into a pumpkin at midnight. But right now? There's a man who wants me. A man I want.

I didn't come here for a guy. But now that he's found me—this other version of me—I want him to keep talking, keep touching, and keep going.

Now I truly understand why all the heroines in those

historical romances craved masquerades so much. You can let down your guard, talk freely, tease. It's so much easier to be who you are when no one knows who you are.

I'm not a woman with an unused wedding dress. I'm this other version of me. Tonight's me. A woman with no past. And the man in my present is so damn handsome—at least, what I can see of him. His square jaw, his lush lips, and his green eyes captivate me.

He glances down at the book, as if reading from it, then back up at me. "She had the prettiest lips," he says, and my stomach swoops.

Then, because we're playing our parts, I imagine what comes next in my script, and I do it. No holding back. I blow an almost imperceptible kiss in his direction, whispering into the air, "Did she?"

He hums an appreciative sound then tosses the book onto the desk. Closing the distance between us, he runs a finger over my top lip. I gasp.

His gaze pins me, and the butterflies in my belly escalate to full-blown dives. "And the most mischievous eyes he'd ever seen."

He runs a hand along my hip, and I ignite. Fire burns everywhere. I shudder as he touches me.

"And an absolutely addictive body," he adds.

I think I want him addicted to me. "How do you know I'm addictive?"

"I don't. But I want to find out. That's why I'm telling the story."

"What happens next?" My voice sounds breathless, maybe even a little giddy.

"The narrator isn't finished extolling the virtues of the woman who wanted to be kissed."

"What are the other virtues?" I ask, gobbling up his

compliments like they're a bowlful of candy. I want to eat them all then take another handful too.

"Her lips aren't just pretty. All these words that spilled from her wicked mouth, and her wicked mind, had a particular effect on a certain man."

I arch a brow above the outline of my mask. "What sort of effect?"

He moves closer. "I think you know."

"And this man, I wonder who he is."

He's inches away, and I'm on the edge. My whole body vibrates with anticipation. "I think you like not knowing who he is," he says.

I shake my head, as the confident, masked me answers, "You're wrong."

He wrenches back. "Why am I wrong?"

Time to go for Boardwalk. Time to make my move. I loop my hands around his neck, jerking him closer. "I *love* not knowing."

I go for it. I'm soft at first, but not tentative. I brush my lips to his, dusting across his mouth.

We're not soft for long.

He shifts the kiss to hard. Rough. A little desperate. A lot needy. And full of promise.

It's one of those kisses that doesn't exist on its own, but as part of a continuum. It will become a mouth over skin, a tongue tracing the softest parts of me. It will lead into hotter, wetter kisses that don't stop. It will turn sloppy and wild as we fuck.

He's kissing me that way, his hand running up my neck, traveling along the braided section of my hair. I moan into his mouth because it feels so damn good the way he sweeps his thumb over my cheekbone as if he's imprinting the feel of me, memorizing me.

We kiss harder and deeper, our tongues tangling. Our bodies press and grind, and I wonder if he's curious why I'm a jack-in-the-box tonight, wound up, full of a desperate need to get closer.

But maybe he's not thinking of why, because it's enough for him to be the object of all my pent-up desire, this unknown man, this stranger. Briefly, a neon sign flashes in my brain—who is this man behind all this black? He could be anyone.

But I know enough. He's in this field. He's a venture capitalist of sorts. That's more than I need to know.

Besides, I don't truly care what he does for a living.

I care how he makes me feel.

His kisses should be labeled "known to induce swooning." His touch should be listed as the kind that can melt me into a puddle. Because that's who I am right now. I'm dissolving into sugary-sweet pleasure as he touches me.

Names don't matter. Jobs don't matter.

All I need to know is *this man can kiss.*

He can flirt.

He can dance.

He can talk.

He can play along with the fantasy I always knew I had but never pursued.

And there's one more thing I want to know.

I break the kiss, murmuring, "And what happens next in the story?"

His green eyes are blazing, wild almost. But his voice is calm and confident as he holds my gaze. "The woman at the party wanted the duke to fuck her."

I groan, my knees buckling as electricity skates wildly over my skin.

"She does want that," I whisper. "*I* want that."

He hisses in pleasure as I drag my fingers down his black pullover, exploring his firm chest through the fabric, then tiptoeing along the hard planes of his abs. I raise my fingers and run the backs of them over his chin. Holding his jaw in my right hand, I stare through the slits of his mask into those delicious green eyes. "You're adorable, and I want you to fuck me." I pause for effect. "In a fuck-me-senseless kind of way."

He groans, and the sound seems to hum through him, rumbling up his chest, escaping his lips, which rise in a cocky, boyish grin. It's like a wolf met a tiger cub and they spar for supremacy inside him.

"That's exactly what I plan to do, Angel."

He grabs my hands from his face and spins me around, raising my wrists above my head. The next thing I know, his long, lean frame is pressed against me, his chest to my back, his hard length pushing against the fabric covering my ass.

Ribbons flutter from my arms. My wings are spread. My dress is indeed giving me a whole new start.

Gently, he brushes loose strands of hair from my shoulder, exposing my neck. I tremble in anticipation, waiting, so eagerly. He presses a kiss to the back of my neck, and I shudder in its wake. One soft kiss there makes me weak and ravenous at the same time.

He kisses a trail to my earlobe, nibbling on it. My breath hitches as bursts of pleasure zip through me. There isn't a part of my body, not a single molecule, not a solitary cell that doesn't want whatever he's going to give me.

He traces my neck with the tip of his tongue, and my murmurs turn into pleas. My body begs for him with an ache that vibrates from the very center of me.

I feel his hands move lower, down my sides, over my

belly, along the front of my skirt, then under the hem. His fingers graze up my thighs, and a pulse beats between my legs.

"Masks on or off?"

I shake my head. "On. Leave them on. I like it like this."

He kisses my earlobe once more, whispering, "As you wish."

His fingers feather over my thighs, reaching the apex between them, traveling across my panties. It's his turn to groan as he touches the wet lace that leaves nothing to the imagination. "You do like it, Angel."

I nod on a ragged pant. "So much."

His fingers dip under the fabric as he presses harder against my back, crowding me to the wall, caging me in. I tremble as he touches me for the first time.

He groans roughly, grinding his body against me. "So slippery."

I'm already seeing stars. I'm hovering on the cusp of coming so very soon. I whimper as he runs his fingers across me, gliding, flying. It's so delicious, every stolen touch from my stranger.

He moves faster, making me shudder, making me moan. I drop my head to the wall, my forehead hitting under a picture frame of a man on a horse, I think. Galloping away. That's how I feel. Like I'm racing so fast toward something beyond the frame.

Pleasure winds its way up my legs, spirals down my chest, radiates in and out. *Everywhere.*

He pushes a finger inside me, then another, and I moan wildly, sounding like an animal as I grind down on him, seeking more friction, seeking my release. He rubs against me, fucking me with his fingers, stroking me with his thumb.

I'm so wet, so slick, and everything feels outrageously sinful.

The wild sensations coil into an exquisite tightening in my belly. Once, twice, and I'm there. I'm racing to the edge as he strokes, grinding his body against my ass as his fingers take me all the way.

My brain is static, a wonderful white-out, a blizzard with the snow blurring everything else in the world as I come. I tingle everywhere—my skin, my lips, my legs.

I'm panting, murmuring, as he spins me around, facing him.

When I open my eyes, drunk on my orgasm, he's licking his fingers. He looks possessed. His eyes blaze as he stares at me, sucking me off his index finger. He presses his thumb against my jaw. "You taste like dessert. Next time I want to spread you out before me and devour you, but right now I'm going to fuck you just the way you want."

He can do anything to me. "Take me. Have me."

He reaches into his pocket and grabs a condom. Somewhere in the back of my mind I want to ask if he just carries it around, but then, he seems like the type of man who's prepared for anything—a joke, a dance, or a fuck in a library at a boutique hotel on the Upper East Side.

As he opens the packet, my fingers busy themselves with his zipper, sliding it down until I reach the top of his boxer briefs. When his black jeans hang low on his hips, I push down his briefs, freeing his cock.

My mouth waters as I gaze at his length, hard and heavy and so thick. I run my hand across his shaft, and he stops opening the packet, his eyes floating closed, his lips parting, a shudder moving through his body.

Power.

This feels like power.

Like something I haven't experienced in the longest time. It's intoxicating, and I want so much more of it—of his reaction, of the vulnerability in the set of his jaw and the parting of his lips as I stroke him, feeling how aroused he is. His skin is hot and so hard, and I'm going to take him inside me. "I want to feel all of you."

His eyes open. He shakes his head in wonder. "Who are you?"

I smile because I know he doesn't actually want an answer, but I love that he's asked the question. "Your mystery girl."

He blinks, like he has to shake off the lust to finish the job of rolling on the protection. As he pinches the top of the condom, I slide out of my panties. He positions himself between my legs and hikes up my thigh around his hip. Guiding him, I rub the tip against all that wetness.

"God, you feel so fucking good and I'm not even inside you yet."

He pushes in, and for the briefest second, I feel stretched in ways I haven't felt stretched in too long. He's so deep in me, I draw a sharp inhale, then I sigh blissfully.

I want to use his name. I want to say Duke, or Ninja, or John, or David, or Mr. Venture Fund, or whoever he is. Instead, I blurt out, "I don't think it's going to take me long at all."

He moves inside me, stroking in and out, filling me. I'm vaguely aware of the sounds of the party from far beyond the door, the low beat of the music, the chatter of the crowd, and then us, all the sensations.

My pants. His groans.

The wet slickness of me taking him in deep.

His lips sliding across mine.

His breath on my neck.

The press of my back on the wall.

We're in our own cocoon of one-night lust, of crazy, instant chemistry here in the library as the stealth start-up screws the angel investor against the wall. I band my arms around his neck, all the chiffon and funny money hitting his arms, his shoulders.

I look up at what I can see of his face, the cut of his jaw, the shape of his full lips, the brightness of his eyes, wondering who I let into my body.

But then a thrill races through me because I don't know the answer. I bring my mouth to his, brushing our lips together. As he thrusts inside me, he whispers against my face, "I don't think it'll take me long either. You feel too good."

I bring my mouth to his ear. "Fuck me harder. Fuck me so hard I forget where I am."

His groan sounds like it's ripped from his throat as he hikes my thigh higher. He grabs my other leg, lifts me, and wraps both around his back. "Hold on tight," he says, keeping me pinned like that, holding me up as he takes me.

I can't move like this, and I'm sure the wall is bruising my back where it digs into the wall. I'm equally sure I don't care as he fills me, pounds me, and delivers me to a place I haven't been in the longest time.

A deep pull of desire tugs in the center of my belly. It pulses again, then another time.

"So close," I cry out.

"Yes," he grunts. He unleashes wild thrusts on me, groaning, "Want to watch you come."

My eyes are closed, but I swear I can feel him staring at me as a wave of pleasure sweeps over, pulls me under, and overwhelms me.

Is he as turned on as I am? Is he falling apart watching me shatter? I hope so, oh God, I hope so. Because I'm breaking, and it's intense. I part my lips, I cry out, and then my world spins away as pleasure spills over me, crashing across my skin.

I feel it everywhere. I don't know if I'm quiet or loud. I don't know if anyone can hear me, or if no one can.

But I can't stop saying *I'm coming, oh God, I'm coming* over and over, because it feels like an endless orgasm. Like never-ending bliss.

With his hands digging into my hips, he slams into me, filling me deep as he trembles all over. When I open my eyes, I catch the tail-end of his orgasm. His face is contorted, his lips twisted and his jaw tight. After one final deep thrust, he tenses, grunts a primal moan of pleasure. Then, he relaxes.

I let my legs fall, my feet touching the floor. I'm wobbly at first. My bones need to shift from a liquid state to a solid one again. He pulls out, grabbing a tissue from the desk, and quickly disposing of the condom in a nearby trash can.

When he returns to me, there's one more kiss coming my way.

A soft, sweet, after-the-fire kind of kiss.

A kiss that tells me this was rough and hot, but tender too.

A kiss that says he'd like another, and so would I.

"What's your number?" he asks, and I grin, like a

happy commoner, because the duke wants to see me again.

I start to tell him, then stop to ask if he wants to enter it in his cell.

Shaking his head, he dusts his lips to my neck. "I have an amazing memory."

I shiver from the kiss, then rattle off all but the last three digits for him, when my phone chirps.

And chirps.

And chirps.

Then it hits me.

Bob Galloway.

Fear stabs at me—the worry that I'll miss a big chance.

I blink, drop to my knees, grab my clutch, and rip it open, hunting for my mobile phone. It's him.

I slide my thumb over the screen. "I have to take this call," I whisper to my non-ninja duke.

I grab a bill from the halo on the desk, a five hundred. Waving it, I thrust it at him, mouthing, *The last three digits of my number*. I need to be alone for this call. I want to talk to a potential editor without looking at the man who fucked me, so I run for the door, clear my throat, and say, "Hello, Mr. Galloway," once I reach the hallway.

By the time I'm outside, I realize I left my panties behind.

7

Flynn

A swath of white shimmers on the floor.

Must be one of the ribbons from her wings. Maybe it fell off, or it was ripped off, or it was manhandled during what was an absolutely unexpected but thoroughly fantastic screw against the wall. And hey, how awesome is it to meet someone who likes hot up-against-the-wall sex as much as I do? It is awesome by a factor of ten to the twenty-seventh power.

Figuring I ought to straighten this library before I leave, I bend to pick up the stray ribbon so I can toss it in the trash can.

As I touch it, a wicked grin spreads on my face. It's not a piece of her wings. It's her panties, and I tuck them into my pocket, laughing quietly. This is better than finding a glass slipper. Maybe she's my dirty Cinderella. But then I'm no prince, unless Prince Charming ravaged the heroine in a library.

Hell, maybe that's why the guy is so damn popular.

Maybe that's why men have to live up to Prince Charming —because he was secretly a dirty bastard.

I stand, patting my pocket where I've safely stowed the panties, as well as her number, since it's now stored in my phone.

I head to the door when out of the corner of my eye I spot something else she forgot to grab in her mad dash. On the desk is her homemade halo with its headband, wire, and all the dollar bills wrapped around it.

I run a finger over the band, wondering if she needs this. Maybe this is her favorite headband and she'll be glad to have that back along with the panties. Guess this gives me a double excuse to see her again.

I grab it and run a hand through my hair, hoping I don't entirely look like I just had the best sex of my life.

Wait. Where the hell did that thought come from? Not the best sex part. Clearly, I'm well aware of how I'd rate that encounter on the How'm I Doing scale—at the pinnacle.

But the idea that I don't want anyone to know. That's an interesting thought, and I ruminate for a moment, roll it around in my brain until I realize where it started.

From something I saw in her expression.

Some flash of vulnerability in her eyes, even behind the mask.

I don't know who she is, and I want to protect her. To keep her secrets. Maybe even to keep *her* a secret.

I straighten my shirt, tuck the halo under my arm, and head out of the library. I check my phone. It's eleven thirty. Listening briefly to the thumping music from the ballroom, I decide my team is having a blast still, and there's no need to return to the party. I saw everyone from Haven, chatted with my employees all night long, and endured all their mockery over my *that's-so-lame* costume. Like a good leader, I bore the brunt of the outfit ridicule and gave them a chance to have some fun before we roll up our sleeves and dive into the heavy lifting of market rollout this week.

Plus, if I head home now, that means I can curl up with the newest quantum physics book I downloaded and practice my Japanese, since I have business meetings in Tokyo next month. Last time I flew across the Pacific, I was able to handle the majority of my meetings in the native language of my business partners. This time, my goal is to handle all of them.

Why?

Because. That's why.

As I stroll down the hall, I yank my mask over my head, since I don't need to wear it anymore, and when I turn the corner, I nearly bump into a frog.

When I first met Kermit at a conference last year, he asked me to introduce him to my VCs. Laughing, I told him I hadn't been venture funded in five years. I was past venture funding. My brother and I had already sold our firm, and some of the money from that went to fund Haven. I'm one of the fortunate ones who are self-funded now.

Kermit didn't care for my answer. "But you know everyone, and everyone takes your calls. And this isn't even for me. It's for the tech my network runs on. It's going to blow up."

He was a bold little bastard. Persistent. Dogged. Determined. I suppose that's part of why he played a big role in securing his network's money in the end. Tenacity—he has it in spades.

Now in the hall, he lifts his chin. "Flynn. How's it hanging?"

"Hey, Kermit. It's hanging well. How's your night?"

"It's been interesting." His muddy brown eyes narrow, and he roams them over me, like he's cataloging every detail. Briefly, I flash back to something Jennica told me about his podcast network—the guy is ferocious. He wants to smash down barriers, get everything out in the open, and let consumers decide on tech. In short—"tread carefully because he does what he wants. He's rogue," Jennica had warned.

"Did you enjoy the event?" I ask, keeping it innocuous.

He scratches his jaw, considering the question. "I did. Met a *ton* of people who want to work with me. You know what that's like, right, man?"

I clear my throat. "Sounds like a good problem to have."

"The best problem," he says, puffing out his chest, then he takes a beat, narrowing his eyes. "When are you going to sit down for an interview with me?"

"You know how to reach Jennica. She's in charge of all that."

"You could say yes to me right now."

Persistent, indeed. "Jennica's the one though. She'll have my head if I go around her. It all goes through her."

"But you could say yes, right?"

Damn, she was right about him. I clasp my hands together. "Been hearing great things about your company, Kermit. That's always a good thing."

Deflection, may you please work?

His eyes narrow. "Flynn . . ."

"Kermit."

He sighs, holds up his hands, then shoots me a smile. "Fine. You win. I'll call Jennica."

"Good plan."

I take a step to leave at the same time he does.

"You go first," I say. "So we don't do one of those awkward dances."

Kermit laughs. "Definitely let's avoid awkward dances."

As he steps around me, his eyes stray down then widen. He raises them, staring at me as he runs a hand over his beard, smirking. "Did you have fun with your angel investor?"

I jerk my head. "Excuse me?"

His eyes linger on the halo, and red flushes over my face. Damn, I wish I had a better poker face. But I can bluff. "I think it fell off, and I'm trying to find her to return it."

"Ah," he says with a nod. "Good luck with the department of lost and found."

Yes, I'd very much like to find her again.

8

Sabrina

I end the call with Mr. Galloway, standing under a gorgeous tree bursting with emerald-green leaves. I turn to the right. I'm next to a glittering stoop in front of a red brick brownstone. I glance at the street, picturesque with no traffic.

I laugh happily. So damn happily.

This is a perfect New York night.

There might as well be a soundtrack. Cue it, because I'm ready.

I'm ready to lift my face to the sky and give all of New York City a kiss to say *thank you*. If you'd asked me eight months ago if a night like this would come my way, I'd have scoffed a big fat no.

Eight months ago, Ray called me.

"Hey, babe," he'd said. "I'm ready. Are you?"

"Of course," I'd told him, barely able to contain a grin. In two days, we'd be tying the knot. I'd met Ray two years before, via a matchmaking site. We'd seemed like a good fit, bonding over a shared love of Goldfish crackers, the

Knicks, and our belief that New York City was the greatest place on earth.

As workaholics, we'd both implicitly understood that sometimes we were tethered to our laptops and our phones. But we'd made plenty of time to see each other too, and Ray had fancied himself something of a gourmet chef, whipping up tasty meals for us and hosting dinner parties for our friends. He'd worked in the export business, coached basketball at the community center, and played poker every Thursday with his buddies. He would come home flush with cash—because he was a lucky bastard, he'd said. Then he would take those same friends out the next night or over the weekend. Mr. Generous, they'd called him.

There had been no red flags.

Except maybe the poker. But that's still the great unknown.

Even in retrospect, even with my twenty-twenty hindsight, I'm not sure I'd have seen it coming. The change was inside him. It was veiled. It was deeply secret.

We were rolling along, ready to say *I do*. The church was booked, the venue secured, and my brother was going to walk me down the aisle.

Until Ray called from the office.

"Hey, babe. I'm ready."

"Me too."

But he was ready for something else.

"Ready for a change," he added. "See, I love you, but . . "

My heart skittered up my chest, my skin chilling as the hair on my arms stood on end. No good sentence ever began with *I love you, but* . . .

His *I love you, but* was that he was moving to Macau in

China. He'd landed a job there and would be moving out, putting the apartment up for sublet, and going away.

That was that.

There was no invitation to come along.

There was no explanation.

It was a clean break, and I was sliced from his life.

Neatly, without any blood spilled.

He did as promised. He left immediately.

Like any modern woman, I turned to my girlfriends, to my Singer sewing machine (which I used to make voodoo dolls of Ray, between crying and drowning my frustration in mojitos supplied by Courtney), and to the great World Wide Web for answers. As if I could find a hidden letter from him online. Like he might have pinned a postcard to Google explaining his departure.

But that's the crazy thing about the internet.

We turn to it for answers. We think the answers exist. The internet has trained us to ask it anything. The search bar is filled with questions that we want the machine to tell us—*why am I here, is my wife cheating on me, is he the one?*

I tried every permutation of *why did my fiancé move to Macau two days before our wedding*, and shockingly, Google gave no answers.

All I could figure was he'd been lured by gambling. As soon as I dug into the search for any shred of comfort, I was reminded that Macau is the new gambling capital of the world. It's rife with casinos and high rollers. Maybe he decided to roll the dice. To ante up bigger bets. For weeks, I clung to the possibility, but I found no closure online or in real life.

No matter where I turned to understand why I'd suddenly become the owner of an unused wedding dress and the seller of a modest diamond ring, I came up with a goose egg for an answer.

I moved out of the apartment I'd shared with him and into my cousin Daisy's place, returned the gifts that had arrived in advance of the wedding, and buried myself in work until I lost my job.

Now, months later, I stare at a phone call, a dumb smile still splashed on my face, and think maybe I am on the other side at last.

As I head for the train, a nearly foreign sensation bounces around inside my chest.

Something I haven't felt in a long time but do now, thanks to that phone call.

Hope.

A little later, that hope turns into the next course the universe is serving to me on its silver platter, when a text message arrives.

9

Flynn

Duke: I have your halo and your panties.

Angel: You're taking excellent care of them, I trust.

Duke: Yes, I'm quite the keeper of angel accoutrements and lingerie.

Angel: Lucky you. All I wound up with is your start-up button.

Duke: You have my button?

Angel: I wanted something to remember you by. That's not weird at all to be reminded of someone because of a button, is it? It did start you up, after all.

Laughing, I slip my hand into my pocket, confirming the

button is where I left it earlier. It's also right next to her panties. I place them both on the table as I sink onto my couch by the floor-to-ceiling windows that afford a stunning view of Gramercy Park and beyond. Lights from high-rise buildings flicker in the dark sky, and I wonder where in this city she is. If she's looking at the same view. If she lives in Manhattan, even.

Duke: Not weird at all. I hope the button brings fun memories. Also, did you slip your hand in my pocket while I was fucking you against the wall?

Angel: Is it an issue that my hands were in your pants while your cock was inside me?

Her directness makes me chuckle as I set my bare feet on the glass table in front of me, next to a signed copy of *Astrophysics for People in a Hurry*.

Duke: Not when you phrase it like that.

Angel: Also . . . kidding. Completely kidding. I have nothing to remember you by. Except, well, I'm not likely to forget the hottest ever sex in my entire life.

Pride surges through me as I read her text again. This is a message worth saving. Maybe soon I'll know the name that goes with Angel, but for tonight, I'm fine keeping up our masked identities. Some part of me is damn curious who she is in my world. It'd be ironic if she worked at my biggest competitor, so I'll hope she's truly an angel investor.

Duke: Glad the orgasms were so memorable you don't need the button.

Angel: Everything was memorable: the dancing, the sex, the talking . . .

Duke: Personally, the talking is what made the sex fantastic. Well, it was part of it. A big part of it.

Angel: I have to agree, and I have to agree that other big parts played their role ably, as well.

Duke: Now I'll have to revise my earlier assessment to clever, handy, and good with wordplay. But then, I kind of knew that.

Angel: And does that make you even more powerless to resist my charms?

Duke: Considering I'm texting you an hour after you ran away from me, Dirty Cinderella–style, I'd say you have all the power.

Angel: Ha. Doubtful. But thank you for saving my undies. There's something rather noble about rescuing a damsel's underthings.

Duke: You're into this whole nobility thing, aren't you? Duke and whatnot. Perhaps you should just call me *your grace* next time. Or Prince Charming.

Angel: Next time, Prince Charming? That seems presumptuous. I don't believe you arranged a next time.

Duke: No? Does asking for your number and using it sixty minutes later not count?

Angel: Should I be impressed with that timing? Is that some new sort of land speed record?

Duke: You should be impressed I remembered your number. Who can remember numbers anymore these days?

Angel: You.

Duke: It's amazing what I can recall when I really want to.

Angel: Like?

A visceral memory of earlier in the evening flashes before me, so real I swear I can taste her. I can recall perfectly how she felt against me. I'm parked here on my couch, alone in my dark apartment, the whole of the city keeping me quiet company beyond the glass, and yet, I'm back in time to an hour ago.

Duke: The taste of your lips.

Angel: How did they taste?

Duke: Like champagne. Also, the feel of your body.

Angel: How did I feel?

Duke: Addictive, as I predicted. I want another hit.

Angel: All this talk about next times, and another time.

Duke: I'm getting there. But first, I can recall your eyes perfectly.

Angel: What about them?

Duke: Warm, glittering hazel eyes with bronze and green flecks.

She doesn't answer right away. There are no indicator dots on my phone, and I resign myself to the possibility that she fell asleep, or reconsidered. As I click over to my Japanese app, though, her nickname flashes on my screen.

The excitement in my chest is out of proportion to what it should be. I know that, but even so, it's there. It's real. I feel it.

Angel: I tried to think of a clever and witty and perfect reply. But all I want to say is this—your eyes are beautiful too, and I really want to see you again. Maybe that's too forward. Maybe in this modern world of dating in New York City, I'm supposed to let you make the first move. But I don't care because I want to see you again. Which I already said. But it's the truth. You're adorable and hot at the same time.

Duke: Same to you, and I want that too. Also, I seriously can't believe I only met you tonight. I spent all that time with you, and it was the best unexpected date in ages.

Angel: I like that you consider it a date. But please know I don't do that.

Duke: Date?

Angel: Ha! Lately, the answer to that is no. But I meant sleep with a man I've just met. Everything about tonight was entirely new to me. One-night stand, sleeping with a stranger and not knowing his name.

Duke: It's not going to be a one-night stand, Angel. Also, is it weird that I'm really happy to hear that? Especially because I've never done that either.

Angel: Is it weird for me to be really happy to hear that too?

Duke: Can I take you out tomorrow night?

Angel: Why, I thought you'd never ask, Prince Charming. :)

Duke: You always knew I was going to ask, Dirty Cinderella.

Angel: I don't like to be presumptuous. But all kidding aside, I was hoping you'd make good and fast use of my number. I've also been on a high since I left you—not just because of the O, but also the work call that came in. It was something I've been hoping to hear about, and I'm really excited to get all the details. But I can be free shortly after my meeting. Meet at six p.m.?

Duke: Let's do it. Do you have a favorite place?

Angel: Have you ever been to The Dollhouse?

Duke: No, but if it's your favorite, I'm there. See you tomorrow. Also, I won't be wearing a mask. Will you be okay with that?

Angel: I have a feeling I'm going to like your face.

Duke: I feel the same way about you. I'll tell you my name when I see you.

Angel: I'll tell you mine then too—that way, we won't be tempted to google each other. I'd rather see your face for real first, rather than in a picture.

Duke: I was going to say the same thing. I couldn't agree more.

Angel: For now, I picture you like this.

She sends emoticons of a tiger cub and a wolf, and the grin on my face is too wide, the lightness in my chest too much. But I'll take it because I think I could really like this woman, my Dirty Cinderella, and I want to know more.

As I hold my phone, not wanting to say good night, I decide I better wait for tomorrow to learn any more about her.

10

Sabrina

It's like a movie scene, when the plucky heroine from the Midwest gawks at the brand-new office building in the city, amazed at its size.

That's understandable since the high-rise in the heart of pulsing midtown is sky-high. New Yorkers scurry past me on Monday afternoon, barking into phones, lugging messenger bags, and hefting huge purses full of everything anyone could possibly need to do battle during a day in the city.

The afternoon sun shines brightly, reflecting off the brushed black and gold skyscraper. I stare at the towering structure. Not because it's new to me, but because I've always wanted to be a part of what's inside.

A woman in a sharp gray suit pushes on the gleaming revolving door, her heels click-clacking purposefully across the sidewalk as she vacates the power center. She's a woman on a mission. Of course, she is, if she works here in this sleek, modern castle, home to legions of media outlets, TV networks, ad agencies, and many other businesses that make the media go round.

When I started as a journalist fresh out of college, I imagined working here someday, writing in-depth features, rich narratives full of color and detail, shining a light on the people behind the Standard Oils and Ford Motor Companies of today—the Googles, the YouTubes, the Apples.

I never craved covering politics or news of the day. No, thank you when it comes to wars, murders, or Washington shenanigans. Business, however, always intrigued me, in part because I have a mind for numbers and a head for strategy, but also because I've always believed business is more than a profit-and-loss report. It's a story. It has a beginning, a middle, and an end. And the good ones have twists.

They have zigzags you don't see coming.

Raising my index finger, I touch my right earlobe then my left. Both are bare today. No triple hoop earrings, nor my kitschy black spider studs either. I'm in the costume of professional reporter Sabrina Granger, with a knee-length black skirt and a short-sleeved white blouse. Two-inch pumps complete the basic, timeless look.

Lois Lane has nothing on me.

I step into a pie section of the door and swish into a lobby with marble floors so polished I swear I can see up my skirt.

But I don't self-perv.

With my chin high, I stride to the security desk and show my ID to a man in a navy suit. He places a call, checking with the receptionist, I presume, at *Up Next*.

He nods at me, giving a yes.

I nearly bounce in my shoes. I'm being admitted into a club I've always wanted to join.

Once the guard checks me in, I paste my name tag sticker onto my shirt and head to the nineteenth floor. Soon, the elevator doors whoosh open into the cool, air-conditioned offices of *Up Next*, showing off walls lined with framed magazine covers from over the years, introspective faces of artists and business leaders taken by some of the best-known shutterbugs in the world, as well as iconic images of New York and photos that capture flashpoints in history and culture.

The magazine itself is powered by ads for expensive watches, sophisticated colognes, tailored suits, boats, homes in the Hamptons, and more. Thanks to those advertisers, the offices are opulent. It's like this magazine doesn't know that journalism has changed in the last decade, that the internet, social media, and real-time news has upended all our work.

The receptionist whisks me to Mr. Galloway's office in the corner, where he waves me in.

Gray-haired and weathered, but dapper in a Ted Danson way, he wears charcoal slacks, a white shirt, and a yellow tie. His tailored suit jacket is slung over his leather chair. He stands and heads around a massive mahogany desk to greet me. We shake hands, and he gestures to a soft leather couch with ornate arms after we exchange hellos.

His office screams money and considering my paper laid me off because ad dollars were way down, I can't help but breathe a sigh of relief that somehow *Up Next* is largely immune to the seismic changes roiling journalism.

Mr. Galloway parks himself in a burgundy chair, rubs

his hands together, and says, "Let's get straight to business."

"Yes, let's," I say, loving that he's efficient. That's a good sign in my field.

"I've been watching your work. I've been reading your stories recently, and when the paper cut half its staff, I knew it was a chance to nab you for an assignment. I have an important feature I want you to write."

I smile, nodding deferentially, delighted he's had his eye on my work. "I can't wait to hear what you have in mind."

"We're expanding our business coverage. That's what our readers care about. We want to look at the men and women who will become the next generation of business leaders. Who is the next Mark Zuckerberg, Jeff Bezos, Larry Page? That's what I want to do. To profile the rising stars and give our readers a true sense of who the business leaders of tomorrow will be."

A burst of excitement whips through me. He's talking my language. "That's exactly the type of story I love writing. Something deep, where I can dig into what makes a person tick."

"That's what I'm looking for, and that's why I want you to profile Flynn Parker."

I smile when he mentions the internet boy wonder. I've never met him before, but I know of him, of course. "Mr. Parker has something of the Midas touch, doesn't he? After selling his first company for a record high valuation and then starting the hottest new tech in home automation, he's absolutely one to watch. Especially since Haven is poised to be at the forefront of a whole new and exciting sector."

Mr. Galloway nods, a sage look in his gray eyes telling

me he likes my response. "Exactly. Get in there and dive into who he is and what drives him. That's what I want you to uncover. He's thought to be the next Zuckerberg. Find out what makes him tick. I want to understand who the next business visionary is."

I nod enthusiastically as ideas for questions to ask Flynn ping-pong in my head. "I've never had the chance to interview him, but I think that can benefit the piece since I'll come into it with a fresh start. No preconceived notions," I say, wanting to be frank with Mr. Galloway. Even though I've covered a lot of people in business, that doesn't mean I've interviewed everyone in New York yet.

He slashes a hand through the air for emphasis. "That's what I want. A clean slate. You don't bring anything to the table about Mr. Parker."

I arch an eyebrow. "Should I bring something to the table when it comes to him?" I drop my voice to a conspiratorial whisper. "Are there skeletons in his closet you want me to discover?"

Mr. Galloway chuckles, a deep, scratchy sound. "If he does have any skeletons I would very much like to know about them, but I suspect he's one of those squeaky-clean people."

I laugh. "Sometimes they're the ones with the most to hide." I fix on a more serious expression. "But regardless, I'm your woman. I'll find out what excites him, what scares him, what keeps him up at night, and what motivates him to get out of bed in the morning."

"Exactly. Learn his keys for success. That's what our readers want to know. And I don't want those *top five points* he shares at conferences." He scoffs derisively. "Get me something fresh. Roll up your sleeves and find the real story behind his success."

I mime rolling up my sleeves, even though I don't have any. "Will do."

Mr. Galloway rises, brushing his hands over his slacks. "My assistant will send you the name of Parker's PR person, and you can start there to schedule with him. The company is open to the piece, and Parker knows about it, so scheduling won't be a problem. You should be able to get some good interviews with him. You might need a few meetings."

"Consider it done." I stand, shoulder my bag, and shake his hand.

"I'll need the piece in two weeks."

"I'll have it to you on time."

We firm up the final details, like word count and pay. I suppress a squeal when he tells me the fee—much higher than I expected, much higher than is the industry norm too. It'll give me breathing room and let me help my brother.

"I'll have the piece to you in two weeks."

"Brilliant." Taking a seat at his desk, he taps his keyboard, presumably to move on to the next item on his list. "And if this works out, we might be able to start covering that sector on a regular basis. You'd be first in line for the beat."

"That's great," I say, reining in a big fat grin.

As I leave, I resist the impulse to run down the magazine's hallway, smacking the walls as I hoot and holler because, holy smokes, from the party, to the guy, to the gig, my luck is changing.

Once I'm in the elevator, I start my research, googling Flynn Parker, eager to talk to him for the first time. When his picture pops up, a *whoa* slips from my mouth. Damn, he is fine-looking. Even though I've never interviewed him, I'm well aware he's been named a most eligible bachelor, given his fortune, but I wasn't aware he was quite this handsome. Now I see another reason he's earned that title —that face. For the flash of a second, there's something eerily familiar in the set of his jaw, and his eyes remind me of someone. But then, I can't get a good look at them since he's wearing glasses.

Not that it matters—I'm sure I'd remember meeting someone this fine in the flesh.

But who cares if he's hot? I'm not interested in his looks. I'm interested in his story. Besides, I'm a professional. I'm going to treat this professionally because this is a tremendous opportunity that could lead to an even bigger one. That's why I won't let myself think twice about how good-looking he is, even though there's a soft rap on the door in the back of my brain, telling me I've met him. I cycle through parties and conferences, keynotes and events. Surely, I'm remembering seeing him in passing somewhere, or saying hello after a presentation he made. That has to be it.

I shove him out of my mind for the moment. I'll return to him tonight as I dive into my prep. When I reach the lobby I duck into the restroom, change out of my superreporter outfit, and slip into something that feels more like me.

The me who met the duke.

Do-it-yourself Sabrina.

Since it's easier to change here than go home, I tug on a short polka-dot skirt I made and a pair of red ankle boots, tucking my work skirt and pumps into my bag. I leave on the blouse since there's just something about a cute white blouse that works with nearly any outfit.

As I look in the mirror, I consider my hair, scooping it

up. Will he kiss my neck again today? Will he nibble on my earlobe? Grab my hands, steal me down a hallway, and press those lush lips to mine?

I shiver as the delicious memories dance before my eyes.

I'll say yes. I'll say yes to whatever he wants to do to me.

I let go of my hair, leaving it down, then clip one side with a small rose-gold barrette with a tiny crown design at the top. I pair them with little crown stud earrings, then I layer tiny pink hoops above them.

My stomach flips nervously. I'm going to see him in person. Without masks and with names. Will we still like each other?

Part of me wishes we could keep up the charade, but another part wants to know him for real.

As I catch the subway to The Dollhouse in Tribeca, my phone lights up with a message—the contact for Mr. Parker. I send her an email as the train rumbles under Manhattan, and when I arrive at the station, her reply lands in my inbox.

Tomorrow, I have my first interview.

A few minutes later, I enter The Dollhouse, grab a stool at the bar, and do a double take when I see Flynn Parker walking toward me.

11

Flynn

  An hour earlier

"There you are."

As I wait for the elevator—and "wait" is a generous description, because it's more like I tap my foot and count down every single second because I am so amped up—I turn to see Jennica marching to me, pink sunglasses perched on her head, a huge purse weighing down her arm.

"Here I am," I reply.

"You're leaving early?"

"It's five thirty."

She arches a brow. "That's early for you, Flynn."

I shrug, taking off my glasses, wiping the lenses on a shirtsleeve, and putting them back on. They're as clean as they were ... well, before I cleaned them. "Anyway, you're looking for me?"

"I want to let you know I'm ready to accept my badge

of awesome right now." She pats her chest.

"And to what do we owe the honor of your awesomeness today?"

She thrusts an arm in the air, victory-style, as the elevator arrives. We step in together, and I press the button for the lobby. "I was on the phone a few minutes ago with none other than Bob Galloway. He has officially assigned a reporter at *Up Next* to do an in-depth feature piece on you." Her voice rises high on the last word as she pokes my shoulder with affection.

"Cool," I say, checking my reflection in the elevator panel to make sure all the buttons are lined up on my shirt. You never know if you've misbuttoned something. Not that I did that in my senior year of high school before a speech. Not that I've ever forgotten that moment of embarrassment either. In my defense, buttons are hard.

"Cool? That's more than cool. That's amazing."

"Right," I say, nodding as I study the alignment. I bare my teeth next, making sure the choppers look sharp and lunch-free.

"I talked to the reporter too. The piece is going to pivot a bit from what I pitched them, but I think it'll be even better. Get this—it's going to be about you as one of the next generations of business visionaries." She rattles off more details on the piece, telling me the reporter is Sabrina Granger, my assistant has scheduled a meeting, and tomorrow is our first interview.

I run a hand through my hair. Yup. Just the right amount of floppy mess.

"It's going to be a fantastic piece," Jennica adds.

"That's great."

The elevator goes silent.

Jennica clears her throat, catching my attention with

the sound. I snap my gaze to her. Her hands are parked on her hips. "You're barely paying attention."

"Visionary, check. Tomorrow, check. Sabrina, check. Piece will be great, check." I tap my temple. "I listened."

"Hardly. You were distracted, and I'm willing to bet it's because you have a hot date."

I scoff.

She laughs, shaking her head. "Flynn Parker, you've been checking your reflection, and you're making sure you don't have lettuce in your teeth, even though it was five hours ago that we went to the salad bar for lunch, and you've probably also brushed your teeth twenty times since then."

I blow out a breath of air. "Minty fresh. Guilty as charged."

"Who is the lucky lady, and does she know you're a certified dork?"

"Correction. It's not yet official. But the Adorkable Committee assures me the certificate should arrive any day."

"Excellent. We'll frame it," she says as we reach the lobby, and she shoves her bag higher on her shoulder. "Now, fess up. Who is the lovely you're lettuce-free for?"

I laugh, shaking my head. Jennica wouldn't believe me if I said I didn't know who she is. I hardly believe me. "She's a bit of a mystery."

Her eyebrows shoot up, and she hums her approval. "A mystery girl. How intriguing. What do we know about her?"

Let's see. I don't know her name, her occupation, her family background, where she lives, or any of the usual details. But I do know some key traits already. "She's smart, independent, clever, and likes my jokes."

Also, she's great in bed—or against the wall, as the case may be—and feels spectacular in my arms. But I keep those key attributes to myself.

"Sounds like a keeper."

"Plus, she hasn't proposed to me yet."

"There's still time tonight for her to get down on one knee. And on that note, I need to get to the year-end open house at my daughter's first-grade classroom. My husband is making me attend. The torture. Dear God, the torture of an open house."

"Have fun with Steve, and be sure to take Taylor out for frozen hot chocolate at Serendipity when you're done."

"Her? How about someone taking me out for enduring an open house?"

We say goodbye, and I head in the direction of The Dollhouse. When I looked up the description online, I immediately thought, *Aha, it's perfect for her.*

On the way downtown, I check my reflection in the subway window. When I exit in Tribeca and carve a path through the trendy streets, I peer into shop windows to make sure my glasses aren't sliding down my nose. Jennica was right to note my distractedness—I am nervous, and that's unusual, especially considering I don't break a sweat when I deliver a keynote speech, negotiate with business partners, or go out on dates.

But this date feels different. It's like we've done things entirely backward. Like we're assembling a jigsaw puzzle from the middle out. But we both seem to like it this way. She likes the intrigue as much as I do, and that makes me want to know her even more, learn what makes her tick, what excites her. But more than that, I want her to keep wanting to see me, the guy she called Duke, not the dude everyone wants a piece of.

Then I'd know if it was real. Then I'd know it was about me, and not about anything else I might bring to the table. I almost wish I could keep up the ruse.

Because it's not merely that I'm tired of the random women, the catfishers, the gold-diggers, and the money-hunters. I can handle a woman hitting on me at a conference, a bar, or the gym because she's figured out I could be a meal ticket. I can shake that off and move on. Other things are harder to let go. I know what it's like to give my heart to someone thinking she wants it, but then learn she only wants all the zeros attached to my name.

That was Annie.

She was a math nerd too, and we went to college together. I had the biggest crush on Annie, with her big blue eyes and equally blue hair, and her badass coder attitude. She didn't give me the time of day romantically, but friend-wise, absolutely. I was the guy she leaned on, the one she told her man woes to. Yeah, I was *that* guy, and then I finally found the guts to ask her out.

But her answer was clear—I was friend-zoned forever. "But we're so much better off as friends, don't you think?"

"Sure," I'd said because some of her was better than nothing.

We stayed buddies, keeping in touch even though we moved to separate coasts after graduation. A few years ago, she returned to New York and asked, ever-so-sweetly, if she could have a do-over on the "let's just be friends" bit.

Hell to the yes. I hadn't forgotten why I'd liked Annie. She was cool and smart.

We went out for several months, and it felt like sweet victory. Revenge of the nerds, indeed. Finally, the girl I'd wanted, wanted me too. And boy, did she ever. The praise flowed in. How good it was to finally be with me. The sex was plentiful, like she couldn't get enough. Plus, she liked to sleep naked. Can you say kryptonite for a guy?

The closer we grew, the more often she floated the idea of moving in, maybe getting engaged.

I wasn't opposed to bumping things to the next level, but my radar went off when she became not only overly interested in me, but keenly curious about my bank accounts. *Where do you park all the money? Who manages it? What sort of investments do you have?*

"The kind that requires a prenup."

Yes, I told her that.

Because I'm not stupid.

"I can't believe you'd want a prenup," she said, like I was the jerk.

"Annie, we're not even engaged."

"But you're well and truly saying you'd want a prenup?"

"Um, yeah."

"I can't believe you don't trust me."

I certainly didn't after that. It didn't take a genius to figure out why I'd been laddered up to the *Let's Be More Than Friends* category. The more she pressed, the more evident it became. I hadn't been promoted from the friend zone. I was skyrocketed into the green belt, and she watered the Flynn plant with compliments and nudity. A hungry ficus tree, I guzzled it up.

I suppose in the end I'm simply grateful that she showed her cards before I fell any deeper for her.

That's why I wish Angel and I could keep up the masquerade. Because it's honest. It's freeing. I don't have to worry about getting hurt. I don't have time for another heartbreak. I have a company to run and employees to provide for.

I do, however, have time for a fantastic night out or two or three, and that's exactly what I want.

As I glance up at the numbers above the storefronts, a window full of old-fashioned toys comes into view. There's a spinning top, a hobby horse, and some wooden blocks that spell the name of the establishment. *The Dollhouse.*

It's one of those places that doesn't need to rely on a flashing neon sign or scads of scantily dressed ladies out front to lure anyone in. It's like a speakeasy. You need the secret language to enter, and the code is knowing this isn't a storefront for old-fashioned toys.

Smiling, I push open the door and head into a bar. One wall is lined with shelves holding rooms from doll-houses—sitting areas decorated with pint-size couches, sleeping dens with beds that would hold a teaspoon and pillows no bigger than a fingernail. At the bar, the napkin holders are actual upside-down doll-size tables, that would, I think, fit inside one of those little homes.

Patrons sip drinks from teacups in shades of pastel blue and pink.

It's so retro, it's beyond retro. It's like a fiesta of quirki-ness, and as I look around, I hope I'll recognize the woman from the party instantly. But then, I'm not sure how I *won't* recognize her. I ran my fingers up her legs, slid them between her thighs, felt her tremble, kissed her lips.

I'll know her.

The hostess strolls over and asks me if I'm meeting someone. I survey the tables and the bar, hunting for caramel hair, green eyes, pink lips. There's a sign by the taps that says: *Lollipops for good boys and girls.*

My gaze drifts past the sign, and a smile tugs at my lips.

Damn, I've got it bad already.

"Yeah," I say, and my voice sounds a little dreamy, a little dopey when my eyes land on a woman wearing a polka-dot skirt. I zero in on her hair, a warm shade of brown.

The woman whose underwear is in my pocket.

The woman whose scent has been in my head for the last twenty-four hours.

It's like a blind date fantasy come true.

She's even prettier now that I can look at all of her.

The problem is, she doesn't smile when she sees me.

12

Flynn

If I were offered ten emotions and asked to point to the one for her expression, it wouldn't be excited, angry, annoyed, or thanking-her-lucky-stars-that-I'm-a-handsome-devil.

Too bad.

The word I'd pick would be *vexed*.

Like she doesn't remember me. Her brow narrows and she studies me. It's like the moment when a record scratches and all the good vibrations come to a halt. This wasn't entirely the greeting I imagined—honestly, I was hoping she'd saunter over, wrap her arms around my neck, and kiss the hell out of me—but I tell myself to go with the moment.

I head to the bar.

"Hi," I say, tapping the wooden sign on the taps. "I think I deserve a lollipop. Do you?"

Her lips part, but no sound comes. She blinks. Shit.

She doesn't like me in person. What the hell? I'm damn cute. I'm a hottie.

"I didn't think we were meeting yet." There it is, that voice from last night. Sexy and throaty, with honey notes.

But she's talking nonsense. She's supposed to say, "Hi, Duke. May I have another?"

Or something like that.

"You didn't think we were getting together?" I rub my ear. Maybe I'm hearing things.

She narrows her brow. "I thought our meeting was tomorrow?"

Did I get the location wrong? The date wrong? I thought we were damn clear on both, but I've been preoccupied. "I thought it was tonight. Isn't that what we agreed on?"

She shakes her head. "I'm pretty sure we're meeting tomorrow. I just set it up." She peers around me, looking for something, or someone. "I'm waiting for someone else now, but . . ."

My brain sputters, trying to make sense of her flummoxed face. Did she make another date tonight? "Who are you waiting for?"

She laughs, an embarrassed sound. "Just someone." She waves a hand across her face. "Sorry, I don't mean to be unprofessional. I'm really looking forward to interviewing you tomorrow." She takes a beat and licks her lips. "And I can't shake how much you look like someone else I know." Standing up from the stool, she extends a hand and says, "I apologize for my confusion. I'm Sabrina Granger. Nice to meet you, Flynn. I can't wait to chat with you for the story."

My brain clicks and whirs, and for a nanosecond, I think—or hope—I mixed up the names. Sabrina is the

reporter interviewing me, but Sabrina can't possibly be . .
.

Or can she?

Those lips, that hair, those hazel eyes . . .

The universe has just dropped an anvil on me, Acme-style, flattening my excitement. This is the whoopee cushion, the hand buzzer, the "kick me" sign on my back. That would be fitting, after all, in this gin joint. Perhaps the toy storefront was more of a promise of what's to come for me —a game where I don't win.

This can't fucking be.

"You're the reporter?" I ask heavily, still hoping against hope I've gotten it wrong somehow.

She nods. "I'm Sabrina Granger."

All at once, awareness seems to dawn on her, and she gasps, "Oh, hell. You're . . ." She points at me, like I have the plague. "You're . . ." She gulps and doesn't finish.

I laugh incredulously, sketching air quotes. "Yes, I'm *just someone.*"

Her eyes widen to moon pies. "I can't believe," she begins, her words coming out staccato. "I thought. My brain. Cognitive dissonance," she says. She knew I was Flynn, but she also figured I couldn't possibly be her mystery guy. Newsflash—I'm both the winner and the loser of the masquerade contest. "I thought you were . . . but I didn't think you could be."

I sigh so damn heavily it's going to require its own weight class. "I didn't think you'd be the reporter, Angel."

She flaps her hands around. "I assumed I had the times wrong for my interview, rather than you were my . . ." She lets her voice trail off like she can't bring herself to say what we are.

I pick up the dropped words. "Your duke? Your dirty

Prince Charming? The guy who made you forget where you were?" I toss out, repeating her request from last night. One I followed to the O.

She drops her face in her hands, moaning in frustration. "I can't believe this," she mutters, shaking her head. Her shoulders rise and fall. She raises her face like a cat poking its ears out from beneath a blanket. "Say you're kidding."

"I wish I were. But nope, I'm Flynn Parker, the guy from last night. The guy from tomorrow. The guy who texted you. The guy who has your panties. And, evidently, the guy you're interviewing."

She shushes me then leans her head back and sighs, raising her eyes to the ceiling, talking to the roof. "I came here to meet the guy from the party—the guy I had this crazy-amazing connection with—and it turns out he's the man I'm interviewing for my first big break at a magazine I'm dying to work for. The universe seriously loves to laugh at me."

I nod, signaling the bartender for a drink. "And I can't believe the first woman I had a crazy-amazing connection with is now off-limits since she's writing a critical piece on my company during an important time in our market rollout."

Her lips quirk up into a delicious grin, as pink splashes across her cheeks. Her blush is magnificently alluring. It reminds me of how her skin flushes when she comes, how the color crawls up her chest when she nears the edge.

The memory is like a serving of lust, and my response to it is instant and hard.

"What can I get you?" the goateed bartender asks as he arrives.

"Something strong," I tell him, since I can't very well ask for the drink I really need—The Boner Killer.

"Coming right up."

"Do you want something?" I ask Sabrina.

She shakes her head and points to her cup.

When the bartender leaves, I gesture to Sabrina, unmasked. "If it's any consolation, you're even prettier like this." My eyes roam her face, cataloging cheeks I held, eyes I stared into, lips I bruised.

Her expression softens. A faint smile tugs at her mouth. "You too," she whispers, and for a moment, I can see how this night would have unspooled. A drink, a conversation, a laugh. The laughter would have led to kissing, the kissing would have led to stumbling out of here, hailing a cab, making out as the city blurred by, then a hot, sweaty night at my place that went by far too fast.

That can't happen anymore, yet the promise of a night like that is powerful. I tap the bar, drumming my fingers as I soak in the ambiance of this quirky joint. "I'm not surprised you like this place. I bet you had a dollhouse when you were younger."

A faint smile plays on her lips. Those lush, sweet lips. "That's how I learned to sew. For dolls."

I laugh, wishing this conversation was the prelude to our evening. "Yep. Pegged it."

"The first time I took needle to thread, I made a terrible frock for a four-inch-high blond toy woman." She dips her hand into her purse, and fishes around. She grabs a swath of fabric and holds out her hand to show me a green paisley triangle. "Here it is. I keep it with me, like a good-luck charm."

"That is awful, and I say this as someone who made his first robot out of cardboard, so it was equally abysmal."

Tucking the dress away, she asks, "Do you make better robots now?"

I shake my head. "I gave up the robot trade in high school. Decided to make radios instead."

She studies me. "Funny, I would have pegged you for model toys, airplanes, and RC cars."

I bring my hand to my heart, pretending to look affronted. "I'm offended that you don't realize I'm weirdly practical. I have no interest in things that don't do . . . *anything*. But I do love the radio."

"Do you have your own radio?"

"Of course. Built it from old parts. Listen to it at night. Works like a charm."

She shrugs playfully. "Maybe you can tune in to little green men on it."

I wiggle my eyebrows. "One can hope."

Hope. Just like a sad part of me is hoping this night can keep ticking along in the direction of paisley dresses, cardboard robots, little green men, and cabs hailed hastily. I want to turn on the radio, then turn her on, as sultry music plays and moonlight streams in through the penthouse windows.

She laughs as she lifts her yellow teacup and takes a drink of her beverage. But when she sets it down, a lightning bolt of anger flashes across her eyes. "Wait," she whispers sharply, and there goes the hope. "Did you know I was going to be covering you? Did Mr. Galloway tell you first?"

I wrench back, getting out of the way of her ambush. "Are you crazy?" I slash a hand through the air in certain denial. The interlude is over. Officially. "I had no idea who you were. I had no clue you were working on a story on me."

"I was literally just assigned the piece today. My editor told me you knew about it," she says with narrowed eyes, as if she's trying to catch me in a fib.

"And you think that means I knew who you were at the party?"

"Maybe you were feeling me out. Trying to get a sense of what I was like."

I scoff. "Angel, I'm not that nefarious nor so desperate that I need to conduct recon for a magazine article I agreed to do. And I don't need to sleep with a reporter to try to sway her view of me."

"Then why did you say you were a VC last night? See? You were trying to throw me off then. I thought you were a venture capitalist. Were you just saying that so I wouldn't know who you were?"

I hold up my hands. "I didn't say it. You assumed it."

"And you didn't correct. Why?"

I sigh, rubbing a hand across my neck. "Because I didn't want you to know who I was. Because we were role-playing. Because it was part of the game. I thought you liked the game."

"I did," she says, her tone vulnerable once again. "But why didn't you want me to know who you were?"

"Because I wanted you to like me for me."

She exhales deeply. "I guess I wanted the same." She holds up a finger, a sign she has to ask another question. "But if you didn't know who I was last night, if you truly didn't know it was me, how did you recognize me as the girl from last night when you came in?"

I furrow my brow as the bartender brings me a pink teacup. It's a frilly-looking porcelain cup, meant for proper ladies sipping tea. I swear this drink better be as strong as steel.

"This ought to do the trick," he says, then whispers, *tequila*.

I thank him and swallow a thirsty gulp of the fiery liquor from the prissy cup. The burn intensifies as it goes down, then it spreads through my lungs. I draw a deep breath, and when that cuts-like-a-knife sensation starts to fade, I say, "Seriously, Angel? Is that a serious question? You think I'd only recognize you if I had planned in advance to seduce the reporter assigned to cover me?"

She lifts her chin, nodding, as if she believes that line of bullshit.

I lean closer to her, raise a hand, and finger a curl of her hair. Her breath catches. "Angel, I recognized you because you're wearing polka dots, because you said you make your clothes and something about polka dots seems uniquely you and uniquely DIY. I recognized you because your hair is the same gorgeous shade, because I had my lips on your face, on your earlobe, on these pink lips." A shudder moves through her as I go on. "I knew your voice because it was the same husky, sexy voice that the woman used last night when she begged me to fuck her against a wall. To fuck her hard." A tremble is her answer. "I knew it was you because you match my mystery girl, and you smell as delicious as she did." I move back, letting my words linger. "But perhaps I didn't make a memorable enough impression."

"You did," she whispers, her voice wobbly. She doesn't meet my eyes. She runs a hand over her skirt and crosses her legs. Taking a deep breath, she raises her face. "I swear you did."

I like her response. Hell, I needed her response. But once it's voiced, a kernel of doubt wiggles insidiously through me, burrowing into my chest.

What if she's setting me up?

I throw her question back at her. "But how can I be sure you didn't know who I was?"

She rolls her eyes. "Please. I already said I thought you were a VC."

But what if she's lying? What if she knew who I was and seduced me to soften me up for the piece, like Annie came back to me to try to pry open my accounts? "How do I know?"

She arches a brow and straightens her shoulders. "How do you know? I guess you don't. You'll have to take my word for it. All I knew was you were a guy I liked spending time with. I had no idea what you did for a living. I didn't care. I liked dancing with you. I like talking to you. And I really liked kissing you. I liked that the best."

Dammit, she's making my heart roll over, and there's no time and space for that.

"I liked it too," I say, but I can't let myself be fooled. I can't be Annie-fished again. I need to zero in on boundaries. "But obviously we're not going to do it again."

"Obviously." She agrees almost too quickly. "I don't sleep with sources, or people I interview."

She takes a drink from her yellow teacup then sets it down. Her drink has a sprig of mint in it. Mojito. Yeah, she obviously likes torturing the bartender, since those drinks are hard as hell to make. I tended bar briefly after college while working on my first start-up, and anyone who ordered that drink might as well have used me as a voodoo doll. It's best that I learn now she's an evil bartender-torturer.

She pushes the teacup away and lifts her chin, her jaw set hard. "And I'm *not* going to recuse myself from the story."

"I don't think you should recuse yourself."

"Good. Because I don't need to. I didn't know who you were when last night happened, so I wasn't sleeping with a subject then. And now that I do know, we'll proceed as if it's business as usual. Plus, I could wind up covering your company or your sector on an ongoing basis for this magazine, or honestly, for any publication, so it's best if we just move on." Her tone is all-business, no flirting, and no soft underside.

I nod in agreement because, hell yeah, do I agree. "Business as usual means I also don't sleep with people I work with." Though, to be fair, I've never confronted a situation where I considered sleeping with a reporter covering my company. Nonetheless, I get that it falls in the same Very Bad Idea category as sleeping with a business partner, investor, banker, or lawyer.

I haven't done those either.

See? I do deserve a lollipop.

"Besides," she adds as she lifts her teacup, "I can't risk this story. I have bills to pay, and I *need* this assignment . . ." Her voice trails off in a waft of desperation.

And the red warning buzzer goes off.

Money troubles.

She needs money.

Instinctively, my hand goes to my back pocket, covering my wallet. I'm a generous guy. I donate to charity, I've funded scholarships at my alma mater, and I have no problem sharing the wealth.

But it's good I'm learning her deal now. If she's mentioning money this early, then how would I ever know going forward if she likes me for me? I wouldn't. It's good the universe is looking out for me, giving me this info before I fall harder for her. Last night was one night, one moment, and that's all it'll ever amount to. I need to be ruthless about who I let into my heart.

"I have your halo still," I say, cool and businesslike.

She waves a hand dismissively. "I don't really need it."

"So I'll just toss it?"

"Sure," she answers, then furrows her brow. "But I do like the headband I used. Can you just hold on to it for me, and I'll get it next time?"

"I'll bring you the headband."

"You can just toss the other parts."

That feels fitting. I'll dismantle her halo, trash the fake money, and bring her the only part that matters. Just rip to pieces the thing she left behind.

There's one more item she discarded though.

I finish off the tequila, then reach into my pocket. "Here are your panties."

She stuffs them into her purse.

Like I said, I'm no Prince Charming.

Dirty or clean.

Prince Charming would have gotten the girl. Dirty Prince Charming would have found a way to take her home again, spread her out on the bed, and take her all night long.

Me? I'll be heading home alone to listen for little green men on the radio.

Before I leave, she lifts her chin and taps the bar. "By the way, I like your glasses."

13

Sabrina

If something is too good to be true, it usually is. That's what I've always taught my brother.

That's why I'm not in the least bit surprised.

Luck doesn't twirl around in spectacular fashion, transforming the beast into the prince before the last enchanted petal falls. Nope. That's the stuff of fairy tales. In real life, you don't get the gig, the guy, *and* the great sex.

You get one night with someone like Flynn Parker. The fairy tale ends when he returns your slipper. My panties are back, the story is over, and happily-ever-after is for fictional gals.

This is what happens next. The after-the-glass-slipper moment, when real life, real bills, and real responsibilities trump fairy-sparkle magic.

As I lock the door to my pipsqueak apartment, I sink against the wall, sliding to the floor on my butt.

I groan in frustration. I wish he was anyone else. I

wish he was the trash collector, the guy who runs the flower shop at the corner of my street, a product manager for an enterprise software company.

Anyone but the man I have to cover.

The cardinal rule of journalism is to be fair and get it right.

You can't be fair if you're sleeping with the subject.

You simply cannot.

And the story matters more to me than the guy, than the sex, than the stupendous spark, and the sizzle I felt with him last night and again tonight. Like when he leaned in close and told me all he remembered, and when he asked me about the first outfit I ever stitched together. When I shuddered from his nearness, from the way he seemed to want to own me. And, truth be told, the way I want to be owned. I want to hand over the keys to my body to someone who knows what to do with me.

To Flynn.

"Stupid fate," I grumble.

I dig my hand into my purse and take out my panties. They're clean. Freshly washed. I narrow my eyes. How the hell did the dude have time to launder my underwear? This is New York City. No one has a washer and dryer. We go to laundromats, or we send out our laundry.

Unless we're rich.

Super rich.

Lucky bastard probably has three washer-dryer combos.

Now I'm jealous, but it's also a reminder. Flynn and I live in different worlds. We're from opposite sides of the tracks. He's millions and I'm pennies, and it's for the best I learned this now. Opposites don't attract. They repel.

After I make myself a cheese sandwich—I do know

how to rock it when it comes to cheap eats—I FaceTime my brother.

"Want to hear a funny story?" I ask him on the screen.

"Of course I do."

"The guy I like?" I ask, since I told him this morning I met someone.

Kevin wiggles his eyebrows. "Oooh, guy talk. I was hoping for some guy talk before I returned to St. Thomas Aquinas."

"Oh stop. My guy talk has always been more interesting than a philosopher's mumbo-jumbo," I tease.

"Perhaps because it often requires me to be philosophical," he says, then flashes me his dimpled smile.

"I wish I could give you a knuckle sandwich through FaceTime."

"No, you don't. You love me and my non-knuckle-sandwiched face. So, tell me what happened. Did this one take off for Chile? Nova Scotia? The Arctic Circle?"

"He might as well have," I say with a sigh. "It turns out he's the guy I'm covering for my new article."

"Ouch," he says, frowning. "That would be a bit of an ethical quandary. Are you going to recuse yourself?"

I recoil, staring at him as if he were speaking in tongues. "No! I didn't know who he was when I met him at the party. I'm going to start this with a clean slate."

He nods, a thoughtful look in his eyes.

My chest squeezes. I need the money from this piece. My bills are looming. "Don't tell me you think that's a bad idea," I say, nerves thick in my voice.

He holds up his hands in surrender. "Of course I'm not going to say that. I'm simply processing the news. Trying to consider all the angles."

"Do you think I'm crossing a line?"

He sighs, and I brace myself for a yes. Kevin has always been a barometer for doing the right thing, and I've needed that, especially since our mom rarely does. Hell, our mom is the reason I don't eat roast beef. For my twelfth birthday, she asked what I wanted for a special dinner, and I told her I would love one of her delicious roast beef sandwiches.

"Consider it done," she said, then took me to the grocery store, snagged some cold cuts, stuffed them in her purse, and proceeded to earn her first shoplifting arrest.

It wasn't her last.

I stare at Kevin, swallowing as I wait for his answer.

"I don't think it's an issue," he says, and I picture him as a pastor, doling out advice to a congregant. "Just keep things on the business level with him going forward and that's the best you can do. You're not at fault for something you didn't know and I have faith you can do a fair, and fantastic, interview."

I smile. "Me too."

When I say goodbye to Kevin, I send an email to Flynn.

Not to Duke.

Not to Prince Charming. But to my source. To the man I'm interviewing.

I send it from my work address.

From: Sabrina G
To: Flynn Parker

Hello! I see we're meeting at your office, but can we change the location? I find people are more comfortable and open up more easily if we're not talking at their office.

We can have a thoughtful conversation if we're someplace else. Do you have a favorite spot?

From: Flynn Parker
To: Sabrina G

How much time do you need? I have lots of favorite places.

From: Sabrina G
To: Flynn Parker

An hour or two? Let me know one of your favorites.

Ten minutes later, he sends me an address that strikes my curiosity.

I haven't been there. Ever.

And that's saying something, because New York is *mine*.

I write back telling him I've never been there before, but that I'm looking forward to it.

I have a feeling that Flynn Parker is going to be one hell of an interesting guy to get to know over the next few days.

That's all he'll be though.

He's not the duke. He's not the guy from last night. I'll need to erase those fun, fond, flirty memories from the banks of my mind. These last few messages should help— they're so professional. So *worky, worky, work*.

I flop down on my bed, grab my laptop, and bury myself in research for the piece. A little later, my phone lights up with an alert. Probably an email from a friend, or a note about a new yard of fabric for sale at my favorite discount shop.

But some insistent little voice nudges me. Tells me to check it now because . . . what if?

I slide open the inbox, a flutter of excitement racing through me. The email is from Flynn, and it's not about the interview. It's a simple question: *Why should you never date an apostrophe?*

I scrunch my brow and then shout, "Aha!"

My fingers fly on the keys, tapping out a reply before I risk him sending me the answer: *Because they're too possessive!*

He answers swiftly, but this time his note zips over the transom of text. He's switched gears, shifting back to who we were last night.

The name I gave him on my text blinks.

Duke.

My heart dares to skitter in my chest, to bounce around madly.

Duke: What do you call Santa's elves?

Clutching my phone as if it's a source of joy, I squeeze my shoulders in delight, my grammar nerd heart lighting up. I swear it's glowing in my chest, and the warmth from it spreads to my toes, then my fingers. I think and think, and then the answer materializes, and I grin as I reply. This is more fun than 80s Trivial Pursuit. This is better than Boardwalk.

Angel: Subordinate Clauses!!

I'm rewarded with another grammar riddle seconds later.

Duke: What should you say to comfort a grammar nerd?

I narrow my eyes and chew on my lip, considering. Then, it hits me, like a bucket of social media grammatical errors slamming into me all at once.

Angel: They're, their, there.

I feel like we could go on all night. I want to, even though I know it's silly. Even though I know it's pointless.

But maybe that's the point of us flirting.

That it goes nowhere.

That it's a momentary buzz.

It's a quick whiff of expensive perfume in the department store. A nibble on a bite of decadent chocolate. A dance with the best-looking guy you've ever met.

You take your snippet of pleasure and you move on. That's all you get.

Angel: Did you know the last four letters in queue aren't silent?

I wait, and I wait, and three minutes later, his name appears.

Duke: I bet they're just waiting their turn.

Now it's my turn to move on.

14

Flynn

"In retrospect, maybe I shouldn't have sent that apostrophe email."

I wait for a response from my audience. She gives me none. I pace across the living room, checking out the view of Gramercy Park. "But in my defense, it was a good joke."

Still no answer.

"She liked it. I swear, she liked it," I insist.

Silence.

"Look, you'd have done the same, Zoe."

A delicious smile is my reward. My niece coos at me.

This kid. This sweet little baby. She melts me. "See? I knew you would laugh! You love my jokes. You cracked up when I told you the broccoli joke the first time I met you in the hospital room."

She smiles again, like the Mona Lisa, and I'm ready to give this little blonde baby anything in the cosmos she wants. I bounce my niece higher in my arms then drop a kiss to her soft forehead, taking a moment to inhale her baby scent as I pace around my sister's place, waiting for her to return from her morning workout.

"Knock, knock," I say, then answer for Zoe. "Who's there? Broccoli. Broccoli who? Broccoli doesn't have a last name, silly."

She emits a gurgling sound that makes it clear she remains my number-one fan, enjoying the joke as much as she did on her Birth day.

A lock clicks and the door to my sister's home opens. Olivia returns, her face flushed, her hair a little damp from sweating. "Who is my favorite brother in the entire universe?" She points both hands at me as Zoe squirms at the sound of her mom's voice. "I knew you'd win the Best of the Twin Brothers Olympics today."

I wipe my free hand over my forehead dramatically. "All I've ever wanted is to win the gold over Dylan."

She strides across the living room, reaching for her little girl, who squeals when she sees her mom. "Hello, my little love bug," Olivia says to the baby, then to me, she says, "If you keep babysitting in the wee hours of the morning when my husband has to spay a dozen Chihuahuas, you could pull far ahead in the brother race."

"A dozen?"

"Crazy, right? They were rescued from a puppy mill. Herb spayed them all, and now they're going to Little Friends to find homes," she says, naming one of the dog rescue shelters in the city.

"That's fantastic. Now, can you two stop being such do-gooders? You make the rest of us look bad."

She nudges me. "Speaking of doing good, how did your face-lift go the other night? I'm waiting for all the details."

I groan and drag a hand through my hair. "Too well."

"What does that mean?"

I give my sister the quick update, minus the wall-sex details, but including the I-met-this-awesome-woman-who-I-can't-see-again part.

"And you really like this girl?"

"I do. I mean, I did. Is that weird?"

"Why would it be weird that you liked her?"

"I only spent one evening with her. Isn't that too soon to really like somebody?" I stare at the ceiling, considering. "Okay, fine we texted later that night. And we did talk a little bit last night at the bar, even though we really weren't supposed to."

"So, it was almost like three dates."

I seesaw my hand. "Technically, one could make a case for a trio, yes."

She laughs, shooting me a warm smile, stripping her tone of our usual teasing. "You don't have to convince me. I knew after my first date with Herb that I was crazy for him. We just clicked."

I hold up my hands. "Whoa. I didn't say it was love at first sight."

She arches a brow. "It wasn't love at first sight. It was chemistry. It was attraction. It was mutual respect. Then, the more I got to know him, the more all of my initial first impressions were confirmed. Sometimes it happens quickly. Sometimes it happens over the course of years." She runs her hand over her daughter's hair as the baby snuggles closer to her. "Is there really no way you can make this work?"

I shake my head, adamant that, in spite of the grammar games, I can't go there again with Sabrina. "She's covering my company. I have to focus on Haven right now, and the huge opportunity we have in front of us," I say, and point to the door. "On that note, I should make my way to the office."

"Wait. Why can't you just see her when the story is over in a couple weeks?"

I stop with my hand on the doorknob, considering.

That's a good question.

I suppose we *could* do that.

But doing *that*, or rather, planning for it, sounds a little shady. A bit like hoodwinkery. Like we might as well be getting together.

And that's what we're trying to avoid.

Plus, a bigger reason looms.

A reason that I can't avoid. I can't let my desire to chat with Sabrina from the masquerade party make me forget that Sabrina the reporter might not have my best interests at heart.

She might only have hers front and center.

I shake my head. "I don't even know if I trust her. There's a part of me that wonders if she knew who I was all along."

Olivia stares at me, her expression soft. "You really think she was deceiving you?"

I shrug. "I don't know. That's the issue."

I power through work, focused on the three o'clock meet-up time. I cruise through contracts, review more marketing plans, make calls, and even conduct some of the other phone interviews Jennica has set up for the rollout.

Later that day, Carson and I go over the early numbers

in my office. He's nervous, shaking his knee as we chat. "We can stave off ShopForAnything. It's looking good so far, and I want everything to go well."

"Yeah, me too." I give him a curious look. "Hey, are you okay? You seem out of sorts today."

He sighs heavily. "Yeah, sorry. My mom is starting radiation next week."

My heart sinks. "Sorry, man. How is she doing? Do you need to take some time off to help her out?"

He shakes his head. "No, she'll be okay. I just want to make sure everything here launches without a hitch. I can't afford to let ShopForAnything chase us down right now, know what I mean?"

I nod. I do know. He's worried about his job. He doesn't want to lose it at a time like this in his personal life. He doesn't want us to be stomped on by the competition.

"We are going to crush it," I say with confidence. Complete and utter confidence.

When he leaves my office, I renew that promise.

"We're going to crush it," I say to myself.

That's the reason I can't dally around with *what happens in two weeks* scenarios, and I can't keep firing off flirty texts to the woman from the masquerade party.

I need to zero in on the goal—leading my company through these rougher waters.

There will be time, eventually, to think about women, about trust, and about falling for someone.

But that time isn't now.

The trouble is, when I see Sabrina that afternoon at the subway station, I wish she'd stop smiling at me like she was also wanting all the things we can't have.

15

Sabrina

His green eyes gleam as he walks to me on the sidewalk by the Fifty-first Street subway station. He's holding something in his hand. I can't quite tell what it is, since his fist is closed. He stops inches away and for a brief moment, I imagine him kissing me on the cheek, or perhaps embracing me with a hello hug.

My heart beats a little faster. Stupid hopeful thing.

Instead, he simply smiles. "Hey."

"Hi."

"I have something for you."

"What do you have?"

"I conducted a very daring halo-dismantling mission last night. The wire nearly nicked my hand, and the Monopoly money tried to give me paper cuts, but I soldiered on." Flynn uncurls his fist and hands me the headband.

I tuck it into my purse. "Thank you. I appreciate you

risking life and limb for a hair accessory." I lower my voice to a whisper. "It's a favorite of mine."

"A duke always tackles dangerous tasks for a lady's lovely hair," he says and tingles spread down my chest from that private little reminder.

I curtsy and nod in a demure thank you.

His eyes drift toward the subway entrance. "And look. We won't even have to *queue* up for the train." He winks.

I laugh at the reminder of our clandestine exchange last night, as I give him a furtive once-over. It's hard not to, since I like looking at him so much now that I can see all of him. Of course, I liked looking at him on Sunday night too, even shrouded by the mask. With it removed, he's so handsome it hurts, but it hurts so good.

He wears jeans, brown shoes, and a dark-blue button-down, untucked. The cuffs are rolled up, revealing his forearms. Racquetball arms, I think. When I researched him, I read that he plays racquetball for a hobby, as well as softball, and I wonder if those sports have made him lean and ropey.

I raise my gaze quickly to his face, cataloging his features.

Flynn Parker has a boyish charm about him, with his clean-shaven jaw, twinkling eyes behind simple black frames, and flawless skin. But I doubt he shaved this morning. Stubble lines his square jaw and makes me wonder deliciously dirty things about how his face would feel against my thighs.

Things I should not entertain.

Especially since the prospect of his scruff near my lady parts is dangerously arousing.

I conduct a clean sweep and focus on the article, donning my imaginary super-reporter cape. "Thank you for making time for me. I'm curious about your favorite place."

He gestures toward the stairwell that leads underground. "Let us go then, you and I."

I grab his arm. "Did you just quote T.S. Eliot to me?"

"Hmm. Seems I did."

I shake my head, amused and turned on. "I was an English major. That's not fair."

An impish grin appears. "What's not fair about it?"

"You can't quote the first line of a great love poem to an English major. Shame on you," I admonish playfully, but I'm being honest too. He sounds too seductive reciting poetry.

"*Let us go then, you and I, when the evening is spread out against the sky,*" he whispers, and my skin tingles.

"Bad boy."

"Do you like bad boys?"

"Now I do."

I'm flirting. I'm flirting times ten. I should stop. I really should.

"I'll keep it up, then. *She walks in beauty like the night.*"

My pulse beats faster, and it's too hard to stop when he quotes poetry. "You're very bad, Lord Byron."

"*Shall I compare thee to a summer's day?*" he begins, and the little hairs on my arms rise in excitement, anticipation.

"You. Must. Stop."

He tilts his head, and screws up the corner of his lips, fixing on a comical expression. "Arr, I'll talk like a pirate then, ahoy, matey."

I roll my eyes. "You're terrible."

Laughing, he tips his forehead to my skirt as we head down the stairwell. "I'll shift gears for you. Is today's outfit homemade?"

I'm wearing a simple black skirt with a pale pink satin ribbon down one side. "Yes. I suppose I'm predictable." I glance at my skirt, which hits mid-thigh. I like them short, always have. Flynn seems to, as well, since his gaze follows mine and lingers on my legs.

"You're hardly predictable. It's more like a fun discovery each time I see you."

"You're kind of weirdly fascinated with my clothes," I say as our shoes smack against the concrete, but truth be told, I like his interest in my wardrobe. I care about what I wear. I love making my clothes, and the fact that he notices—well, it delights me.

"It's not so much that I'm fascinated. I'm more curious and impressed with how handy you are. I suppose, in a post-apocalyptic world, you'd have a seriously usable skill to barter with."

I crack up. "That's exactly why I learned to sew. To trade services at the end of the world. Speaking of, how will *you* manage, Mr. CEO? Will you organize the first company to sell post-apocalyptic supplies?"

"Maybe." He scratches his jaw. "Or perhaps I'd start an escort business."

My eyebrows shoot up. "You'd have time for an escort business?"

"I'd make time for it. One, pleasure would be at a premium when the fate of the world hangs in the balance. Two, what if it's not really the end of the world? It'd be good to have a business that can transition. Three, I have a feeling I'd be excellent at it, and it would make my final days brighter."

"You are indeed prepared for a doomsday scenario. I'm impressed."

We head past the turnstiles and into the muggy

station, waiting for the 6 train. "Also, I assume you're good with us chatting for the piece as we ride the subway?"

"Absolutely. It was my idea, after all." He taps his chest, a look of pride in his eyes. "And I'm pretty damn proud of myself for finding something you haven't done."

"Me too," I say, bouncing on the toes of my short gray boots. "Especially since I've lived in New York or around it my entire life, and I've never actually seen the abandoned City Hall subway station."

He wiggles his eyebrows. "There's a first time for everything, then."

Like sex with a stranger at a masquerade party.

But that night was both a first and a last time, I remind myself.

I take out my phone, hit record on my voice recorder app, and clear my throat. "Tell me about the robot you made when you were a kid."

He shoots me a curious look. "Why are you asking about the robot?"

"I suspect Mr. Cardboard Robot has significance in the story I want to tell about Flynn Parker, the next generations business visionary." I peer down the tracks. No sign of the train. "The robot was one of the first things you made. Did you always want to create?"

He strokes his chin. "Ah, she assembles the clues, like Inspector Poirot."

My eyebrows shoot up. "I love him."

"He's badass," Flynn says of Agatha Christie's Belgian detective. Flynn strokes an imaginary mustache, the crime solver's trademark.

I lean in closer and whisper, "So glad you don't have one of those curlicue mustaches."

He mirrors me, sliding near and dropping his volume.

"Me too." He steps back. "So, you want to understand the role of the robot in my life story."

"I do." I've started the interview with a relatively easy question, but at the same time, it's one that I hope will open a door, that will give me a chance to look around, to shine a flashlight into the corners of his mind that he might not normally share.

I want to find out who he is. Yes, he's a man who creates—experiences, products, companies. But what led him in that direction?

He lifts his chin. "Why do you ask that question?"

I grin. "You're turning the tables around and interviewing me?"

"I'll answer, but I like knowing the reason."

I like being asked. I like that he makes me think, that he seems to poke and prod at me too. "I ask because at the heart of it, being a visionary is often pictured as thinking deep thoughts about what's to come. But most true visionaries aren't only gazing at the future. They're not afraid to get their hands dirty either. Do you agree?"

"I'm definitely not afraid to get my hands dirty at all," he says, skirting this close to the naughty line, but not quite stepping over it.

I must steer clear of the line, too, so I stay the course. "I want to know if there was a lightbulb moment when you knew what you wanted to do in life. When everything clicked into place."

With his eyes locked with mine, he shakes his head. "No."

I shoot him a skeptical stare. "That surprises me."

"It's the truth. I can't isolate a moment when the lightbulb went off because it's always going off. I can't remember a time when I didn't want to build something big. Something exciting. Something innovative."

My skepticism vanishes. "It's as if that drive in you was pre-memory. Before you were even aware of *wanting* it."

He taps his nose. "Exactly. I've always built things. I've always wanted to. I don't know how not to."

"What sort of things did you make when you were a kid?" I hold my phone, soaking up the details that he shares as we wait for the train.

"Everything. Jigsaw puzzles. A huge Lego pirate boat sculpture. A catapult. A candy dispenser. After that, I made a tree house, a doghouse, and a swing set at my home in Connecticut."

"Wow," I say, my eyes widening as he lists his projects, and I ask what his inspiration was for each.

"Pirates are cool. Catapults are cooler. Candy is the coolest."

"Good, better, best."

"Exactly. Plus, tree houses are the definition of fun."

"And the robot? What inspired that?"

A sheepish grin spreads on his face. "Naturally, *Star Wars* did. After I saw that flick for the first time I wanted my own R2-D2, so I built one out of cardboard."

"Did it talk in a sort of boop-beep way and hold all of the secret plans of the rebellion?"

"I wish," he says, a look of pure desire in his eyes, as if that truly would have been the greatest thing ever. "But even though it was cardboard and flimsy, I was hooked. I couldn't stop making things."

There's a tightness in his voice, but it's not tension. It's excitement. It's determination.

"You lived with intention from an early age," I say as I absorb what he's telling me.

"I suppose I did."

A loud rattle echoes down the tunnel as the train approaches. We talk as it chugs into the station and creaks to a stop. Once we board and the doors close, I ask more questions and he answers, and as we travel downtown I begin to see the watercolor of Flynn Parker filling in. Colors, shapes, details. I start to understand the picture of who he is.

On the outside, he's the math nerd. The smarty pants. The tall guy with glasses who aced all his classes, can recite pi to a hundred digits, and has taught himself Japanese.

But he's more than that.

His drive isn't about numbers or circuit breakers. His drive is passion. The kind that insists on being heard, like a drumbeat. It's a flame that can't be extinguished.

He tips his chin toward me. "What about you and writing? Did you have a nose for news at a young age?"

"When I was a little girl, I wanted to be a fashion designer."

"Why aren't you, then?" His tone is completely earnest, and curious as well.

The answer is easy. "I don't think I have the vision for it."

He frowns. "Don't say that."

I hold up a hand and shake that thought away. "No, it's okay. I'm not putting myself down. I'm really okay with it. I have no regrets. I'd much rather play around with somebody else's pattern. It's what I thought I wanted to do, but it wasn't what I *actually* wanted to do, even though I do love making outfits."

"But you don't have the passion for it as a career?"

"Exactly. But being a reporter absolutely feeds something I love."

He leans closer, his palms on his thighs, his eyes holding mine. "What's that, Sabrina?"

I love that he's asking me these questions. I adore that he's curious. Because that's what I'm enamored of.

"I love curiosity," I answer. "I love understanding things. I desperately want to understand people, what makes them tick. That's why I do what I do."

"Desperation can be a good thing. We should love our careers desperately if we're going to give so much to them."

"Desperate love," I repeat, liking the sound of that. "Yes, we should love desperately. Especially work, since it's often more reliable than the romantic kind."

He laughs lightly, one of those *you're preaching to the choir* laughs, and I wonder if he's had the shit kicked out of him by love too. If perhaps he's so passionate about work because, like me, he's been on the receiving end of a steel-toed boot. Maybe someday I'll ask, but it doesn't feel like it should be an interview question.

"So, you do love what you do?" he asks.

"I do, Inspector Poirot."

"And you also love understanding new things?"

"I do."

A slow grin forms, and he strokes an imaginary mustache. "You'll like where I'm taking you, then."

"The abandoned subway station, you mean? I read that we can see it on the train at the turnaround. You can catch a glimpse as the train loops around before it heads back uptown."

"That's true. You can absolutely see it through the

window. But you can also take a tour if you know the right people."

My eyes widen as surprise courses through me. "You arranged for a tour?"

He shrugs happily. "I thought you might like that."

I do. I do like it.

And I like him.

Which is the thing I most can't afford right now, and the list of things I can't afford is miles long.

16

Sabrina

Scads of New Yorkers scurry off the six line at the last stop. They exit, heading above ground or making connections, continuing with their day. But we stay on.

"Come here," Flynn says, offering his hand as the doors close.

I take his palm, standing, and he guides me to the scratched, dirty window of the closed door. We peer out, staring at the tiled wall of the platform, his hand pressed to the small of my back. It's hard for me to not think about his touch. It's gentle and firm at the same time, and my mind can't help but assemble images of his hand sliding under my shirt, along my flesh.

I suppress a tremble as the train chugs out of the station, heading into the curving loop at the bottom of the line. "You have to smush your face against the window to get a really good view."

"Commencing smushing," I say mechanically. I look at him. "Am I like the robot you built as a kid?"

He scoffs. "If I'd designed a robot that looked and sounded like you, I would still be building robots."

A blush creeps across my cheeks. A flutter skids down my chest. I will them away, doing my best to ignore these sensations. It's pointless to linger on them. When this story ends, I'll still need to focus on work, finding a job, and perhaps covering his business regularly—a direct conflict of interest to any flutters, no matter how they make me feel. I can't entertain the idea of whether we could try again then, because it's not a possibility. I'm simply going to enjoy the time with him for what it is.

An interview. A fun interview. The phone in my hand, recording us, is a reminder of that.

We stand by the window as the train rumbles forward at a more leisurely pace this time, as if it knows that its job is to let us catch a glimpse of the past.

"Look," he whispers, almost reverently, pointing to what's beyond the scratched glass as the train curves into the loop.

I gasp quietly. It's like entering a time warp. We've slipped back decades. The old, abandoned station is a marvel of days gone by. It's New York in another era, with vaulted ceilings made of glittering tiles, and stained-glass windows, with mosaics lining the walls. Brass chandeliers hang from the ceiling, hearkening to days when New York was a city of splendor and gold.

"It reminds me of where we met. The hotel. It had that olden glamour feel," I say.

"Yes. This is the same. The city in days gone by. This station was the crown jewel of the transit system, designed by a renowned architect, and yet they had to shutter the station because it couldn't accommodate the longer trains. It could only handle five-car trains. It was too curved, too round, so in 1945, they shut it down," he tells me as we circle past it, the tracks serving as a mere turnaround, offering a now-you-see-me-now-you-don't view into what once was.

"Why is this your favorite place? Because you only catch a glimpse of it?" I offer, trying to understand what excites him about the abandoned stop.

He shakes his head. "It reminds me that we can all become obsolete at any moment. It reminds me that success is fleeting." He sweeps his arm out wide, gesturing to the grandeur that has no purpose anymore. "You can have the best transit system in the entire world, and if you don't plan for the future it can be shut down."

Nodding, I let that little nugget of insight soak into my brain. A part of me almost hates how quickly I agree with him. I want to quiz him, to poke a hole in his argument, like a good journalist. But I can't because his observation rings wholly true. "I can see that. It's like a beautiful warning."

"Precisely. A reminder that at any moment we might be shut down."

"Haven?"

He nods. "This station is incredible, and I love it, but I don't want my company to become a relic."

"Can I quote you on that?" I ask, because this feels personal, as if we're diving into territory that needs the consent confirmed.

"Of course."

He points to the station as we leave it in the rearview. "This is a recognition that there is so much to look out for —the past, the present, and the future. You have to adapt to the changes so that your train can keep using the tracks."

"Love the metaphor." I study his face for a moment. "You kind of remind me of old New York."

"I should be shut down?"

"No," I say, adamantly. "I mean *you*. There's something about you. You're thoroughly modern, but I could see you fitting into the Gatsby era."

"*So we beat on, boats against the current, borne back ceaselessly into the past*," he says, quoting the last line in F. Scott Fitzgerald's most famous work. "Another warning not to repeat the mistakes of the past. Or, wait. Should I not quote Fitzgerald? Same rule as T.S. Eliot for you, Miss English major?"

"Exactly. You're asking for trouble," I say, smiling, since I'm amused, maybe even overwhelmed by Flynn. He has so many layers. I want to keep peeling away at them, peeking at what lurks inside. "You're an interesting man. You're not just a math nerd. You're a Renaissance man."

"Is that so?"

I nod resolutely. "You are."

He shrugs, and his lips curve into a smile. It's one of those *I'll take it* grins, and I love it.

When we exit, I turn off the recorder and tuck my phone away. I've accomplished some of what I've come to do today. I understand what motivates him. He's a man of learning, not only a numbers guy. He finds inspiration everywhere. That's what makes him tick.

Perhaps he's figured out it's my jam, too, because I love the tour.

He's a member of the New York City Transit Museum, and they offer private tours for its members. A docent shows a small group of us through the once splendid subway station and I drink in the mosaics, the architecture, the feel of old New York, as well as the stories of the master artisans and the architect who worked on this station.

For an hour or so, I feel as if I'm transported to another era, as if I'm in New York before my own time and before all my own troubles. On this fine June evening, I've made my great escape and I'm existing in a slip of the past, a whisper amidst the storm.

When we're done, I thank the docent and we head aboveground.

"That was amazing," I say, practically bouncing. "I'm almost ashamed I've lived here so long and I haven't done that."

"Don't be ashamed. Be glad you did it. I think there are so many things right in front of us that we don't do. We don't always take advantage of what we have. I try as much as I can, but you can't get to everything."

"Do you try because a great idea for work might come from doing something unexpected?"

He shakes his head vigorously. "I suppose it's a welcome by-product if it happens, but no. I like new experiences in and of themselves. I like learning for learning's sake. I do it for that reason, whether it has an obvious benefit or not."

There he goes again, amassing points he isn't even trying to earn as he stimulates my mind with his thirst for knowledge. He's everything I like, and exactly what I must avoid.

He's a risk I can't take.

But he'd be a risk no matter what. Even if it wasn't a conflict of interest to date him, it would be a hell of a conflict to my wounded heart. I already like Flynn Parker too much for my own good. I can only imagine how much it would hurt when he left me.

Because he would. We'd date, and laugh, and screw, and talk, and visit all the hidden spots in New York.

Then he'd leave.

He'd be done.

He'd break my heart.

"By the way," he says, "do you know there are several other abandoned subway stops around the city? You can see some of them when you ride the train if you know where to look."

"I'd love to see them," I say wistfully, hoping I'll do as he suggests, hoping I'll take advantage of everything that's truly in front of me.

I'll be doing it alone, but I'll do it. I want to experience all that the city has to offer. Now that I've ditched the dress, it's time to immerse myself in living again, experiencing things anew.

He looks at his watch. "Come to think of it, I don't have anything going on at the moment. Do you want to check them out now?"

My skin tingles. The birds sing. The sun kicks its heels in the sky.

But a voice reminds me—*he's a risk you can't take.*

I silence the voice. There's nothing risky about doing this because nothing will happen with Flynn. Not now, and not in two weeks.

"I do want to."

I'm not dating him, and we're not together, nor can we be, so he can't hurt me. He can't stab me in the back with a rusty serrated knife and move halfway around the world, going radio silent.

Flynn is work, and we are professionals who like

spending time together. There's nothing more to it, and my heart is safely locked in the steel cage I built for it with the remains of my failed un-wedding.

That's what I tell myself as we ride past the Worth Street stop and he points out the shuttered station's name on the tiled columns, then the closed Eighteenth Street station that's now merely a home for graffiti.

When we finish checking out the hidden treasures of the city's transit system, I feel refreshed and vibrant, like I've gone on a great date.

In an alternate world, this date would lead to me taking him back to my tiny place, grabbing the collar of his shirt, and yanking him close. He'd push me against my kitchen counter, spread my legs, and fuck me. A spark tears through me like a fire lit and roaring as I imagine Flynn parting my thighs, tearing off my panties, and filling me.

So deep.

So good.

I could get lost in him. I could get lost in his kiss, his rough and tender touch. I could disappear into bliss, and let it consume my hurt. The pleasure would burn away any lingering ache from the past.

We could be Angel and Duke again for a night.

But us too. I want to know how it feels to be us *and* to be them.

I want that because this feels like the best date I've been on in ages.

That's why when I'm home that night, I resist every urge to text him and tell him what fun I had. I abstain from sending him math jokes or grammar puns. That would be something I'd do post-date and this—this was work.

That echoes through my mind as we set a time for our next interview. Because that will only be work as well.

That way, he can't become Ray.

He can't leave me for no reason.

Because I won't let him in.

But he texts me the next day. As the duke.

17

Flynn

Duke: What's your favorite place?

Angel: Too many to name.

Duke: You made me pick.

Angel: Made you pick? Did I twist your arm?

Duke: Yes. My wrist still hurts from your sheer, brute strength.

Angel: I'm powerful.

Duke: Like a genie. Incidentally, you'd look good in a genie costume. Just saying.

Angel: You'd look good in many costumes—an earl, a prince, a pirate, a bandit, a highwayman . . .

Duke: You have such a fascination with olden times.

Angel: Yes, I do. Regency, Victorian, historical—give me breeches and I'm a-swooning.

Duke: Next time, I'll be donning a waistcoat and a top hat.

Angel: I fainted in a most ladylike fashion. See? It really does work.

Duke: Excellent, m'lady.

Angel: Also, I'm so sorry I hurt your wrist with that hard twist I gave. That was cruel of me.

Duke: Now that I think of it, maybe that's *not* why my wrist hurts. :)

Angel: You're naughty.

Duke: Naughty? Me? Why would you say that?

Angel: Your wrist hurts? Okay, my fingers hurt!

Duke: My wrist hurts from racquetball. Did you think I meant something else?

Angel: You know what I think you meant.

Duke: Spell it out for me. What did you think I was doing that made my wrist sore?

Angel: Gee. I wonder.

Duke: You need to get your mind out of the gutter, Angel.

Angel: You led it there, Duke.

Duke: Somehow, I think you can find the gutter on your own.

Angel: Guilty as charged. But back to favorite places. Why do you want me to pick one?

Duke: Hello? Our next interview. You're allergic to offices, and since I took you to one of my favorite spots, it's your turn to choose one for our next chat. Name some.

Angel: My favorite place in all of New York City is New York City. :)

Duke: Clever.

Angel: But I'd also have to add Central Park, the hidden underground gin joint in Chelsea, the small Elevator Museum in Tribeca, the Starry Night locksmith in the West Village, one of the street artists in the East Village, the Met, and I think I would probably also love Gramercy Park.

Duke: Tomorrow, let's do the Elevator Museum. I've never been.

Angel: I'll be there.

Duke: Also, why did you say you think you'd like Gramercy Park?

Angel: It sounds lovely, but I've never been there.

Duke: You haven't?

Angel: It's a private park. You need a key.

Duke: I have one.

* * *

I stare in disbelief at the former freight elevator shaft that's now a strange museum. "It's actually an elevator. And it's the size of a car."

She nods, a hint of mischief in her eyes as she bounces on her pink-booted feet. Pink boots I want to see on my shoulders.

I blink away the filthy thought, even though it'll surely return in seconds.

"It's the smallest museum in all of New York. It's five square meters," she says as we step inside and ogle the odd displays lining all three walls.

"And it's weird. Admit it. This is intensely weird." I spin in a circle, gesturing to the tubes of toothpaste on the shelves, the crushed coffee cups and bags of potato chips. Each object has a letter and a number in front of it, like you could enter it on a vending machine keypad.

Only the tubes and bags and cups aren't for sale.

They're crushed, stepped on, trampled. The exhibit placard reads *"Found objects from the streets of Manhattan."*

I study the objects, searching for hidden meaning but find none. I shrug and glance at Sabrina. "I don't want to be one of those 'why is this art' people, but . . . why is this art?"

"I don't know that it's art, so much as it's odd," she says, crossing her arms as she regards the display here in Tribeca on the tip of Chinatown.

I scrub a hand over my jaw, thinking. Trying to connect the dots. "So it's odd. Is that why we're supposed to like it?"

"I don't even know if we have to like it." She waves a hand at a shelf of discarded honey-roasted chip bags. "I like that it's entertaining. That it's strange. It makes me think about all sorts of things."

"Okay, Rodin," I say, naming the sculptor whose most famous work was dubbed The Thinker. "What do these trampled-on toothpaste tubes make you marinate on up there?"

Smiling, she studies a wrinkled bag. *Fire-hot*, it promises. "It makes me think about things we overlook. Things we ignore."

"But shouldn't an empty bag of chips be ignored?"

"No." Her tone is strong, laced with unexpected emotion.

I step back, giving her some space. "No?"

"You should clean it up. Throw it out."

"Fine, true," I concede. "I wasn't advocating being a slob. And I'm totally against litter. But why do old tubes of toothpaste and empty bags of chips affect you?"

As she stares at the display, sadness flickers across her eyes. Her lips form a straight line, then she breathes in deep. "I think people, places, and things get ignored. And this exhibit forces us to see what we'd rather ignore. Every day, we walk past uncomfortable sights, we weave around painful conversations. And other people ignore us. I guess I like this place because it reminds me *not* to do that."

As I study a coffee cup with tire tracks on it, I suspect she might be onto something—a universal sort of truth about human nature. "How to be a better human," I say.

"Yes." Her lips curve into a grin. "That's what I would call this exhibit."

"So you're saying that perhaps looking at trash—displaced objects—makes us think how we can treat each other better?"

"I do believe that. Is that cheesy?" she asks nervously, her right hand fluttering to her hair, patting her silver bow-shaped barrette. Her phone's not recording, and I like that we can enjoy a few moments just for us, not for print.

"No. You actually made sense of something that I saw as kind of pointless, to tell the truth. I don't know that I now consider it art, but I guess it does make me think a little more deeply about what we ignore. I'd like to believe I don't ignore the people who matter. I went to see my sister and her baby earlier this week. I try to see them every week," I say, maybe because I'm looking for points.

Sabrina's warm smile tells me I've tallied several with that. But her smile disappears as she returns her focus to the display. "That's good, because no one wants to be ignored. I don't like it. I don't like being discarded."

I draw a deep breath to ask a hard question, since I think she wants me to ask it. "Did someone do that to you?"

"Yes," she says sharply, then fixes a pinched smile on

her face as she spins and faces me. "And I didn't like it. But that's that. I've moved on."

As I wonder who he was, a spark of anger ignites in my chest. Because some guy hurt her, and that pisses me off. What kind of idiot would let a woman like Sabrina become displaced?

Whether she wants to talk in detail or not, I won't stand by and let her think I don't care, when I care deeply —more than I expected I would.

I touch her shoulder. "I'm glad you've moved on and I feel one hundred percent confident that whoever he was, he's a complete jerk who tramples on people, and tubes of toothpaste."

Her smile is genuine now, and she whispers a wobbly "thank you" then squares her shoulders. "Speaking of discarded things, let's put your brainpower to use." She raps her knuckles against my head.

"Activating brain power for your usage," I say robotically.

Her laughter is pretty, like bells. "Want to chat about your college days now?" She holds up the phone, ready to record.

"I was wondering why you haven't hit that button yet."

"We were just talking for fun before." She shrugs playfully. "Besides, I figure all this pre-talking will get you buttered up and ready to spill all."

I laugh. "Thanks for the warning. So the museum is a warm-up act to me sharing everything about college?"

"It sort of frees both our minds from the usual grind, don't you think?"

I consider this, then nod my agreement. She does make a good point.

"By all means." I gesture to the sidewalk and we stroll

through Tribeca, passing shops and bakeries, boutiques and hip stores. I tell her about my days as a math major, the things I learned, and how that set the stage for starting my first company, and at a corner bodega, I stop, pointing to a pineapple for sale.

"Do you like pineapple?"

"Duh. Isn't it impossible to dislike pineapple?"

"It is. But did you know pineapples are math?"

She squints. "Explain."

I grab a spiky fruit, hand a few bills to the vendor, then spot an artichoke and a cauliflower. I add those to the order, and soon we find a table at a café up the street.

She shoots me a quizzical look. "We're making artichoke, pineapple, and cauliflower salad? I'm admittedly a little skeptical."

"No salad is forthcoming. But this pineapple is why I studied math," I say, spinning the fruit in a circle.

She takes out her phone and hits the record button once again.

This is the interview portion, the reminder that even though the time at the museum felt like a quirky little date, Sabrina and I are now on the clock for her article. Hell, I need the reminder because it's too easy to get lost in how I feel with her.

Carefree. Happy. Easy.

As if I'm simply enjoying getting to know someone I like.

Someone I like a lot.

I can't have that someone, though, and that's why I need these moments. These reminders of who we are when she clicks on her recording app. But maybe these not-dates, these work-slash-fun slivers of time, are what I need more than falling for someone. Maybe I need to have fun with a woman and not worry about what she's after.

With Sabrina, I haven't felt that worry since the night at The Dollhouse. I didn't experience it on the subway, and I don't feel it tonight either. The time with her is like a rejuvenation. It's refreshing, as if her curious spirit and inquisitive mind are restoring my faith in humanity.

She pokes the pineapple and looks at me expectantly, waiting for my explanation.

I turn the pineapple around, showing her the spirals that comprise its hard, rough skin. "See? They fall in patterns."

"They do?"

Enthusiasm courses through me, and my geekery emerges in full force. This shit is awesome. "Mother Nature is amazing. Mother Nature loves math. Plants love sequences. The Fibonacci sequence is one, two, three, five, eight, thirteen, twenty-one, and so on. Basically, you add up the prior two numbers to get to the next one. And what you have here is the Fibonacci sequence. Pineapple spirals only appear in one of the numbers in this sequence."

I take her hand and bring her index finger to one of the spirals, dragging it down the scales. Silently, her lips move, counting. A row of five. A row of eight. A row of thirteen.

Slowly, she raises her face, her eyes sparkling with astonishment, as if she's found buried treasure. "Mind. Blown."

"Nature is actually completely dependent on math. You see these beautiful patterns all across the world. The same is true for the cauliflower spirals," I say, running her fingers across the florets in the vegetable. "And the artichoke too. Sunflowers follow the same pattern. Math is literally all around us."

She shakes her head in amazement. "I had no idea."

"It's cool, isn't it? Math doesn't dwell in a quiet little separate space, but it can intersect with nature and ideas."

"Evidently." Her eyes drift down to my hand still on hers, and maybe because I'm amped up on the Fibonacci sequence, I don't analyze what I do next.

I do it.

I thread our fingers together, and a spark of pleasure rips through me. From *that*. From that bit of contact. From the thrill of holding her hand.

A quiet gasp escapes her lips, and then she tightens her fingers around mine, grasping. She nibbles on the corner of her lips, something she did the night we spent together, and it shoots me back in time to those seconds before we kissed in the library.

I swallow. My throat is dry. Somehow, I manage to keep talking. "Math is the foundation of my business, in a lot of ways. Numbers serve as the core, and I build ideas on that. I've always taken that approach. That's what excites me in business—taking patterns and numbers and then marrying them with what people might want next."

"I know what I want next," she whispers.

Her sultry tone is like a dart of lust straight to my chest. It stokes the fire in me. "You do?"

"I can't have it, but I want it."

She laces her fingers tighter, running her thumb along my skin, triggering a fresh wave of sparks within me.

From her thumb stroking my flesh.

One simple touch and I don't know if we're talking about the interview, or business, or math, or what we like. But I don't care, because talking to her is what I like.

"You," she whispers, her honeyed voice like a caress. "I probably shouldn't say this, but it turns me on to no end that you're this math god and that's your foundation, and then you layer T.S. Eliot on top of it, or you put *Gatsby* on top of it, and you think about whether random things are art or ethics."

I lean closer. "If it's any consolation, you're not the only one turned on."

She draws a breath, then lets it out in a sexy, needy moan.

"Sabrina," I warn. "This is dangerous."

She squeezes my hand. "So dangerous," she says, lowering her face, averting her gaze. "I'm trying not to launch myself at you right now."

"I suppose I ought to be a gentleman and say I'd resist you . . . but I wouldn't."

She looks up and lets go of my hand. "Okay, you're too tempting. You practically seduced me with a pineapple and the Fibonacci sequence."

I pump a fist. "Nerds for the win."

She laughs and turns off the recorder. "Okay, hot nerd. Let's get out of here before you seduce me with a cauliflower next."

"Don't forget the artichoke. It's willing to offer services for seduction."

"And the artichoke would probably render me helpless to resist too. Ergo," she says, pausing to press her hands against the table as she rises, breaking the moment for good, "we should go. I have one more favorite place for us today."

I don't say no. I want this next non-date, artichoke or not. "Take me where you want to go."

"I'm going to take you to the locksmith in the Village."

It sounds quaint and provincial, but when we arrive I see it's more than that. The front of the shop in the Village is covered in a replica of Van Gogh's *Starry Night* made entirely of keys, forming swirls and spirals like the famous painting.

"The guy who owns this shop recreated *Starry Night* with twenty thousand keys that he kept over the years," she explains as I step toward the wall, raising my hand.

I run my finger over the bumpy metallic surface. "It's like he wanted to leave his mark on the neighborhood."

"Yes," Sabrina says. "That's what I think too. The Village has become home to condos and fancy restaurants, but this is a sort of homage to days gone by, when this place was an artist's enclave. And this craftsman, whose business could have been kicked out or shut down, has turned his storefront into a sculpture."

"Found art, like found math in nature," I say, musing on the possibilities.

"Or maybe a reminder of change? The artists who used to live in the Village can't afford it anymore. Hardly anyone can afford to live in Manhattan."

Her observation raises another question—how can she afford it?

I don't even have to ask. The question must be in my eyes, because she jumps in. "If you're wondering, I can only afford to live in Manhattan because I'm staying in my cousin's apartment. She's gallivanting around Europe, and she lets me stay there for basically a nickel, and God knows I need her generosity."

The money talk again. I tense, a bolt of worry slamming down my spine as she mentions the very thing that often separates people. Money is a dividing line. Is she trying to figure out how it divides us? How money changes what people want from you?

Once again, I'm left wondering if it plays a part in her wants. That warning voice speaks louder, a reminder that trust must be earned.

Fully.

"I love that you're kind of obsessed with what New York was. Its past," I say, so I can dodge the thorny subject of incomes, and how I can afford to live in New York twenty times over and how she's living off her cousin's kindness.

"I am, and it's probably a pointless obsession. We can't really cling to the past. God knows I've had to move on from so many other things."

That's an issue I don't want to dodge though. I want to know what holds her back, beyond work. I want to understand where that sadness comes from. "Do you mean ex-boyfriends or family?"

"Both," she says heavily. "My ex was pretty much the worst, and my mother is pretty much the worst too."

"The ex—he's totally out of the picture?"

She tucks a strand of hair behind her ear. "He's so far out of the picture he lives in China. We were supposed to be married, and he left me two days before the wedding."

"Jesus," I mutter. "He's not fit to pick up the potato chip bags you walk on."

She smiles. "I know. And I'm glad I'm over him."

A warm, golden feeling spreads through my chest, blatantly ignoring my concerns about trust, overtaking them, even. "I'm glad you're over him too."

* * *

The next day, Jennica pops into my office. "Any chance you'd want to talk to Kermit?"

I remember the halo from the party, and him hard pitching me on an interview, then commenting on the halo, like he knew what had happened.

I shake my head. "I'd rather not."

She presses her palms together in a plea. "He's pretty insistent, and he does have a great reach. Will you reconsider?"

Sighing heavily, I lean back in my leather chair, thinking. I need to make sure my focus remains on Haven— always on Haven. These people depend on me. As much as the guy irked me with his offhand comment, if I have to sweep it under the rug, I will, and keep my emotions out of the equation. "Will it help the marketing? Is it important to the company?"

"I think it'll help our rollout. The more publicity we get, the better. His network is expanding. His work is getting great pickup—not just the shows he hosts, but all his shows. His podcasts and reports are carried everywhere."

When I started the interview with Sabrina, I promised myself I wouldn't let my feelings for her get in the way of that piece. While she has more on the line than I do when it comes to this story, I can't afford any missteps either. Not with her, and not with anyone. It would definitely be a misstep to piss off Kermit.

I look at my watch. "I'm pretty focused on this piece with Sabrina right now. It takes up a lot of time. Could we set something for when it's done?"

She bounces on her tiptoes. "I can do that."

"Glad I could make you happy."

She smiles. "I know he's a pain in the butt, but he's also a rising star, and he's somebody we can't overlook."

That's what irks me. I feel like he has something to lord over me. Something he'll whip out at any moment. That's another reason why I personally can't afford to ignore him.

18

Sabrina

This is cruel and unusual punishment.

The icing calls to me. It speaks to me in sweet, sugary tones. *Lick me, take me, touch me.*

"This isn't fair. This is like going to a shelter full of big-eyed pups needing homes. I want to give them all a home," I say to Courtney as I gawk at the polished glass case in the Sunshine Bakery on the Upper West Side.

Marble cakes and slices of tropical coconut pies whisper sweet nothings to me. Pink strawberry-shortcake cupcakes wink in my direction. A mouth-watering seven-layer bar talks dirty to me—*eat me.*

Oh yes, I believe I will.

Courtney taps her finger against her chin. "We're having a celebration today since one of our start-ups hit a big milestone, and I need to bring cake to the office."

"Cake is the universal currency."

"It's also the universal motivator. People will do anything for cake."

"You're going to use cake to tell your team you need them to work sixty-hour weeks? You're a cruel mistress."

"Ha. Not quite. But you know what else cake does?"

"Tell me."

"It weeds out the animals in your office. I brought a sheet cake in once, left it in the break room, and when I went to get it ten minutes later, it looked like a family of bear cubs had come through."

"Cake transforms people into bear cubs. It's a proven fact."

She returns to the glass, perusing the offerings and stopping at a vanilla cake with confetti frosting. "Ohh, look at the celebration cake."

I do, and my eyes pop out. "It's eight dollars a slice. It better give me celebratory orgasms at that price."

The woman behind the counter laughs. "It just might. I've been told my cake is quite orgasmic."

I laugh, but I can't bring myself to shell out that much dough for a slice of dough.

"Too pricey for my pauper budget," I whisper to my friend.

"I'll get it for you."

"You'll do no such thing. I'm not taking your cake handouts. Besides, I'd rather come to the office and act like a bear cub in your break room without you knowing."

My friend places her order for two-dozen cupcakes, and as the woman packs the box, Courtney smacks her forehead. "I can't believe I forgot to tell you."

"Forgot to tell me what?"

"Your name came up the other day."

"Was it for a fabulous job at a tech publication?"

She laughs, shaking her head. "It was just in passing. I had my regular check-in call with Kermit, and he mentioned you."

My spidey-sense tingles with suspicion. "What did he say? It can't have been good since he told me he thought I was a hack."

"I don't think he thinks you're a hack. I think he's jealous of you."

I scoff. "For what?"

"He wanted to know how your story with Flynn was going. He heard through the grapevine that *Up Next* was doing a feature, and that you were writing it, and he said, 'That angel investor stole my scoop with Flynn.'"

I arch a brow. "Stole his scoop?"

She waves a hand dismissively. "You know how boys are. They're so territorial. Peeing on everything. Marking it like it's theirs."

"It's not his scoop. It's *my* story."

She pokes my shoulder. "You're like a bear cub with a cake when it comes to that piece."

"Damn straight."

As she finishes her purchase, my attention wanders to a mini pink cupcake for a dollar fifty.

"I'll take that one," I say, and the woman drops it into a bag for me.

* * *

Later that day, I head to Flynn's office. Even though we're doing most of the interviews off-site, I do want to see a demo of Haven in action. As I walk to midtown, I toggle over to my podcast app and cue up one of Kermit's shows.

Keep your friends close, and your enemies closer.

With my earbuds in, I listen as I march across town. I catch a snippet of Kermit interviewing a CEO at a search giant, then tune in to a piece of another show about the top ten companies to watch. Next, I try a segment on trends in consumer technology.

I grit my teeth, frustrated.

Because they're good.

All of them.

They're compelling, fascinating, and I can't believe how much I'm learning as I listen to Kermit and his team of reporters.

How much I'm enjoying their work. It's irksome.

And so is the name that flashes on my screen.

Maureen.

Tension floods every molecule in my body.

My mother.

As I stop at a red light, I briefly weigh whether to look at her text now or later. But it'll nag at me during my time at Flynn's office, so I slide my thumb across to view it.

Maureen: Hey, baby! What's shaking? I feel like I never talk to you anymore. Call your mom now and then, would you?

I draw a deep, calming breath, pretending I'm a bird soaring in the sky. My wings are spread, and I'm free of her. Free of hiding, free of lying, free of any hold she might have on me. Hell, I've been free for years, ever since she left Kevin and me, barely making time for us when I was in high school, leaving me to be the surrogate parent for her son.

Sabrina: Hi. Life is good. I've been busy with work! I'll call soon.

I won't call soon, but it's easier to type than telling her the truth. I haven't called her in years, and if she hasn't realized that, she's the foolish one.

As I cross the street, I kick her far out of my mind. I do the same to Kermit and his podcasts.

* * *

Flynn meets me at reception, then guides me through the offices. As he passes employees in the hall, he peppers them with questions about school plays and book clubs, remembering their kids' names, their wives' names, and so on.

When we reach his office, I say, "You planned that, didn't you?"

"Planned what?"

"To wander through the halls looking like the genial, amazing boss who everybody loves."

"Yes, Sabrina, that's exactly what I did. I'm really a horrible ass, but I want you to think I'm a wonderful guy, so I told my employees in advance to act like they like me. Are you fooled?"

I wink. "Completely." I pause then add, "Also, my job is to be skeptical."

He shakes his head, and his tone is intensely serious. "Don't be skeptical about that. I do care deeply for them."

When he walks me through the whiz-bang features of

the smart home, including a British voice that talks back to me in a sexy-as-sin accent, I have to say, I'm suitably impressed.

"Want Daniel to make you tea or coffee?" Flynn gestures to the coffee grinder and the tea kettle on the counter of the demo home setup in the offices.

"Daniel, please make me some green tea," I say to the white device on the table.

"Of course. Would you like anything with that? Some music, perhaps, as you wait?"

Laughing, I answer him, "Yes, please play the Broadway soundtrack to *Aladdin*."

As "Arabian Nights" sounds softly through the speakers, I shrug at Flynn. "Guess I had genies on my mind."

"Or genie costumes," he says, wiggling his eyebrows at the reminder of another private exchange of ours.

Soon, my green tea is ready, and we head to Flynn's office where I ask him a few more questions as I drink my tea.

After we finish, I stand, ready to head for the door, lest I be distracted by another magnificent meandering conversation with him that stimulates my mind and my heart. But before I go, I reach into my purse and take out a white bag with a pink sticker on it. I place it on his desk.

"Do you like cupcakes?" I ask nervously.

He blinks. "What kind of question is that? Are you testing to see if I'm secretly an alien?"

"Are you?"

"No, I'm not an alien, because I love cupcakes."

"I picked this up for you." I slide the bag closer.

His smile does funny things to my heart, makes it cartwheel as my skin heats, and I wonder what compelled me to buy him a sweet treat.

"I have no idea what you like to eat," I say, explaining myself. "But it looked really good, so I took a guess."

He peers into the bag and removes the treat. "Looks amazing. Are you trying to bribe me with cupcakes to give up all my secrets?"

"Is that all it'll take?"

"Depends how good the cupcake is."

"Then, please by all means, devour it."

He drums his fingers on his desk, his eyes never straying from mine. "That isn't what I want to devour."

"It's not?" I ask, feigning innocence.

"Not in the least. But it might be a substitute."

"I hope it tastes as good as what you really want," I say breathily.

"I doubt anything tastes as good as what I really want."

As he brings the cupcake to his lips, he stares at me. His expression is full of rampant lust and desire, and it almost feels like a dirty promise that at some point he'll have me. He flicks the tip of his tongue over the icing and heat flares low in my belly.

I want to be that cupcake.

That cupcake really is orgasmic.

* * *

After I leave, I call Mr. Galloway and update him.

"Glad to hear it's going well, and don't forget, we have that opening coming up soon. If you deliver, we can create a beat. You could be the reporter to make it happen."

That's exactly what I want. "I'll make it happen, sir."

"Excellent. I'm told the advertising team is working overtime on the cause. As long as we get the ad support, we can start regular coverage."

Images of watchmakers and cologne purveyors flash before my eyes. If there's any publication that can drum up the necessary ad money, it's *Up Next*. That's what they do—land big money in sponsors, making it possible to write these deep features and hopefully keep covering technology.

"It's going to be an exciting industry to follow," I say, then I take stock of that comment for a second. Do I think it's exciting because I care for Flynn? Or is it exciting in and of itself?

But the memory of the tea brewing and the sound-track to *Aladdin* playing flashes before me, calling for attention. They were cool, plain and simple. This is a huge growth area. "I should have the piece done shortly. I've finished all the interviews with people who have worked with him and those who compete with him, as well as analysts and experts. I just need two more short interviews with him, and one with his brother. I should be finished shortly after. I'll turn it in a few days early."

"Excellent. I hope you'll impress me. If you do, that will go a long way."

I terribly want to impress him, to win him over.

The trouble is, every time I see the subject of my article, it's harder and harder for me to be objective as I write about the man I'm falling for.

19

Flynn

We are officially freaking her out. It's a trick we've employed since we were kids, and we probably will till the end of time. It honestly never gets old.

Sabrina's eyes drift from Dylan to me and back as we stand near the bleachers at the softball field in Central Park. We are the spitting image of each other. Being identical twins, it's not hard to look exactly like my brother.

But today, since we're on the same softball team, the doppelgänger effect is operating at full power. We're in matching outfits—white shirts, blue sleeves, with the Katherine's jeweler's logo on the back of our gear. We both wear cargo shorts.

Sabrina's hazel eyes are painted with the astonishment I've seen so many times when people meet us together.

Her index finger drifts from me to him and back. "If you didn't have black glasses, I'm not entirely sure I could tell you apart. But I think I could."

Naturally, that's the cue for our next trick, something we did to our mom and our sister. We turn around, exchange eyeglasses, switch spots, do it again, then pivot once more to face Sabrina, playing our own game of three-card Monte. Two-Card twins.

She makes a stop sign with her hand. "Stop. It's too freaky."

"We freaked our Mom out all the time too," Dylan says, laughing.

Sabrina peers studiously at my twin. Her lips curve up. She points to Dylan's wedding band. "Another way I can tell you apart is the wedding band. I hope you don't pull the twin switcheroo trick on your wife?"

He cracks up. "I would never do that to Evie. Plus, I feel like she could tell us apart because I'm ultimately more strapping and studly than my brother. I have more in certain areas."

I scoff at my brother, clapping him on the back. "Oh, that's a good one."

"Wait." Sabrina lowers her voice to a whisper. "Do identical twins have the same size . . .?"

I laugh. "Actually, I don't know because we haven't compared. *Ever.*"

Chuckling, she turns away from us briefly, perhaps to cover up that she's laughing harder now. She tamps it down, clears her throat and taps her watch. "Love the party tricks, but can we chat now?"

The game starts in thirty minutes, so we sit with Sabrina on the metal bleachers, and she interviews us about starting and selling our first company, and what we learned. Sometimes, we finish each other's sentences.

"What do you think makes Flynn a visionary?" she asks Dylan.

He tries to suppress a smile. "He has twenty—"

I jump in, shaking my head. "—eight thousand vision."

"Just like—"

I point at Dylan. "—him."

Sabrina's lips twitch like she's trying to rein in a grin.

When we're done, Dylan says he needs to stretch before the game, so he heads to the field. She watches him then swings her gaze to me. "It's funny to meet him after knowing you."

I arch an eyebrow, curious. "How so?"

"This might sound weird, but you don't seem like a twin when it's just us chatting. But with him, you absolutely are."

"Did you expect me to seem like a twin?"

"I think I did. Because it's so much a part of your identity, or at least what's been written about you. You're always identified online as the Parker twins because of your first company, but when I'm with you, I don't think of you that way."

"How do you think of me?"

She nibbles on the corner of her lip, considering the question, it seems. "When it's just you and me, I can see who you are shining through. You're this fascinating, brilliant, thoughtful, creative man, and it's hard for me to see how you ever shared credit with anyone."

"Keep thinking of me that way. I did everything on my own. It was all me." I wink.

"It's more that you're so uniquely you, from the pineapple to the poetry to the wordplay to your jokes. That's *you*. Flynn Parker. Not Flynn the twin." She holds her palms like scales, raising then lowering. "Then when I see you with your brother, you have this whole other twin-ness to you. It's not a bad thing; it's just different."

"Would you be different if I met your brother?"

"We're not twins. I'm five years older. He's twenty-three."

"Right, but you're close, aren't you?"

"Very much so. He's amazing. He's one of the reasons I wanted this opportunity so badly."

"In what way?"

"I support my brother. I help pay his bills for school."

"You do?"

She nods, a smile spreading instantly. "He's going to divinity school, getting a master's."

I take a moment to absorb the enormity of what she does for him. It's hard enough to pay bills on her own, but to help the person she adores? "That's amazing. I'm floored. What an incredible thing to do."

"I kind of raised him," she says, a note of pride in her voice.

"You did?"

"We never knew our dad. He didn't ever live with us. I suspect he knocked up our mom twice, and that was the extent of his role in her life. As for her, she started to check out when my brother was ten or eleven. I looked out for him after that."

"How did she check out?"

She swallows and looks away. "She . . . well, let's just say she doesn't have the best track record with the law."

My eyes widen. "What happened, may I ask?"

She counts off on her fingers. "Petty theft, shoplifting, then grand theft. She started by stealing small items from stores, then from rich neighborhoods—silver, china, expensive objects. Soon, she moved on to jewelry."

She says it all so matter-of-factly, but as someone raised by a happily married couple in a crime-free family, it's hard to imagine this upbringing as normal. But that's what's shocking to me—this is Sabrina's normal. It's also what she's strived to separate herself from, I surmise.

"That must have been incredibly hard."

"She's been in and out of jail most of my adult life. If she's not in jail, she's asking me for money. She gambles a lot. She does what she wants, and she blasts into town asking for more. I do everything I can to avoid her, but she usually finds a way to show up when I least want her to."

I drag a hand over my jaw. "Damn. That's tough, but it's amazing that you help your brother."

The mention of her brother brings a radiance to her eyes. They sparkle when she talks about him. "She left for good when he was fifteen. He's the reason I went to school in New York. I had a bunch of scholarships, but I needed to stay close and look after him. The only thing she left was the tiny condo she'd owned. I lived there with him when I was in college since he was still in high school. He was the most important thing to me—he still is—and he wound up doing a beautiful thing with his life."

Her smile is so warm and earnest it reaches someplace far inside me, finding a home. It makes me care even more for her, when I'm already wading into the deep end, so deep that my *don't-get-involved-with-work-associates* rule is close to breaking. "Kevin is my hero. He has the biggest heart, and the strongest sense of right and wrong."

As she tells me about him, a stone of guilt digs against my ribs. Guilt for thinking she was after me for money. Guilt for wondering about her motives. She's so genuinely focused on her brother, so giving of herself, and with the short straw she drew with her mom, I can't see her in the same category as the women in my past.

"You're good people," I say, silently exonerating myself from doubting her a week ago. I don't doubt her anymore. I know who she is.

She blushes. "Thanks. Speaking of good people and maybe not-so-good people, what do you think of Kermit La Franchi? He asked my best friend how the story was going. Isn't that odd?"

I swallow hard, the pleasant balloon of our conversation now popped. "Sabrina, I think he knows about us."

She cringes. "What?"

I tell her what happened in the hall after she hightailed it from the party, wishing I didn't have to be the bearer of bad news. "He asked me for an interview too. I held him off, but he called Jennica and is trying to weasel his way in."

"That's why he said I stole his scoop. Which is ridiculous. But are you going to do one with him?"

"He's determined, and Jennica convinced me since he's becoming quite a playmaker in this space. But I won't be talking to him until we're done."

She fidgets with her earring, twisting a daisy-petal stud back and forth. "What if he knows Bob Galloway? What if he says something to him about what he thinks happened with us at the party?"

"Why would he do that?"

Fear seems to flash across her eyes. "He's Evil Kermit."

"That was just a part he played," I say, trying to reassure her, though I'm not entirely sure there's nothing to worry about.

"I don't trust him. I don't trust anyone."

And that—that I understand. "We'll deny it. He has no

evidence. All he knows is I had your halo, and that doesn't prove anything. I don't want you to lose this chance with the article and *Up Next*. I know how much it means to you."

Her lips quiver, then she presses them together. Her voice is a feather when she speaks again. "Stop it. Stop being so sweet and thoughtful."

"I'm not being sweet and thoughtful. It's just how I feel."

"And how you feel is because you're good and generous, and I wish I didn't have a job on the line."

"Me too." As I glance at the field where Carson tosses the softball to Jennica as they warm up, I know we all have something on the line.

I do my best at Haven to take away my employees' worries by treating them well, treating them like family. I wish I could take away Sabrina's worries. I wish I could do something to make her life easier. I don't know what it would be though.

Grabbing my glove, I vow to try and figure it out as I play the game today.

"Wait." She reaches for my shirtsleeve, her voice dropping to that low, sultry tone that absolutely obliterates my resolve. "Do you want to know how I could tell you and your brother apart?"

"How?"

She zeroes in on my face, her voice barely audible. "Your lips. I'd recognize them anywhere."

"Why's that?"

"Because they drew me to you. They're the reason I talked to you that night. I wanted to kiss you as soon as I saw you."

I ache with desire. It fills every cell in my body. "I wanted to kiss you. I wanted it so fucking much."

And God, I want it again.

I want it again so badly that I strike out all three times I'm at the plate, because my mind is on what I can't have.

The woman I'm falling for.

When the softball game is over, we head to a café. Ostensibly, she wants to talk about the future of tech, and we touch on that briefly, but mostly we just chat. She tells me more about her mom. She talks about Ray too, how devastated she was when he left her but how her work as a reporter was critical to her moving on. She poured herself into her job, and as she tells me this, I understand even more of what makes her tick —who she is beneath the mask she wore the night I met her.

"Remember the dress I wore to the costume party? The angel wings?"

"Yes. They were satin or something soft."

"Chiffon. That was my unused wedding dress. Every-thing was ready, then he called and said he was leaving the country."

My jaw tightens. "Do you think he was cheating on you?"

"It's possible. He might have been lured by gambling, by another woman, or by his own unhappiness. I don't actually know."

"Do you want to know?"

She pauses, seeming to consider the question. "For the longest time, I did. I wanted to understand. But ultimately, I had to accept that maybe this is one of those things I won't ever have an answer to, just questions. So, I've learned to let it go. It's an unsolved mystery, and I learned from it."

"What did you learn?" I ask, hoping she doesn't say that she never wants to get involved with a man again.

"I learned I won't always have the answers, and that's okay." She offers a small smile. "What about you?"

"I learned to be cautious about who I trust." I take a breath and tell her about Annie, and how the end of that relationship hurt but how I walked away from it knowing that leaving was the only choice.

Sabrina meets my gaze, her hazel eyes fierce. She stabs the table with her finger. "She did not deserve you. I mean that, Flynn. She didn't deserve you at all. No one does unless they love you for you. Unless they love you no matter what you have or don't have."

When she says that, I start to believe we could be that way—we could be a no-matter-what. That's what scares me and, honestly, kind of thrills me at the same time. A no-matter-what with her—I feel the potent possibility in my chest, thrumming in my veins.

As we drain our iced coffees, her phone rings. It's Face-Time. She glances at the screen, and her face lights up. I've never seen her like this. Absolute delight spreads across her features as she declares, "It's Kevin!"

I tip my chin to the phone. "Answer it."

She shakes her head. "No, I can call him back later."

"Sabrina, you can talk to your brother. It's totally fine. I get it."

"Are you sure?" she asks nervously.

The phone rings again. "Answer it, or I'll answer it for you."

With a grin, she slides her thumb across the screen and says, "Hey, Kevin. I'm here with Flynn."

The fact that she didn't need to introduce me says she's already told him about me. That has to be a good sign. I sit a little taller. She shows me the phone, and I say hello to her brother, a baby-faced blond with a straight nose and kind eyes.

"Hey, Flynn. Nice to finally meet you."

"Good to meet you. Sabrina has told me a lot about you," I say. "She thinks you're the cat's meow."

Kevin meows. "And the pajamas too. Also, thank you. I'm glad to hear she said good things to you."

Sabrina peers at the screen. "Hey, can I call you later when I finish this interview?"

"Sure." Kevin scratches his head. "You're doing another one?"

Her answer comes at the speed of light. "Yes."

"How often do you guys do interviews? Hasn't this kind of been going on for forever?"

Sabrina glances at me over the top of the phone, a guilty-as-charged look in her eyes before she returns her focus to her brother. "Kevin, stop saying things you shouldn't be saying right now. I love you, and I'll talk to you later."

When she clicks end, I cluck my tongue. "We don't really need to talk this much for the story. Do we?"

Sabrina shakes her head. "I don't think we do. I kind of have everything I need already."

"Really?" Perhaps she can hear the disappointment in my voice. If she can't, she should have her hearing checked.

"Well," she says, tapping her chin, "I suppose there are a couple more things I wanted to ask you."

"I guess we should talk again tomorrow?"

"Definitely."

We make plans for the next day.

20

Sabrina

Since I've had so many interviews with other people, it's only natural that I need to talk to Flynn after I speak with the others.

To check for his reaction.

To glean his response.

Or, really, to spend more time with him.

Flynn is a pattern I want to make over and over. He's a word I never tire of using. He's a song I can blast in my earbuds all night long.

All day too.

With Flynn, it's like we have an endless well of topics for conversation. Dip a hand in it, pick another item, and chat, chat, chat.

The next evening, when we leave the café where we've been talking, we wander past a store window display that catches my eye.

A zombie mask. A gangster suit. A cheerleader.

Dorothy, complete with her blue gingham dress and ruby-red slippers.

I point to the glittery shoes. "I want the slippers. I'll click my heels."

"Where will you go?"

"I would go back to the costume party."

His eyes lock with mine. His aren't green now. Longing is their shade, and I want to capture the way he looks. He stares at me like I'm worth everything. Like I'm emeralds and rubies. God, how I want that. How I wish I could have it with him—everything in his eyes.

He tips his chin toward the door. "We should see what masks are in the store, don't you think?"

"Absolutely."

We say hello to the shopkeeper who glances up from the counter and smiles, letting us know she's here if we need anything. She's dressed as Rita Hayworth, with a bust-exposing dress and a red wig.

We head toward the masks.

"Now that you've seen me, would you recognize me in, say, this?" He covers his face with a fox mask.

"You're foxy, but yes, I can tell it's you."

"Good." He reaches for a dog. "As Fido?"

I smile. "Absolutely."

"What about this?" He tries to sound silky and sultry as he slides a pink pig mask over his face, adding a most unsexy *oink, oink*.

"Still you."

He locates a mask of a clown with a tear sliding down its face and a big red ball for a nose. He positions it over my eyes then peers at me, studying me. "Yup, it's you."

He holds the mask to his face. "And now? Can you tell it's me?"

I slug his arm. "Yes, yes, yes. Of course, I'd recognize you."

"Just like you 'recognized' me at The Dollhouse?" His tone is somewhat challenging.

"I told you, I recognized you, but I didn't want it to be *you*," I say wistfully.

He wraps a hand around my arm, and flames lick my body. "Sometimes I still feel that way. Sometimes I see you, and I wish you were someone else."

"Me too," I admit.

"Do you want me to be the duke?"

I nod. "Yes, and we'll go to costume parties. Maybe I'll dress as Marilyn Monroe at one."

He groans and steps closer to me. It's dark here in the corner of the shop—we're out of sight of the windows. Red velvet lines the wall, and masks, swords, and shields hang from it. "You'd look so hot as Marilyn Monroe."

"I'd get a mask just for my eyes. You could cup my cheek while you kissed me."

"Fuck," he says in a long, low rumble. "And what would I be?" He rests his hand on a rack of poodle skirts.

"You'd be Joe DiMaggio, of course."

He pumps a fist. "I always wanted to be a star athlete."

I lift my hand and run it up his arm, grateful he's wearing a T-shirt today. I trace a path to his bicep. His breath hisses as I travel higher then squeeze his muscle. "You'd wear your Yankees uniform, and I'd admire how it fits you. I'd admire your arms too. I'd touch them."

He swallows harshly. His eyes are fire. His voice is sandpaper as he whispers, "And I'd slide in for a dance and wrap my arm around your waist while you had on that white satin dress. And nobody would know who we were because we'd wear masks."

"We'd know."

"But we'd pretend."

"Can we pretend now? That we're at a costume party?"

He glances over his shoulder. Rita is on the phone. She's looking the other way, and we're partially hidden behind the racks. "Let's pretend. If we pretend, it's not really happening."

Permission. We're giving each other the permission we both so desperately want.

"We're at a make-believe party," I say, as we move closer to each other, and he glides his hand around my waist.

I want to melt into him. My bones dissolve into honey as I raise my hands to his shoulders, sliding over them, looping around his neck, then drawing him near. "You never know what might happen at a costume party," I whisper as we glide closer. Inches separate us. Inches and air and restraint that's frayed so thin it's unraveling at breakneck speed.

"One dance, maybe more."

Music plays softly in the background, and I swear it's Linda Ronstadt crooning the opening notes to "Someone to Watch Over Me." Or maybe that's how my body feels. Like it's become a torch song. Like I'm living inside the lyrics to a smoky, sexy tune of desperation and wanting.

My eyes flutter closed for a second, and warmth spreads from the center of my chest all the way to the tips of my fingers. A shiver runs through me as his hands tighten around my hips.

Once again, we exist on two planes. We seem to slip back and forth in time like we did when we visited the subway station. Like we exist here as Flynn and Sabrina, and we exist in the past as Angel and Duke.

I dance, though I shouldn't.

I sway, though it's risky.

I look into his eyes, though that only makes me want him more. Wanting is such a painful emotion. It aches and throbs and hurts even as it asks for more of the torture. More of the things that I can't have. A real chance with this man. A real date. A real love.

"Sometimes you look at me like you did the other night," I whisper.

"How did I look at you the other night?"

"As if you liked being kind of dominant."

"I think you liked it when I was kind of dominant."

"I liked it when you raised my hands over my head."

"And you liked it when I hiked your legs around my waist."

"I did," I say breathily.

"Why?"

"Because I didn't have to think. I didn't have to worry. I could get lost in the moment."

"Do you want to get lost again?" he asks, in a voice that betrays his want for me. It makes me dizzy. It makes me high.

I'm swallowed whole by a new kind of desire that floods my body. I want to lose myself in him. I don't want to be found.

"I do," I whisper as my skin prickles with the clawing need to get closer to him. My pulse spikes. "I wish we didn't have to pretend."

"So do I."

I stop pretending. I lean in, part my lips, and give in.

He brushes his lips across mine and hums as he kisses me.

It's a soft, aching kiss. Like the song. Like my need for him.

It's sad and it's intoxicating at the same time. It's the way we kiss when we're saying goodbye, when we're borrowing time, when we know we can't be.

The kiss is born of longing, forged in a wish that can't come true.

I want it too much. I want to forget all the reasons why he's a mistake. I want to be his Marilyn right now, and his Angel, and his Sabrina.

"Say my name," I whisper, breaking the kiss. "I want to hear you say my name."

"Sabrina," he says. His voice is rougher than I've heard before, and it turns me liquid. I'm silver and gold, and I want him to kiss me forever and ever. This kind of bittersweet kiss, this kind of stolen kiss in a costume shop, hearkens back to our first secret kiss.

But when Rita laughs loudly, the sound of her amusement is a sharp reminder that we're playing with fire.

We break apart.

Because we have to.

I clear my throat, trying to center myself. I can't think. I can't speak. "Maybe I should buy a . . ." I don't know how to finish the sentence.

"A fox mask?"

"If it meant I could have you, I would."

But there's no real way to hide who I am, or what I need.

I need a job, and if I'm in love with the man I'm covering, then my story goes up in smoke, and any possible future with *Up Next* turns to ash.

21

Flynn

"Now, if we can just have this smart home make me eggs and toast in the morning, I'll be all set."

The morning news anchor, Camilla Montes, smiles and laughs in that isn't-it-amazing way that morning news anchors have.

"We're working on that, Camilla, and we hope to get there soon," I tell her, since I've finished showing her all the cool features of Haven.

"Thank you so much for joining us today, Flynn, and we are so excited that our homes are now becoming brilliant robots that can deliver whatever we need at the sound of our voices." She flashes a lipsticked smile, with gleaming white teeth. "Also, I would be remiss if I didn't point out you remain on our list of the most eligible bachelors in New York City. Any chance that'll change soon?"

I laugh lightly. Jennica briefed me that Camilla might toss a curveball with a personal question—the morning news show ran a list of eligible bachelors recently, so I'm not surprised.

"Is there somebody on the horizon?" she adds.

As I briefly consider whether I want to admit anything on air, I picture Sabrina, her sparkling hazel eyes; her mischievous smile; her wild, warm heart; and her sense of adventure. How I want her to be the one on the horizon. I do. I just do.

Even if we hadn't kissed yesterday, I'd want a chance with her with the same fierce desire I had when I first wanted to build this company.

Just as I've marched my way to the top of the tech world with focus and rigor, I need to find a way to make that woman mine no matter what. I'm not someone who sits back and takes no for an answer. "There is someone on the horizon," I say with a smile. "I'll let you know if anything comes of it."

She smiles and speaks to the camera. "You heard it here first, folks. There is a lovely lady for Flynn Parker. Now, stay tuned for our next segment on how to make your own organic butter."

When the camera cuts to a commercial, she thanks me, a technician removes my mic, and I say goodbye. Making my way out of the studio, I meet up with Jennica, who waits in the hallway. She stares at me like a teacher about to reprimand a student. "Who is she? Is it your mystery girl? And how long were you going to keep her from me?"

I smile, a grin that can't truly be contained. "I was going to tell you."

"You were? I'm getting ready to beat you over the head with the broom for not serving up the deets."

I love that Jennica has something of a mom in her, that

she looks out for me. She's taken on this role since we've been working together. She's one of the people I'm lucky to have in my life, and as we stand in the concrete hallway to the TV studio, with crews rushing by, guys with headsets, women with clipboards, I decide it's time to truly understand if I can take this chance.

"Let me ask you a question. How do you think we're doing? With the rollout of Haven? And with the competition?" I need to hear it from her. From someone who won't bullshit me.

"It's going even better than we imagined. Everything is working great. It's coming together, and we're far ahead of ShopForAnything."

"Are they having us for breakfast?"

"Cornflakes we are not."

"Is one article in one magazine going to make or break us?"

She shakes her head. "I don't think we'll live or die by one piece of publicity. But if you're asking me how you're going to deal with the fact that you're falling for the reporter from *Up Next*, I would tell you that, while the story matters, your happiness matters more."

My jaw comes unhinged. "How did you know it was her?"

Her smile is soft and kind. "You've been spending a lot of time with Sabrina. I've never really known any article to require five or six interviews. And when she came by the office the other day, there was a sort of glow in your eyes. I saw it again at the softball game. You've never looked at anyone like that."

"Not Annie?"

Jennica shakes her head. "This seems like something that makes you happy here." She taps my sternum.

I smile. "Yeah, it does. She does."

I wipe away the smile. I have a job to do, and employees to look out for. I've studied our numbers. I know we're doing well. Still, I'm the kind of guy who likes to check and double check. It's what I did on all my math tests, and it served me well. "Does that mean I'm not totally messing up our company if I pursue things with her?"

Jennica leans against the wall, a thoughtful look in her eyes. "We're stronger than that at Haven. We'll be fine."

And if that's the case, that means I can reconsider the approach to this math problem.

My hypothesis has changed when it comes to Sabrina. At first, I'd been so focused on what I might lose at work if I got involved with her. Would our rollout falter? Would we lose ground? Would my edge fade? But at this point, my company is solid and the shark circling us appears to have retreated. Since the hypothesis has changed, the expected result should too. Perhaps falling for her and managing my business can go hand in hand. "You're sure?"

She laughs. "Yes. And listen, I know you've tried not to get involved with people you work with because you love the company so much. I get that. You've wanted to keep everything separate, devote yourself to Haven, and not let anything distract you. But look what you've done," she says, gesturing to the hallway, and presumably to the piece we just finished. "You built another amazing company, and there's a part of you that still believes if you don't give it one hundred percent, we'll get lost or hurt. But Flynn, fifty percent of your focus is the equivalent of two hundred percent of anyone else's."

"Oh stop. You're too good to me."

"You're too good to us. And if she's the one for you, you have to take the chance with her. You've given so much of your heart and your soul to the businesses we've worked on together. I think it's time you take care of yourself." She squeezes my shoulder. "I want you to be happy."

"And this is when I remind myself that whatever your bonus is, it's not big enough."

"Precisely. Just remember that when it's holiday time." She takes a deep breath and fixes me with a serious stare. "But what will happen to her and her story? Frankly, that's a bigger concern at this point—what impact will it have on her?"

"You're right. She has more at stake. I have more cushion."

She squeezes my arm. "Be her cushion, then."

That's the next problem to solve—how to be her cushion. How to turn Sabrina's risk into *our* reward.

22

Sabrina

It's three in the morning. I'm bleary-eyed. I've drunk all my tea. I've consumed enough caffeine to power a small planet.

I'm pretty much done with the first draft of my article. This is a dream. This is what I've always wanted to write. Something deep and rich that tells a thrilling tale, with ups, downs, conflict, and hope.

As I lean back in the tiny chair at my tinier kitchen table, staring at the laptop screen, satisfaction flows through me. This is a good piece. This is a fair piece.

The next step is to show it to my brother. I don't have enough distance to know if I've done the job. If I've been critical enough in my observations.

I email him.

Your mission, should you choose to accept, is to apply those finely tuned ethics to my piece. Let me know if I've been fair. Let me know if it's patently obvious I like the guy, or if you can't tell one iota that I have a massive crush on him.

He must be up late too, because his response is swift.

Mission accepted. I have a test tomorrow, so let me read it later in the day. Also, I knew you had a crush on him. And I'm glad you're being so introspective and thoughtful about whether you can even do this piece.

I blink. *Whether?* No, I'm doing it. I've done it. It's done. All I want to know is if I pulled it off, or if it needs more wordsmithing.

But I don't need to get into those details yet. I send him a thank you.

It's funny how feedback from my little brother is what I needed. He's been my benchmark for how to behave for the last several years, and I needed his input after the kiss with Flynn.

My stomach drops with guilt.

But it's more than a morsel of guilt. It's snowballed into a too-tall boulder.

I don't regret kissing Flynn.

How could I? When he kisses me, I feel it in my bones, it radiates to my soul. He kisses me like I'm cherished. Like I matter. Like I could matter for a long, long time.

My regret comes from the work.

From my fear that somehow my feelings for him could hurt the reputation of *Up Next*. Bob Galloway put his neck on the line for me, and I want to deliver. I don't want to bring scandal or gossip to his publication.

As my stomach dive-bombs in a nervous loop, a part of me thinks I should tell Mr. Galloway I have feelings for the subject of my piece.

But as I stare at the mail on my table, and the bill for divinity school, I can't. I can't risk this assignment, and really, it was only one bone-shatteringly good kiss.

What happened before doesn't count.

What happened at the costume shop was a mistake, and I can't let it happen again.

I can't have both Flynn and the job. Mr. Galloway would ax the piece if he knew I'd been involved with the subject. Editors love to wield their scepters of impartiality and fairness. I get that—it's the foundation of the field.

That's why my best bet is to make sure there's nothing to know. It was one kiss, and it's over. Nothing more will happen now. Maybe one day in the future, a year down the track, if we're both still single. But that's a lot of what-ifs and you can't plan for what-ifs.

I click on the website for *Up Next*, hoping that it will remind me of my new dream—to work there full-time. I read a few articles posted online, including a gripping piece on new trends in wearable technology. That could be me next.

Not wearing technology, per se.

But writing a gripping piece for *Up Next*.

It's a dream job, and I can't let one kiss derail my attempts to land it.

When I'm done, I fire off emails to other editors I know, sending in clips, checking on work, and pitching potential stories. If *Up Next* doesn't pan out, I need to be prepared. No one writes back yet, since it's not even dawn, but at four thirty a new email rolls in.

The name makes me tense.

The message makes me tenser.

To: Sabrina G
From: Kermit LF

Sabrina, I think it would be in your best interest if we set a time to talk.

My stomach dives painfully. I wonder if I can be eaten alive by worry. Maybe it is possible.

I write back, asking when he's free. That ought to buy me some time. That's what I need right now. I shove Kermit out of my mind when he doesn't reply right away.

As the sun begins to rise, I read my article one more time.

I'll be ready to turn this in once I have Kevin's feedback, and after I meet Flynn for my final fact-check.

I have to fact-check in person. There is no other reason for me to see him, especially not the memory of that kiss I can't get out of my mind.

* * *

We are nearly done.

This time he chose another one of my favorite places. We stroll along the Central Park Mall, one of the many beautiful places in this park that's home to countless beautiful places. The walkway runs through the middle of the green land, with huge beds of flowers south of us and a gorgeous bridge north of us. I can imagine that years ago on this path, carriages filled with glittering men and women, perhaps heading to masquerades, clip-clopped across these stones.

We walk and we talk, as has become our custom, while I check the final details for the piece.

"My T's are crossed and my I's are dotted." I turn off the recorder and a wave of sadness wallops me out of nowhere. Like I'm standing on the shore, and a tsunami clobbers me without warning.

This is the last time I can devise a reason to see him. We might run in the same circles, we might even wind up talking more regularly if the job comes through, but this is the end of the line for *us*.

For whatever we've been.

For Angel and Duke.

For this pretend-not-pretend brief little New York love affair. A lump rises in my throat, and I try mightily to swallow it down. But it lodges there, and I hate that a dumb tear forms in the corner of my eye. I glance toward the trees, towering canopies hanging over the walkway, and blink away the thoughts of how much I want this to continue.

I hate my lot in life right now.

I hate my last newspaper and the fact that it couldn't survive.

I hate my mother and her inability to take care of the two of us when she was supposed to. I hate that I had to do it before my own time.

What I hate most, though, is that I was assigned a story that invigorated me professionally and shredded my heart personally.

But I'm a big girl. I've been through tougher times.

Raising my chin, I suck in the emotion and tell myself I'll live off the memories of this man and how he made me feel like my life was easy, because being with him is the easiest thing in the world.

He sighs. "So, this is it."

I smile sadly. "I wish I had something else to fact-check."

He licks his lips and steps closer to me. "Me too. Maybe next time we could fact-check at the Met. Another one of your favorite places."

"I feel like we've gone to all my favorite places these last several days. What about yours?"

"I have new favorite places now." He reaches for a lock of my hair, running his finger over the end as it curls.

Something inside me melts. The final piece of ice that encased my heart when Ray left me cracks, splitting down the middle, leaving me raw but also ready for another chance.

No more ice. My heart is open.

It's telling me to take a chance with him.

I can't let the heart fool me though.

Life isn't a fairy tale. The modern-day maiden must be practical above all. I might want to toss responsibility into the breeze like dandelions, then skip and tra-la-la my way home with him, but I have bills.

And, more importantly, bills have me.

But if I keep looking at his handsome face, his square jaw, his gorgeous green eyes, I'll buckle.

I tear my gaze away from his magnetic eyes, and something catches my attention on a nearby park bench—the plaque on the top slat of wood, shining as if it has been polished today.

I point to it. "What's that?"

We walk closer and we read it together out loud, our voices forming melody and harmony. "*Tony, win, lose, or break even, you always have me. Love, Karen.*"

I look at Flynn. We both shrug then smile.

"One more adventure?" I offer, a note of hope in my voice. "We need to know what that means."

"Clearly."

We whip out our phones in unison, and we google like it's a race.

"It's an inscription," he says excitedly.

"A wife surprised her husband," I say, the words piling up in a rush.

"For his sixty-fifth birthday," he adds.

And we laugh as we each read the details from an article on the many benches in this park. We learn Tony was a retired investment banker. When he came home from work, his wife, Karen, used to ask him if he won, lost, or broke even.

We spend the next hour or two on a treasure hunt around Central Park, searching for more of the four thousand inscribed benches, reading quirky details of the memories and loves and lives carved into plaques in this park, each inscription costing about ten thousand dollars.

"We rarely notice them. We sit on these benches and we read, drink coffee, make phone calls, or maybe we just text or tweet," I say.

"Maybe we feed the pigeons. Or wait to meet a friend and meanwhile, we're surrounded by memories of other people and things that were important to them."

I spot another one with a fantastic inscription and tug his sleeve, pulling him closer to read. "*We would make the same mistake all over again! Vic and Nancy Schiller. Still best friends.*"

He finds the info. "When they told her they were getting married, her mother said it would be a mistake," he says, smiling.

"Guess they had the last laugh. Still together and happy. Okay, this is seriously the coolest thing I've ever discovered in New York City."

"I think so too." He sets his hand on my arm, running his fingers down my bare skin. "I want to keep discovering them. I want to go all over the park and find the best ones. I want to do that with you."

My heart soars, terrifying me with how much longing is in it, so much I feel like I'm going to burst, to drown in it.

I meet his gaze.

The look in his eyes is different than I've seen before. It's vulnerable and hopeful and perhaps the slightest bit nervous.

23

Flynn

In front of the Schillers' bench, I have to float the next question. Despite the risks, despite my own fears, now is the time to ask.

I didn't plan to ask her here. But *here* is the right place.

"Sabrina," I say, my voice gravelly with nerves, "what happens when the story is done?"

The nerves aren't from how I feel for her. They come from whether she'll allow an *us* to happen. Whether she's willing to take a chance. That's the great unknown. That's the uncontrollable factor.

"What do you mean?"

I reach for her hand, sliding my fingers through hers. "Do you think there's any way we could do this?"

"Do what?" Her voice is barely a breath on the air. "I need you to spell it out."

I love that she wants utter clarity. It's so her. "Be

together. You and me." I point from her to me and back. "Have a real go of it."

"Be together," she repeats, as if she's making sense of what I'm saying.

I loop my fingers tighter through hers. "I've had a great time with you over these two weeks, and I want to see where we can go. The article is almost done, so does that mean we can have a new beginning?"

She sighs, a melancholy sound. I want to hit the rewind button, go back in time ten seconds, and turn that sigh into one of contentment.

"Flynn," she says, and my name sounds like an apology. Tension flares through me, and I wonder how I've read this wrong. How I've completely misunderstood yesterday's kiss and everything else. "You know I wish it was different. You have to know that, right?"

There's heartache in her voice.

"Yeah, I know that," I say heavily.

Her fingers slide tighter through mine, and her touch has become an epilogue, the last reminder that we were always pretend. We were each better off not knowing who the other was, when we slipped on our masks and made believe we could be people we weren't.

"I want that more than anything. But this is a big chance for me at *Up Next*. If I can impress Mr. Galloway with this piece, there could be a whole new beat writing deep features on companies—including yours. And you know it's not only my career," she adds, her voice a bare plea. "I have to support Kevin. I *want* to support Kevin. He's my brother, but he also doesn't have anyone else who can look out for him the way I do."

"I understand." And I do. I understand deeply he's the

world to her, and that's how it should be. She has to put him first.

She has to put herself second.

That means we won't turn into anything more. We'll keep fading into less.

If I believed in fate, I'd say it was meant to be this way.

But I believe in math and on the surface, we don't add up.

We're an inequality.

One has more than the other. One needs more than the other. One can't give what the other must have.

But what if I could balance the equation? A surge of energy shoots through me. I've built companies my whole adult life. I create jobs. I can make one for her. I can solve this math problem. "Wait. What if I gave you a job?"

She furrows her brow. "What? Why on earth would you give me a job?"

Be her cushion. "Maybe we can come up with something."

"I don't even understand what that would be."

I hunt for an idea. Anything at all. "Writing a newsletter or marketing copy or something."

She shoots me a look—one that says she can't believe I offered that. One that says she's slightly offended. "You can't solve this for me by coming up with a job you don't have and don't need," she sputters, flapping her hands.

"What if we needed that?" I posit.

She narrows her eyes. "But you don't. You don't really need to hire me. Also, that's not the kind of job I want or am good at."

"I didn't mean to offend you," I say, rubbing a hand over the back of my neck, frustrated as hell to be back to an equation with no answer. "That was kind of ridiculous and insulting."

"It's fine," she says softly. "I know where you're coming from. I just want you to understand. I'm not a marketing writer. Or a newsletter writer. I'm a reporter."

"I know. I wish I could help."

She nods, her expression softening. "I appreciate the sentiment, but right now the job I want is covering your business. I've tried to convince myself every night that I can feel how I do about you and still do my job objectively," she says, and my heart sits up, hoping. "But I can't. And I think maybe it's best if we stop . . ." She takes a beat, swallows, and seems to gird herself to say the harder part. "Stop seeing each other like this."

A kick in the gut. I saw it coming, but it still smarts like a screaming demon. Only, I don't want her to know how much this hurts. I don't want to let on for a second that I'm in pain.

"Absolutely. I absolutely agree." I drop her hand, making it clear I'm 100 percent on board with this.

That's a lie.

But I'm not interested in letting the truth shine through. Not when there's a hole in my chest from the punch she delivered.

24

Sabrina

Kermit writes back that afternoon.

He wants to see me later this week.

To: Sabrina G

From: Kermit LF

Had to catch a flight to Palo Alto. I'll call you, or text you, or really, you should make time for me on Wednesday.

It's not presented as optional.

I don't know why, but I can guess. I suspect he's going to aim that Nerf gun of his in my direction and blow my cover.

Reveal my dirty little secret.

He's going to topple the vase, like a destructive cat, and gleefully watch as the glass shatters.

Writing back, I tell him I'll see him on Wednesday.

It's like scheduling an appointment with the executioner, and the only thing left is to decide how I want my neck sliced. Do I do it myself, or let Kermit the Douche drop the blade?

My stomach churns as I pace my tiny apartment, wishing for answers. Wishing for someone to swoop in and tell me what to do.

But the thing is—that's my job.

It's been my job since I was eighteen and my mom up and left. Since she grabbed her fake Louis Vuitton and said, "See you later, kids, I'm outta here." Once it was clear she wasn't coming back, I secured guardianship of Kevin, somehow juggling college and official surrogate parenthood at the same damn time. The balancing act was no fun at all, but it was so rewarding to see my little brother turn into the finest of men.

I'd do it all over again, even the hard parts, even the not-fun parts.

I've learned something else that's no fun at all.

This.

This is what it feels like to fall in love, have your gut punched, and miss the man you can't be with.

For the record, it feels like complete and utter crap.

As I work on a new design for an adorable skirt made from a dove-gray patterned fabric with script-y French words across it, I cut my finger. I curse, and blood spurts all over my hand, making a beeline for the word *reve*. Fitting, that *dream* should be bloodied.

I jump from the table, run to the sink, and wash the blood off my finger. More crimson pours and the slice hurts. This should feel symbolic, but it mostly feels annoying. Because everything is irksome now.

A man like Flynn Parker came into my life at exactly the moment when I didn't just need him, I wanted him. He came like a beautiful summer day, like blue skies and sunshine, a walk along the beach, and peaceful easy times. He's evenings under the stars too, nights spent dancing, laughing, tumbling together and kissing, hot and fevered and sweaty.

Giving myself to Flynn would be easy because he wouldn't hurt me.

That's what I let slip through my fingers for a possibility.

But I had to. I had no choice.

I keep running the water, and the blood spills into the sink.

I don't think Flynn would hurt me like Ray did. I don't believe he's like that. I believe he's a man of his word, a man I can trust, and saying those words to him—*we need to stop seeing each other*—hurt way more than this sliced finger.

When the blood ceases to flow, I wrap a towel tight around my finger, find a Band-Aid, and put it on the cut. Giving the sewing a break, I settle back in with the article, review Kevin's notes, and make my final tweaks. Then I stand and pace like a lion in the zoo. Cross the kitchen. Walk to the futon. Cover the same path again.

I draw a deep breath and scan my little place. The walls seem to hover, to sway. This apartment is suddenly too tiny. It can't contain me and all these rampant emotions pinballing through my chest.

I call Kevin and tell him I'm taking the next train to come see him.

A couple hours later, the train rattles into the station in the sleepy little New England town where he goes to divinity school. He meets me at the depot, and his smile is magnetic. It hits me in a raw, visceral way. I throw my arms around him, and he hugs me.

A strange relief works its way into me as we reconnect. He's my person. I needed to see him. I desperately need to talk to him. I can't stand trying to sort out all these feelings on my own.

We leave the station and head into town where we settle in at a café and order tea.

He slides my cup toward me. "It must be good if you came all the way out here to see me."

I heave a painful sigh, emotions clogging my throat. "Tell me what to do. Tell me what's the right thing to do."

He leans back in his chair, parking his hands behind his head. "It's the guy, isn't it?"

I give him more details. "I know I won't get the job if I'm seeing him. I can't cover his sector if I'm involved with him. Who would give that gig to me? That's crazy. It's one thing to disclose at the end of a story that you're involved with somebody, the way a publication would disclose you own stock. *Jane Smith has stock in Company X. Jane Smith is in a romantic relationship with Fred Jones.* It's another thing to assign someone to cover an industry on an ongoing basis when their boyfriend or girlfriend is a key player."

Kevin nods thoughtfully. "What happens in other situations though? What if a reporter already has a job, is covering the business, and she falls for somebody she covers?"

I've seen this situation happen at my old paper, and I've seen it happen to journalists I know. "He or she is reassigned usually. Our job is to be fair. Our job is to be accurate. I'm not curing cancer or saving the whales, but at the very least, I'm trying to write something unbiased."

His blue eyes are piercing as he stares at me. "Do you think, then, that you should tell Mr. Galloway?"

He's tossing ethics back at me, perhaps treating me as he would a parishioner someday.

"I have to tell him, don't I?" I squeak out. "Even though I'm not involved with Flynn, I have to tell my editor."

He rests his palm on my hand, giving a gentle squeeze. "I read the piece. I think you did an amazing job. But I'm not unbiased either. I love you to the ends of the earth and back, and I think everything you do is amazing. I tried to give it a critical eye, and I think it's incredible. But what if my take on it is colored by how much I love you? And what if your approach was colored by your feelings for Flynn?"

I groan and drop my forehead onto the table. "This was such a big chance for me. And I blew it by falling for this guy."

He rubs my forearm. "I don't know that falling for someone is ever blowing it. I don't know if I have any answers as to what you should do. But I don't think letting yourself feel something real and true, especially after what happened to you, is a bad thing."

I raise my face. "But it is. I have bills to pay."

"Sabrina," he says, his voice firm and strong. "We'll stretch out the loans longer."

I shake my head vehemently. "No. I made a promise to myself when Mom left that I'd look out for you. I made a promise to the state too. A *legal* promise."

"I can look out for myself. I don't have a ton of debt from college. I can handle all the loans from grad school."

I shake my head. "This is your dream. How many men

today want to be pastors? It's noble and beautiful, and you're mine," I say, pointing at him. "You're mine, and don't you forget it."

He laughs, shaking his head. "I know, but being yours doesn't mean you have to sacrifice your happiness."

I bristle at his characterization. "I'm not sacrificing my happiness. Dude, I have other bills too. Rent, and utilities, and food. That stuff you need to fuel your body every day. You've heard of it?"

He rolls his eyes. "Yes, Sabrina."

"And living. Subways aren't free. Nor is internet access. Who can live without that? See? I need a J-O-B regardless, so don't start thinking it's all about you."

"Your tough-girl big-sister routine is as entertaining as it was when I was fifteen."

I smile and cross my arms, making it clear how sure I am that my decision is my decision. "Good."

He drums his fingers on the table and softens his voice. "My point is, don't do this for me. Don't be so stoic for me. I'll find a way. Schools are flexible. I'm sure we can work out a different payment plan. Would you let me do that? Talk to them and work something out?"

"I'm going to get a job," I say, standing firm.

"You've insisted on the bills going to you. But perhaps I need to do the insisting now that you're giving up something."

"Kevin, give me time," I say, pleading. "Let me see what happens with the job."

"I have faith you'll get it, and when you do, I don't want any more help."

I scoff.

He laughs.

It's a standoff, and soon I catch a train back to Manhattan, staring out the window as it pulls into the station, wondering what Flynn is up to tonight and if his heart feels like a lead weight too.

When I reach my home, I email the article to Mr. Galloway.

25

Flynn

The ball screams toward me, and I lunge for it, slamming it with my racket, sending it reeling against the wall. The blue orb slams the backboard before careening in my sister's direction. She grunts, reaching for it, stretching her entire body perpendicular in a mad effort to reach the whizzing object. But it soars past her and skitters to the ground.

I pump a fist. "Yes."

Panting hard, she offers her hand. "Congrats, you determined bastard."

"Hey, it's at least one thing I got right this week."

"I hardly think beating me in a game of racquetball is the one thing you got right this week."

"It feels that way since I botched asking Sabrina if she wanted to pursue anything more."

Olivia shoots me a sympathetic smile. "It sucks, doesn't it?"

"Royally."

She taps my shoulder with her racket. "What really sucks is that you've finally met somebody who isn't into you for your money, and you can't have her."

"Yes. Thank you for the reminder. Want to rub it in more?"

"I meant that as a good thing."

"How is that good?" I grab a bottle of water and down some.

"Because you knew where you stood with her. She didn't use you. She did the opposite of use you," Olivia says, picking up a towel and wiping her neck with it.

"True," I admit. "I knew where I stood with her heart. And I know where I stand with her life—not in it. I mean, what am I supposed to do?" I force out a laugh. "Buy the magazine?"

Olivia's eyes become billboards, flashing the words *aha*. "That's not a bad idea. That'd be a hell of a big gesture."

"Somehow, I don't think Sabrina will go for that."

"But you could do it. That's kind of crazy and amazing. You could buy the magazine and offer her a job there. Why not?"

I shake my head, dragging a hand through my hair. "She wouldn't want me to. Ironic, isn't it? I've been with a woman who wanted me for money. I finally meet someone who has literally zero interest in my wallet, and I can't even use said wallet to my advantage."

"That means you have to rely on your heart," she says, tapping my chest for emphasis. "And let her know how much you love her."

I straighten my spine at those words. *Let her know how much you love her.*

"You told her you're in love with her, right?" Olivia continues.

I open my mouth to speak, but it turns out I'm speechless.

"Falling in love with her? You told her you're falling in love with her, at least?" she asks.

I shake my head.

My sister rolls her eyes. "*Men.* You never learn."

"You're saying I should have told her that?" Maybe the cushion wasn't what she needed. Or maybe I offered the *wrong* cushion.

Olivia raps the side of my head with her knuckles. "How does anyone think you're a genius? Does the gray matter even work?"

"You don't think it's coming on too strong to tell her I'm falling in love with her?"

"Do you think she's falling in love with you?"

I cycle back through the time we've spent together— our kiss in the costume shop, the way she looked at me at softball, the sound of her voice when we walked and talked.

I smile stupidly. "Yeah."

Olivia moves closer, getting in my face. "Then how do you know what would happen unless you truly put your heart out? You've finally met someone you're crazy about, and that means you need to put everything on the line."

"But I'm not the one who stands to lose so much. How do I convince her? Without, you know, buying the magazine?"

"Hey, I still think that's a fine idea," she says with a wink. Then she turns more serious. "But there are things you could say to her . . ."

And she's right. There are so many things I've left unsaid.

* * *

Sabrina

Courtney encourages me like a coach. "Come on, you can do it."

I crunch higher, my eyes squeezing shut, my core shouting at me to *make it stop.* "Whoever invented core exercises is the devil."

Courtney laughs. "Yes, whoever did is indeed the worst person in the world. But core is so good for you."

I'm at Courtney's gym the next morning, and she's pretending she's a personal trainer. That basically equates to her torturing me endlessly.

Grabbing an exercise mat, she flops down next to me and says it's time for bicycle crunches.

I hold my hands to my cheeks and affect a scream, Edward Munch–style. "Nooooooo. That's the ninth circle of hell."

Laughing, she nudges me as she lifts her knees and embarks on showing off how awesome she is at biking on her back. "You can do it. I have faith in your stomach muscles."

"My stomach muscles are Grumpy Cat today. Just like me. We hate everything."

"You're in a fun mood."

"Oh, sorry. I meant to be more chipper, but I had my heart slaughtered."

Her eyes widen as she crunches. "See? I knew you really liked him."

I groan. "Of course I really like him. I told you everything. He's wonderful, and amazing, and incredible, and this situation is absolutely like some ridiculous curse of the universe. It's like my cursed wedding dress. Like Ray leaving me for no reason."

She crunches as she talks, and it's impressive. That must be some Guinness World Record feat, akin to contortionism or pulling off twenty-four hours' worth of jumping jacks. "It's kind of crazy that you finally met somebody who makes you feel like you can take a chance again, but *you* feel like you can't take a chance with him."

I sigh and drop down on the mat, my entire body going floppy and flat. "I *can't* take a chance with him."

Courtney shrugs as she cycles her legs. "Maybe you can."

"If there was a way, I would've found it. I swear I would have."

"This isn't the Lost City of Atlantis, Sabrina."

I shoot her a look. "I'm not saying it is."

She hums. "You kind of are."

I sigh heavily. "So, what are *you* saying, Courtney?"

"I'm saying that taking a chance with him isn't some great secret mystery to unlock. It's not a code to crack. It's making a choice."

I arch a brow. "It's that easy? Just choose the dish from the appetizer list and have him for dinner?"

Courtney quirks her lips. "I suspect you'd like having him for dinner every night. Which is my point. You can choose Flynn. No one is holding your feet to the fire except you."

I open my mouth to protest, but she holds up a hand

and shakes her head, still crunching. "What are you going to do? Give up perfect guy after perfect guy?"

"He's the only perfect guy I've ever met," I grumble.

"Exactly," she says triumphantly. "And you're letting him go because you think you don't deserve it. Because you can't make time for it. Because you'll never find another job again. Because of your brother. Because of, because of, because of. Jobs come and go, Sabrina. But good men?" She stops mid-cycle and sits up, ceasing crunching. "They don't come around often. More like once in a blue moon."

"He is pretty amazing," I concede.

"Maybe it's time to take care of yourself. Maybe this time, do what you want because you deserve it, not because it's the 'right thing to do.' Do it because this is the *only* thing that makes sense to your heart."

I inhale deeply, processing her advice, then narrow my eyes at her. "Stop being so wise."

"I can't help it. It comes naturally to me. Like crunches."

And just like crunches, following her advice will be hard.

But what if it's worth it?

What if he's the chance I should be taking?

I flash back to my conversation with Kevin yesterday, to the questions he posed, to the truth I've known all along.

I know what I have to do. I have to do the right thing.

But I can also do the *only* thing I want for my heart.

Because she's right. You don't let a once-in-a-blue-moon man pass you by.

* * *

Flynn

I shoot at a cardboard cutout of a building. Dylan rounds the corner and aims at a guy we know who runs a food delivery app. "Take that," he mutters, pointing at the guy's back with his laser gun.

A beam of red light knocks the guy down. The dude falls dramatically and curses at Dylan. My brother simply moves on, hunting the next opponent. He's a competitive bastard, and I'm playing laser tag with him in his CEO game at Chelsea Piers.

Dylan careens around the corner, taking risk after risk, firing and amassing the most points. That's one of the things I've always admired about my brother. He's more fearless than I am. He takes more chances.

He was always the one who was willing to jump. I was the thinker in our partnership.

But as I watch him giving his all, playing his heart out, I realize I could learn from him. Like Sabrina said, there's something to our twin-ness. Maybe I need some of his Wonder Twin power.

When we're done, I smack him on the back and say, "You're freaking awesome. You just go for it."

"Hell, yeah. Balls to the wall. Give it everything."

As we leave, I power my phone back on, intending to click open my text messages and ask Sabrina if she's free to see me. I'm ready to go for it. Give it everything.

Once my phone boots up, I find a note from her.

Angel: Could you meet me at Gramercy Park tonight? I hear you have a key.

26

Sabrina

Dear Mr. Galloway,

Thank you so much for the opportunity to write for Up Next. *I'm so grateful that you gave me this chance. I loved every moment of working on this piece. I've written what I think is a fair and accurate story that dives into who Flynn is and illustrates why he is a next-generation visionary.*

I turned in the piece last night, as you know, but in the interest of full disclosure, I need to inform you that while reporting this story I've developed feelings for Mr. Parker, and I acted upon those feelings. I would like to tell you those emotions didn't affect what I wrote. I hope they didn't, but that is for you to decide.

I want you to know the facts. I will await your decision, and I remain grateful for the opportunity.

Sincerely,

Sabrina Granger

As I read the letter one last time, my stomach swoops, but then everything settles down.

A brand-new calm spreads through me. I'm no longer a caged lion.

Perhaps that's from knowing I'm making the right choice. I might not get the prize. I don't have a safety net. But I hope there's a better prize waiting for me. The best prize.

When I look back on this moment five years from now, whether I'm with Flynn or not, I'll know I took the chance my heart was telling me to take.

Even if your heart has been broken, it doesn't mean you have to put it on ice forever. It can thaw. Mine did, and sometimes it's worth taking the leap without a net.

Flynn is that leap.

He's worth it.

There's no *what-if* about it.

My finger hovers over the *send* button, ready to fire it off, when a new message pops up in my inbox.

It's one from Mr. Galloway.

It startles me, and I actually jump. I look behind me. It's as if I'm being watched, which is a ridiculous thing to think. But there it is—the thought in my head.

Maybe he already knows.

Maybe Kermit got to him.

I click to open the email.

Dear Sabrina,

Could you please come in tomorrow morning? We can discuss the piece then. It's quite good. But there are some things I need to talk to you about.

Sincerely,

Bob Galloway

I wait for the note to hurt. I wait for the fear.

It doesn't come.

Whatever he has to tell me, I can handle it. I've made my choice. I chose love.

I save my note to him in my drafts folder. Some things are better said in person. I will tell him tomorrow.

Tonight is for me.

I slip into an emerald-green dress I finished a few days ago, pop in two pairs of angel-shaped stud earrings, clip one side of my hair in a silver ladybug barrette, and head to what I hope is the first of many dates with Flynn Parker.

27

Sabrina

The wrought iron gates loom before me.

Tall spires let me peek into a world I've never entered.

Not just this park but what it represents: wealth, privilege, money.

A walkway cuts across the land beyond the locked gate, and gloriously high trees, bursting with bottle-green leaves, wrap their arms over the grounds, shielding those rare few who have access.

I breathe it in. It's an enclave. A private square for the privileged.

I've been on the outside looking in, even though I never longed for this much. I've never been a girl who wanted riches showered on her. I simply wanted better choices.

Or really, I wanted choices, period.

But in the end, I wouldn't do anything differently.

I stand by all the decisions I've made, including the one that brought me here tonight.

Shoes click on the sidewalk. It could be anyone—a businessman, a father, a hipster. This is a city of millions.

But what if it's him?

I turn, and he takes my breath away.

Flynn Parker is so handsome. He's lean and tall, and his hair flops deliciously on his forehead, and his green eyes twinkle with excitement when he sees me.

But it's his lips I zero in on.

Those soft, wonderful lips I want on me again.

He closes the distance, and I have to go first, so as soon as he reaches me I say, "I want a do-over. I want a new beginning. I want the chance to say yes to us. It's only been two days, and I miss you like crazy, and I can't stand not having an excuse to see you. I want us to explore park benches and abandoned subways, and visit the Met, and kiss in the Great Hall, and go to costume parties dressed like Marilyn Monroe and Joe DiMaggio." I draw a quick breath, then say the hardest and the easiest words. "Because I love you, Flynn Parker."

He laughs and wraps his arms around me, rubbing his hands on my back. "Well, it's good to see you too." He's grinning from ear to ear, and his eyes dance with happiness.

"I want to be with you," I say, blurting it all out, everything. "I want to have a go at it if you'll have me. I want to do all the things in New York with you, and you can quote poetry to me and show me pineapple math, and we won't have to pretend we need to fact-check anything, and I can take you to the gin joint in Chelsea tomorrow night if you want."

Smiling, he tugs me closer, aligning his body with

mine. "So you can get me drunk?"

"Drunk and naked," I say, giggling, and I'm not a giggler. But right now, I'm so damn happy even though he hasn't said "I love you" back yet. But I'm not worried because I know he will.

This certainty—it's worth every chance.

It's worth the world.

He lifts his hand and runs his fingers across my barrette and over my hair. When he brushes the back of his fingers along my cheek, I melt. Cupping my face, he meets my gaze, holds it, and presses one soft kiss to my lips.

I think I'm going to die of happiness.

He breaks the kiss. "I'm madly in love with you too, Sabrina."

Okay, now it's official. I'm not dying. I've died, and I've gone to heaven, only better, because I'm alive, and my life is incandescent.

It's starlight, and fireworks, and all the diamonds in the night sky.

He runs a finger over my lips. "But what made you change your mind?"

I don't think. I don't contemplate. I tell him the simple truth. "I missed you so much it hurt. And I want you. All of you, because you're worth it to me."

"You're worth everything to me. You need to know that. I know I shouldn't have offered you a job, and I also know there's not much I can give you that you'll let me give," he says, and I smile stubbornly, nodding in acknowledgment. "But I can be there for you. Let me give you the support you need. Let me help you as you look for whatever you want next in your career. If you need an introduction to someone, I'll do that. If you need me to get you a massage or give you a massage, I'll do that. If you want someone to cook you dinner while you talk about your day, I'm your man. But that's not all I can do," he says, and mischief plays in his eyes.

"What other tricks do you have up your sleeve?" I ask, running my hand over his arm, loving the feel of his warm skin, his muscles.

"In the costume shop, you said I helped you to not think about things. You said the way I made love to you made it so you didn't have to think at all," he says, and I tremble as he says *made love*. I'm warm all over thinking about how he'll do it to me tonight. "Let me help you that way. Let me help you whenever you need to not think."

"Like right now?"

He laughs. "But I thought you wanted to see Gramercy Park?"

"I do. I really do. But I want you more."

"We'll come back, then, whenever you want." He leans in close, brushes my hair over my ear, and whispers, "*And now, like amorous birds of prey, rather at once our time devour.*"

I swoon. "You can't quote Andrew Marvell, especially when his words are all randy. I told you poetry is an instant orgasm for me."

He smiles and gestures to the end of the block. "Let's go to my place."

I grab his shirt, shaking my head. "We need to go to mine."

"But I live across the street."

"I know, but if I go into your house, it'll feel like a palace and I'll want to look around and really all I want to do is have you fuck me. No distractions."

He hails a cab, and we go to the East Village.

28

Flynn

Weeks of pent-up desire rises to the surface.

Along with other things.

To be fair, that's been risen for a while. Since I saw her outside Gramercy Park. Hey, my woman gives me wood. It's just the way it is. She makes me happy too, and I couldn't be more thrilled that she's taking a chance with me.

Now though? I'm ready to give her something else she needs, something I need too.

Connection.

The second the door clicks shut, I nibble on her neck. Her arms are still wrapped tight around me. I whisper in her ear, "You like it when I take over, right?"

"I do," she whispers, so husky and sexy. I reach for her hands, removing them from my neck. I drop them to her sides and wrap my hands around her wrists, looking at her gorgeous face. Her hazel eyes pierce mine. Vulnerability, arousal, readiness—that's what I see in her eyes.

"I need you to put your hands on the kitchen table," I tell her as I spin her around, walking her to the table, and pressing a hand on the small of her back so she understands. "And lift your ass."

"Oh, God," she whimpers as she flattens her back and lays her chest against the wood, her arms stretching straight in front of her.

She looks like a jewel in that dress, with the emerald against her creamy, pale flesh and caramel hair. I take off my glasses and set them next to her.

"Stay like that." I bend to my knees and push her skirt up all the way to her ass. A loud groan rips from my throat as I see her panties. Pink. Lace. Barely there. "I don't think anyone can legally sell these as underwear. They barely cover you, and God bless whoever made them."

I glance at her face, pressed to the table, and she smiles wickedly. "There's not much to them."

I stare at her bare legs, every inch of my skin heated, burning with lust for her. I run my hands up the back of her thighs. "Look at you. So beautiful for me." I slide my hands down to her ankles then kiss one cheek. "Do you have any idea how long I've wanted to taste you?"

"How long?"

"Too fucking long. I've gotten off to this so many times. To going down on you."

A full-body shudder shimmies along her legs. As I press a kiss to the back of her knee, a soft little moan falls from her lips. "How did you do it to me? When you fantasized about it?"

"Sometimes I spread you out on the table like this, or I

turned you around and you were flat on your back, your heels at the edge of the wood."

She shudders.

I kiss her right knee. "Sometimes you sat on my desk with your legs wide open and your feet up, and I had you for lunch."

A gasp is her response. "I would come into your office and do that for you."

"I know you would. And I'm going to hold you to that." I run my hand up her thigh, cupping one cheek. "Sometimes you crawled up me and sat on my face, and you rocked your sexy little body against my mouth."

She groans so loud it sends a rumble through my body. It makes my bones shake with lust. This is what it's like to want someone with every fiber of your being. This desire for her, I feel it everywhere—inside me, along my skin, in my heart, in every goddamn cell in my body. It's like a force of its own, obliterating everything else.

"Sometimes I'd set you on the couch, and I'd hold you down with my hands because you wiggled so much."

"Because it was so good," she moans.

I lick the back of her knee then flick my tongue up her thigh, reaching her ass. I lick across that wonderful seam where her ass meets her thigh, and she quivers. Her hands grip the edge of the table, white-knuckling it. "Of course it's so good. It's you and me, Angel."

I bite the soft flesh of her rear, and she gasps, moving closer, trying valiantly to get me to bring my face between her legs.

"God, I want you so much. Please, please," she whimpers. "Please take them off."

I slide a hand between her legs and cup her. She's so

deliciously soaked, it sends a jolt of heat down my spine, and my dick hardens even more. "So wet."

"Please," she begs again.

It's all she can say, and I don't need her to say anything else.

"As you wish." I slide down her panties, leave them on the floor, and press my lips close, but not quite close enough.

She wriggles, trying to get me to the sweet spot. Trying to push herself against my mouth. She's a desperate, wanton thing. I shift to the other thigh and nip her flesh.

She cries out and moans my name. It sounds so fucking filthy and perfect on her lips that it breaks me down. "Do you want me to put you out of your misery, Angel?"

"Yes," she moans, making that one syllable last like the chorus to a song.

At last, I kiss her.

I'm dizzy with desire. She's sweet, salty honey. I lick her, and she cries out. Her taste floods my tongue, coats my lips. I kiss her harder, flicking my tongue across all that slippery heat.

As I go down on her, my brain is mostly a blur. My body is nothing but lust. But three things remain crystal clear.

I'm so fucking happy.

I'm so incredibly turned on.

And I'm deep in filthy, beautiful love with her.

29

Sabrina

It's too much.

Too much pleasure, too much bliss, too much goodness.

I'm lost in the sensations that rocket through me.

Tingles and sparks and wild roller-coaster loops.

I've become a neon woman, a sign blinking brightly against the night. *Pleasure served here.*

He makes love to me with his lips, and he fucks me with his tongue, and he spears my flesh with his fingers. They dig into my thighs, and this is the most intense thing I've ever felt.

I don't have to think. I *get* to feel.

My nerve endings come alive. Heat flares across my skin as his tongue lavishes attention on me. He flicks faster, kisses more deeply, makes love to me with his mouth so wickedly that I fear I might not recover.

I believe I'll be amenable to that.

Gripping the table for dear life, I rock against him, letting him set the pace, letting him control the tempo, knowing he'll get me there.

He'll get me everywhere.

I'm a comet tearing across the night sky, hurtling on a wild thrill ride through the cosmos.

I spin and spiral, and soon, soon everything turns to a blur and I'm soaring. I'm starlight and moonlight, flying so far above the earth.

I didn't know it was possible to come this hard, this thoroughly. I don't want to come down, not ever. I want to live inside these millions of sensations like diamonds in my body.

At some point, I breathe again. I blink open my eyes. I smile like a fool in love. "Thanks. May I have another?" I murmur. I mean it as sort of a joke, but he takes me seriously.

"As you wish."

He scoops me up, carries me to the futon, and lays me down.

We reenact one of his fantasies. He spreads my legs, and in seconds, he has me so wild that he grips my hands, holding them tightly to keep me still.

Or stiller, I should say. Because I'm a live wire, writhing and thrusting as he licks me again and again.

When I near the cliff a second time, I murmur huskily, my throat dry, "Let me touch you, please."

He lets go of my fingers, and I grab his head, holding on to him. Like that, I come again, his face between my legs, my hands wrapped in his hair.

A minute later, or maybe more, I open my eyes to find a gloriously naked and gorgeous Flynn standing at my side, stroking his cock. God, he's stunning.

Reaching out, I trace the grooves of his abs, the cut of his arms, and I feel his hot, hard length in my hands. He shudders when I touch him, thrusting against my palm.

"You're mine," I whisper.

"I'm yours," he murmurs. "And you're mine."

I sit up. I'm still in a daze, but I pull off my dress, and I'm completely naked. "Flynn, can we go bare? I'm clean, and I'm on birth control."

"Fuck, yes. I'm clean."

That's all we need to know. He flips me to my knees, and I want to weep with happiness.

I hate missionary.

I love being taken.

He knows what I need, and he's going to give it to me. He's put me on my hands and knees, spreading my cheeks, rubbing the head of his cock against me.

I ache.

Exquisitely.

Deeply.

My body craves him like a filthy drug.

I am desperate for my fix, and he gives it to me, shoving deep inside with a carnal groan.

I cry out. "God, it's so good."

"It's better than the first time."

"I know," I whisper.

And it's not the position, though I love how he grabs my ass as he moves in me.

It's not the depth either. But I adore how he's reaching the ends of me, how I can feel him everywhere.

It's not even how he pushes on my back, making me lower my chest to the futon. Or how he loops my hair around his fist, though all of that sends me into the stratosphere.

It's how he loves me, even when he fucks me.

It's better because we're Angel and Duke, city explorers, wordsmith and mathematician, poetry reciter and poetry receiver, and most of all, we are us.

Loving and fucking, fucking and loving.

There's no more role-playing tonight. We have no need to pretend because we both want the real thing.

As he goes deep another time, swiveling his hips and stroking me, I'm there again at the edge, coming like it's all my body ever wants to do, like I've been trained to do this, like I can't stop.

He grips me harder, groaning and turning wild. Saying my name. The way it sounds from his lips, like a benediction, like a rock song, like a primal scream of pleasure, is the highest high.

He collapses on me.

His arms slink around me, and he smothers my face in kisses, and I don't know who wins the "I love you" game, but we both play it all night long, saying it, telling the other.

As I curl up in his arms, I know I've never felt this way with anyone else. I've never felt this safe, this content, this wildly, blissfully happy. I have no idea what tomorrow will bring, but I'll be able to get through it with him by my side.

When morning comes we shower, learning how fun it is to get clean with my hands against the wall and his on my breasts as he makes me come again.

Then we dress, and I get ready to see Mr. Galloway. I walk Flynn to the door of the building and wave as he heads down the street.

He waves back, the morning sun haloing his handsome face.

I can't resist.

"Wait!" I call out, racing down the steps and after him.

I run to him, and I throw myself at him, wrapping my arms around his neck, my legs around his waist, like a koala. He laughs and pulls me closer.

"I love you, Flynn Parker."

"I love you, Sabrina Granger."

"I want to kiss you again."

"Kiss me again."

We kiss, and we kiss, and eventually, I let him leave.

As I return to my building, an engine rumbles loudly by the curb. I turn in its direction, spotting an idling red sports car.

As I walk past it, the passenger door opens.

A woman emerges. Red flaming hair. Big sunglasses. Snapping bubblegum. Cowboy boots.

Maureen is here.

30

Sabrina

"Baby!"

I still cringe when she calls me that. When she acts as if she has the right to call me anything other than my name.

Drawing a deep breath, I let it fill me, let it fuel me with calm, with grace. That is the only way I can handle her. "Hello, Maureen."

She holds her arms out wide, scads of silver and gold bracelets jangling up her wrists. Her jeans are painted onto her legs, and her blouse is unbuttoned low enough to reveal the tops of her breasts. "Give your momma a hug."

My skin crawls. I don't want to hug her. I don't want to talk to her. I don't want to see her. But I also don't want to give her the satisfaction of knowing how I feel. I choose blankness with her. That's how I've tried to behave since she left—cool and calm, showing no emotions.

I walk the few feet to her. Steeling myself, I give her a quick hug. The cloying scent of her Britney Spears perfume wafts into my nostrils. She tries to keep me in the embrace, gripping me tight then sniffing my hair.

I peel myself away, smoothing a hand over my blouse —my *Up Next* uniform. My hair is still wet, pulled back in a looped-over ponytail.

"Tell me all the things. What's the dealio?" Her eyes drift in the direction that Flynn walked. "Are you going to tell me about your new main squeeze?"

She hasn't earned the privilege to know a damn thing about the best part of my life. I dodge the question. "How are you, Maureen?"

She blows a pink bubble the size of a small fish. Snapping it into her hot-pink lipsticked mouth, she shakes her head and wags a finger at me. "Don't try to avoid the subject." Her voice is cheery like we always have these kinds of girly conversations when she bursts into town every year.

Oh, wait. We do. Because she bursts into town every year, acting like everything is fine. "When did you start seeing Flynn Parker?"

A blush spreads across my face when she voices his name. I hate how it sounds on her tongue. Gritting my teeth, I remain silent as I wonder how she knows who he is. But then, she probably stays current on all the wealthy men.

She punches my arm. "You got yourself a rich man. Way to go, girl."

"Mom," I say, groaning.

"Good for you, baby. Now, you don't have to worry about a thing."

Sighing heavily, I bite out the words. "Mom, that's not how it works. That's not how it is."

She juts her hip out to the side, tapping the toe of her red cowboy boot. "That's totally the way it is," she whispers and nods at the car. "It's that way for me too. Carlos owns his own business." She scans the block then whispers, "A dispensary. Want to meet him? He loves to shower me with gifts." She flashes a silver bracelet with a turquoise stone in it. "He picked this up for me at the casino."

She turns toward the car and taps the door. "Carlos, show your pretty face to my daughter."

With one hand on the wheel, her new beau leans his head toward the passenger side, flashing a huge grin as he drums his fingers on the dashboard in time to pop music blasting from the radio. He's probably twenty-eight.

"Hi, Carlos," I say flatly.

"Hey, Sabrina, good to finally meet you. You want to hang out with us today?"

"I have a business meeting. But thanks." I turn to my mother. "I have to go. I have an appointment in midtown in thirty minutes, and I need to dry my hair."

"Let us drive you. We can totally help you, and we can chat and catch up."

"No," I say faster than I've ever answered any question. "I don't have time to talk right now."

"How do you not have time for your momma?"

I want to ignore her. I want to play it cool. But this time I can't. The ancient hurt wells up. The frustration that's never far away when it comes to her spills over. "Me? How do I not have time? How did you not have time for us? You left us, Maureen. You left your thirteen-year-old son. You didn't make any time for him."

She laughs, dismissing me with a wave. "You were so much better at taking care of Kevin than I was. I never understood that boy. It was all for the best that you wound up looking out for him. Don't you think so?"

Red billows from my eyes. Fumes roll off my body. How can she do this? That's not how mothering works, handing off a kid you don't understand to your other kid. That's not how family works. "Looking out for him? I raised him, Maureen. You left."

"And it was the right choice."

The temperature in me rises. "It was *only* for the best because I love him unconditionally. Because I treated him better, not because it was an acceptable thing to—"

I cut myself off. My pulse speeds too dangerously for this conversation to continue. Why bother arguing with her? It won't change the past, and it won't alter the future. I absolutely know why my mother left us. Because she wanted to. Because she chose to.

I can make a choice too.

I don't have to give her an audience. I don't have to answer her questions. "I'm leaving, Maureen."

"Fine, fine. Be that way. But since you got yourself a rich, hot thing, can you help your momma out with some greenbacks?" She brushes her thumb and forefinger together. "I just need five thousand dollars for this new venture that Carlos and I want to start. Not too much, right? Surely, you can spare that."

I stare at her incredulously.

This is who she is.

This is how she acts.

It shouldn't surprise me. But it still does. Maybe it always will. But my answer will always be the same.

"No."

"No?" She's equally incredulous. "How can you say no?"

I scoff. "I don't have money for you, and I certainly don't have Flynn's money for you. I barely have my own. I have a business meeting to go to, and I am leaving. Drive safely."

I head inside, slamming the door behind me, my breath coming hard and fast and angry. Latent fury runs through my veins and threatens to overtake me.

But I don't have the time for rage.

I have life to deal with.

I must refuse to let her bother me.

I tell myself to let her go, and I picture her and her boyfriend cruising along the interstate, blasting past the speed limit, getting the hell out of New York and away from me.

I bid them a silent farewell.

She is who she is, and every day I make the choice not to be my mother's daughter.

I dry my hair, run to the subway, and soon I'm back at the building in midtown, heading inside. I do a double take when I reach the nineteenth floor.

The frames of old editions on the walls have been removed. The receptionist is gone. Most of the desks are dismantled.

Bob Galloway strides in my direction. He looks like he hasn't shaved in days.

31

Flynn

I toss the towel into the hamper of the gym locker, grab my wallet, and slide my glasses back on. When I turn to leave, I nearly bump chests with Dale, the locker room attendant.

He flashes a toothy grin. "Hey, Flynn. I've been thinking about what you said, and here's my idea."

He wastes no time, and I do respect that. "Hit me."

Spreading his hands out wide, he makes the universal sign for *I'm-about-to-give-an-elevator-pitch*. "Picture this. Instead of How'm I Doing rating my own sexual performance, what if it's used to rate your partner's?"

I blink, rubbing my ear. That can't possibly be how he's decided to pivot on his idea. "That's your plan?"

He nods proudly. "You'd use the app to write up the person you just got busy with. Like a sexual Yelp."

I part my lips to speak, but I'm not sure words exist to describe how awful that would be.

Dale misinterprets my silence. "Brilliant, right? You could share information about someone. Rate them like an Uber driver. Let the next person know what they're getting into."

"No pun intended," I say drily, recovering speech.

"Right. No pun."

That's the problem.

An expectant look in his eyes, he waits for my blessing. I scratch my head, trying to figure out exactly how to combine the words in the right order to tell him *never do this*, when he holds up a finger and says, "Or, my other idea is something to do with pizza. Because I like pizza, and everybody likes pizza, and maybe I should make an app where you rate your favorite pizza places and share ideas for great and unexpected toppings and combos."

My smile spreads of its own accord, and I clap his shoulder. "Go in that direction. Pizza is awesome. Pizza is good."

I leave the gym and head to my office. In the lobby, Claude raises his face and waves. "Mr. Parker, did I ever tell you about my cousin?"

I stifle a groan but slap on a smile. "The one who wants to play professional miniature golf?"

Claude chuckles and shakes his head. "Not him. I told him he needed to figure that out on his own. No one was going to 'GoFund' him and his dumbass idea," he says, sketching air quotes, and I'm glad Claude set him on the right path. "This is my other cousin. Gracie. She's eleven and goes to school in the Bronx, and they're trying to take a trip to the planetarium next week. You know that one where Neil deGrasse Tyson does his thing?"

"He's the man. I love that guy."

"They're trying to go there. Isn't that cool?" He's beaming, and I don't even wait for him to ask for the money.

"You need me to fund it? I'll do it."

"What?" He jerks back, clearly flummoxed.

"Oh, I thought you were asking."

"No, but I'm sure they do need some help. I was just telling you about it 'cause I knew you liked him. I like that dude as well. I like to watch him on TV."

"Claude, let me take care of it. It would be a pleasure."

As I make the offer officially, an idea blasts into my brain. Unexpected, but completely awesome. Because that's what ideas do. They pop out of nowhere. I'm eager as hell to head upstairs and work out the details.

"Really? That'd be amazing. Gracie will be excited, and so will her class. You're the man."

"It's my pleasure. Anything that exposes young kids to science is a good thing."

As I make my way toward the elevator with a renewed sense of purpose, ready to tackle my plan, another voice calls my name. It's a little gravelly, like it was roughened over the years by too many cigarettes.

When I turn, I see a woman with flaming red hair and too many bracelets. "Yoo-hoo! Sabrina told me to come see you."

32

Sabrina

Even though his face is bedraggled, the suit Bob Galloway wears looks like it cost a mint. The stitching aligns so elegantly across his shoulders that it must have been custom-made.

"Sabrina," he says, extending his hand and shaking mine. "Thanks for coming by. I need to give you a kill fee."

I flinch then swallow hard. "A kill fee?" I ask, in case there's a chance I heard him wrong.

"It was a brilliant piece. One of the best stories I've read in years." He gestures to the disheveled offices, sighing heavily. "But the publication is shutting down."

Swaying, I brace myself against the wall. It's as if the ground has fallen out from under me. "You're shutting down?" I ask, because this makes zero sense.

"Like many other print publications, we don't have enough ad dollars to survive."

"But you had all those fat magazines full of ad pages."

"Those were from last year."

"What about the website?" I ask, grasping for the bow of a sinking boat.

"We didn't move quickly enough to establish a presence, so others have beaten us there." He clears his throat, looking around sheepishly at the emptying offices. "And we might have overspent in a few areas."

In an instant, everything snaps into view. I see where the money went. It went to parties, to his suits, to these opulent offices they didn't need. It went to paying exorbitant fees for articles.

"The story isn't going to run anywhere?" I choke out.

"That's why I wanted to call you in today."

"You could have emailed me," I point out gently.

Genteel till the end, he removes his wallet from his back pocket. "No. I couldn't. I'm paying you the kill fee from my own pocket."

Snapping open his billfold, he fishes out two crisp hundred-dollar bills, less than 5 percent of the finished fee, and hands them to me. "The piece was amazing. Brilliant. Fair. Thoughtful. Entertaining. Beautifully written. Everything I could want," he says, and I beam, a ray of sunshine peeking through a cloudy sky. "I'm sorry we won't have a home for it. But it's yours to do what you want with. You could publish it on your own website. Maybe turn it into a book," he suggests, and both ideas border on outlandish.

One, I don't publish articles on my website, since I don't have one. Two, it's not a book.

Still, I did the work, so I take the money and thank him. "What are you going to do, sir?"

He shrugs happily. "I'm retiring. Sometimes you just have to get out of the business."

I leave in a daze, my feet heavy, my heart leaden once more. I feel useless again. *Used.*

And confused.

Stepping into the elevator, it's as if everything I knew about my business has been turned inside out. Bob Galloway was the exemplar of journalism. He was the man I admired. But even he couldn't keep his ship afloat during trying times.

The elevator chugs downward as my insides churn. I didn't expect to leave today with my original fee and a pending byline. I always knew I'd be leaving empty-handed.

But the part I'm struggling with is that I was fighting for a chance that was never going to materialize. The job here was smoke and mirrors. My actions were meaningless. I didn't even need to confess my sins, since they had no bearing on the story after all.

When I reach the lobby, I take a deep breath and try to make sense of what to do next.

This is a twist I didn't see coming, and even though I'm two hundred dollars richer, I'm walking out the door with more questions.

Where should I go next? What should I do? What sort of work should I pursue?

I'm tempted to head to the nearest coffee shop and fire off clip after clip to other editors. But before I do that, I reflect on last night.

On Flynn's words outside Gramercy Park.

Let me be there for you.

Out on the street, I stare up at the looming skyscraper, the plucky heroine with the new job opportunity no more.

But as I furrow my brow, the wheels start turning. The dots connect. And I can see a way through.

I can see a whole new path.

Maybe the story was never pointless. Maybe the story was always meant to be my way to Flynn.

It's a strange way for me to look at things. I've always been a practical woman. I've always been work-focused, seen things in the context of responsibility.

And yet, even if it was all for nothing, I believe what I went through was all for everything.

I believe it with my whole heart.

This job was never my future.

Because my future includes Flynn.

And maybe, just maybe, there's something else that I can do. I don't have to figure it out alone.

Yes, I have Courtney. Yes, I have Kevin, but now I have someone who is supposed to be by my side as I navigate what's next. I do something that feels crazy, but completely right.

I call my boyfriend to see if he has a few minutes to chat.

Flynn

I shoot her a skeptical stare. "Sabrina told you to come here?"

"My daughter sure did," her mom says, striding up to me and tapping her long red fingernails against my chest. "She said you could help me out."

I tilt my head to the side. "Did she now?"

Her mom shimmies her shoulders back and forth. "Yes, she did. She said you were so generous, and she knew you'd be willing to help the mom of the girl you love."

"Is that so?" I arch a brow.

Her mother smiles—a big fat grin. "She did."

"And what is it that you need, Ms.—" I stop, since I don't know if they have the same last name or not.

"Ms. Maureen Lancaster."

"Nice to meet you."

A voice cuts in. "Everything okay, Mr. Parker?"

I nod to Claude. "I'm all good." I turn back to Sabrina's mom. "You're saying Sabrina told you to come see me today?"

"She sure did. I saw you two kissing like lovebirds on the street, since I was coming to town to visit her. And after my sweet girl and I caught up once you left, she said you'd be so willing to help me out. That all I'd need to do was come see you and give you the details."

I rub a hand over my jaw. This is a brand-new pitch for me. A proposal I never could have expected. "She did?"

Maureen nods, chewing gum and smiling as if it's the last thing she plans to do today. "She told me where you worked, and how generous you are, and how you always like to help her family."

"I do love to help her," I say, studying Maureen's face, trying to see any signs of love for her daughter, for her son.

"And since you're some kind of billionaire, she said it would be easy-peasy for you to give me ten thousand dollars for a new business I'm trying to start. Since that's what you do, right? You start businesses?"

"Is that what Sabrina told you?"

"Of course, and I read all about you on the internet."

"Then you'd know I'm not a billionaire."

She laughs lightly. "Billionaire, multimillionaire. What's the difference?"

"A comma. A very important comma."

She parks a hand on her hip and juts it out to her side in what is likely supposed to be a sexy stance. "What do you say to helping the woman who gave life to your new lady?"

A hundred thoughts run through my head. Someday,

I'm going to write them down and pen a book—*All the Wild Pitches.*

And this pitch would take the top spot. Win the gold medal. The Academy Award.

It would win it since there was once a time when I might have believed this woman. A few months ago, maybe even a few weeks ago. Not because she's believable, but because I trusted no one. I'd been burned by women. My old habits would have died hard in this lobby, and I'd have suspected Sabrina was up to no good.

But I'm not that guy anymore.

I know who to trust. I know who to believe.

"Ms. Lancaster, you want to know what I say to your offer?"

"I sure do," she says, giving a coy little twirl of her hair.

I straighten my shoulders. Draw a deep breath. Speak the truth. "I would say that you have an amazing daughter and an incredible son. Maybe you ought to focus a little bit more on them." I take a beat, hoping to give weight to my last words. "Because she's amazing in spite of you, not because of you. Have a great day."

I walk away, letting Claude know he can see her out. That'll make him happy, since he'll be doing his job.

I need to do mine too. The job of being a great boyfriend.

Once I'm upstairs in the office, I make phone calls. I pull strings. I call in favors.

"Can we get that done by the end of the day?"

The woman on the other end hems and haws. "That's going to be hard."

"I'd really appreciate whatever you can do to rush this."

"I'll do my best."

I don't want to wait to give this to Sabrina. I want to give it to her tonight.

When I hang up, my phone rings, her name flashing on the screen. I answer immediately, and she asks if I have time to meet her.

"Absolutely."

34

Sabrina

I can't help but grin when I see Flynn at the coffee shop by his office.

Here he is looking business handsome in dark jeans and a simple white-and-green-striped button-down that doesn't look like it costs a million bucks. It looks like it costs maybe sixty or seventy dollars and I kind of love that he doesn't have to flaunt anything except his big brain. I do like that part of him.

We order tea and coffee and grab seats at a small table.

"What are you smiling about?" he asks.

"I was thinking about your big brain."

"I was hoping you were thinking about my big dick."

"Trust me, I'm thinking a lot about that too, but right now I'm thinking about something else."

His voice is kind when he says, "Is it your mom? She stopped by this morning."

A bolt of tension slams into me. This is my nightmare

—my gold-digging mom fishing for Flynn. "What? She stopped by to see you?"

Please say no, please say no.

He reaches across the table for my hand. "She asked for money."

I gasp, covering my mouth with my free hand. A fresh, hot wave of embarrassment crashes over me, threatening to pull me under. Mortification has a new definition—me. Flynn detests being used. I can't bear that he might have thought I played a part in her appearance. "I'm so sorry. She showed up this morning out of the blue. I had no idea she was going to do this. I didn't tell her to find you."

"I know." He squeezes my hand. "It's okay, Angel. I told her no. In fact, even when she tried to pretend you'd sent her over, I knew she was lying. I didn't fall for it."

Pinching the bridge of my nose, I shake my head. "This is a new low for her."

"Want to know what I told her?"

"What did you say?" I ask cautiously, as I take a sip of my tea.

"I told her that you're amazing in spite of her, not because of her."

My eyes leak. Twin tears stream down my cheeks, and I don't even bother to stop them. I set down my tea, reach across the table, cup his cheeks, and kiss him hard.

Passionately.

Till my tears stop.

When I let go, his lips look bruised and swollen, and his expression is dazed. "I love you."

"I love you."

Courtney was so right. Flynn is a once-in-a-blue-moon man. That's one of the many reasons why I tell him my new plan. There's something incredibly freeing about having a partner to share ideas with.

"I think it's brilliant. You have nothing to lose, and everything to gain."

That's a brand-new position for me to be in, but I like it. I like this feeling a whole hell of a lot as I head downtown.

35

Sabrina

I'm early for my meeting with Kermit. I read till he arrives.

He's on time, showing up at three on the dot, and I close my e-book.

The spitting image of Seth Rogen down to the glasses, the unruly beard, and the curly hair, he sits across from me at a coffee shop. "It's about fucking time," he barks.

Be cool. Be professional.

"Hello, Kermit. You wanted to meet with me, and I'm here. But the first thing you need to know is I'm involved with Flynn Parker. It's that simple, and my story isn't going to run in *Up Next*."

"Obviously, since they went under yesterday."

I suppress the urge to roll my eyes. "Yes, they did. That means if you were going to try to hold the piece over my head because of something you know about Flynn and me, that's not possible."

He laughs derisively. "You think I have time for that shit?"

His response surprises me, but I stay the course. "I don't know what you have time for," I say, keeping it cool.

"I couldn't care less who you screw."

I blink. "Okay. Good. That's how it should be," I say, as evenly as I can.

He cracks up, scrubbing his hand over his beard. "Is that why you thought I wanted to see you? You can be blowing Mark Zuckerberg and Bill Gates at the same damn time for all I care. I don't give a damn about your personal life."

He really is a dick, but I weirdly admire it. He makes no bones about it. But even though he's gruff, I like his standards—I'm thrilled that my personal life holds zero interest to him.

"Good," I say with a professional smile. "I wanted to get that out of the way because I have a pitch for you."

He raises an eyebrow and crosses his arms. "Go on."

"I believe you were interested in covering Flynn Parker."

"That's fair to say."

"I happen to have a fabulous story on him that's well-researched, well-written, and, as you would say, absolutely fucking awesome."

His brown eyes spark with laughter as I swear. I'm talking his language now. "Is it fucking awesome, Sabrina? Because I think I should be the judge of that."

"Of course you should judge it. I have it with me if you'd like to read it and consider it for your media empire."

He makes grabby hands, and I take the printed copy from my purse, handing it to him.

Ten minutes later, he raises both hands in the air. "Sold."

"You didn't even finish it."

"I don't need to finish it today to know I want to buy it. That's why I've been emailing you. Not everyone has the guts to come up to me at a party and say they want to work for me. In fact, most journalists don't. That's why I gave you a hard time that night. One, because I enjoy giving people a hard time, and two, because I wanted to see if you had thick skin. Seems you do, and after the party, I looked up your work. You're good," he says, and he admits it begrudgingly. I suspect it's hard for him to give compliments.

"Thank you."

He heaves a sigh. "Look, I know I'm an asshole. But I'm good at what I do, and I know talent when I see it, hear it, and read it. You're ballsy. I've been reading your stuff. That's why I reached out to you."

"And you're fine, then, with running my piece on Flynn, as long as we disclose I'm involved with him?" I ask once more, doing my job to fact-check his offer on my pitch.

He waves a hand in the air. "Yeah. Fine. Disclosure. Good. But I want more than a piece on Flynn Parker. I want you working for me."

Must get hearing checked. "Excuse me?"

"News flash. I wasn't emailing you for any other reason. I'm not holding on to old-school notions of journalism. People meet these days in a million ways, including reporters who bang CEOs at parties. I hope you get good stories on Flynn, but the world is much bigger than Flynn Parker." He stabs the paper with his finger. "I want to run this piece on the site, I want you to turn it into a long-form podcast interview, and I want a 'top ten takeaways' piece in video form."

My lips twitch into a grin. "You do?"

"Yes. And then I want you to do that every other week on someone else."

"You want me to do that regularly?"

"Yes. Insurance. Bennies. The whole nine yards. I want you to interview business leaders. I want them raw and unfiltered. I want to run them in their entirety. And then I want you to produce video reports on them too. I want you to work for me because these dinosaur newspapers and magazines are done. They're toast."

"And what about you? Are you un-toast?"

"I have money. I have advertisers and, most important, I have an audience."

An audience. I nearly salivate.

"And you," he adds, pointing to me. "You're a determined Padawan. Will you work for me? I have another meeting in a half hour, and it would be awesome if you'd say yes right about now." He taps his watch.

"What's the pay?"

He answers, giving a highly reasonable rate.

I don't know that I like him.

But I don't really think it matters. I like that he's so straightforward. I know where I stand with Kermit the Douche. I can't believe I'm about to say this, but I hold out my hand.

He shakes.

"I accept."

Sabrina

Flynn opens the door for me. I steel myself, prepared to be dazzled.

When I step into his apartment, my eyes turn into planets. "It's a palace."

He laughs, shaking his head. "It's not. Stop it."

Gawking at his home, I correct him. "It is. This is the entire floor. Your home is the entire top floor of the building."

It's stunning. The living room is the size of a museum gallery, a wide-open space with beautiful wood floors, a navy-blue sectional couch with tons of pillows, and framed photos of cities around the world hanging on the walls.

Floor-to-ceiling windows gaze upon Gramercy Park. I spin around to see his sprawling kitchen. It would be the envy of any chef, with stainless-steel pots hanging from hooks above the counters and a white sink so big I could practically bathe in it. "This is insane."

"It's just home."

For the first time, I'm keenly aware of the differences between us—I live in my cousin's shoebox on the first floor. He lives in his own castle overlooking the city. Everything I have—memo: *nothing*—is paltry compared to his digs. But I'm not jealous. I'm simply impressed and amazed at its beauty.

He grabs my wrist and pulls me close. "It doesn't make you uncomfortable, does it?"

"What? Uncomfortable? No. It's beautiful and stunning, and I've never seen anything like it. Why would it make me uncomfortable?"

He shrugs. "I just picked up on a vibe from you. I want you to like being here."

I run my fingers up the buttons on his shirt. "Flynn, you're here. That's why I'm here. You can show me the rest of the place or you can just kiss me, and I'll be happy either way."

He hauls me in close and kisses the breath out of me. I am happy. I'm happy either way with him. Especially because he's made me dinner, a veggie pasta dish that looks delicious.

I set the white wine I brought on the table, and he brings over the plates. We sit, and he asks how everything went with Kermit as he opens the bottle.

I give him the overview, ending with, "And he's running the piece."

"So it wasn't all for naught?"

"It was definitely not for naught. It was all for naughty if you think about it, since it led me to you," I say with a wink.

Laughing, he points the opened bottle at me. "Nice wordplay."

"But we're not celebrating one mere story." I pause for effect. "We're celebrating a job."

"Seriously? I thought you didn't like him."

"I don't. But I like the work he has for me, and I like that he's forthright and upfront. I can handle the rest."

He pours two glasses and offers a toast. "To a fresh start. And to a genius move on his part—securing the best."

I blush and whisper my thank you.

When we're done, he leaves the dishes on the table and takes me to the couch. He lays me down and climbs over me, kissing me as he grinds against me.

In seconds, I'm hot and bothered. He flips me to my side, moving so he's behind me as he pushes up my skirt. My panties come off, his jeans are down, and we're side to side. He slides into me, his hand slinking between my legs, the other on my breasts as he moves in me, gripping me hard. Electricity crackles under my skin, and I sizzle, burning hotter and brighter with every thrust.

His hold is so tight I can barely move. I feel safe with him, and I feel wanted too. Flynn makes me feel beautiful and sexy and brilliant, and like I don't have to carry the weight of my world on my shoulders. Like he's willing to bear some of it for me, even as he takes me to the edge, bringing me incomparable pleasure again and again and again.

When we're done, he draws me into his arms, pointing through the windows at the sumptuous emerald-green park. "Eventually, I'll get you into the park. You keep distracting me with sex."

"I'll distract you again if you'd like."

Before he can answer, his phone beeps. "Another distraction," he mutters and reaches for it on the coffee table. He clicks open a note, and his expression transforms as he reads it. A wild, delighted grin takes over his face.

"There's something I have to show you."

"You want to show me an email?"

"Yes. It's an important one. It's from your brother's school."

"What?" A strange dread courses through me. "Why would they write to you?"

He smiles impishly. He's good at that. "Because his schooling is paid for."

A shock jolts into me. The hair on my arms stands on end. "You did not just say that."

He nods, proudly. Ridiculously proudly.

"Did you pay for the rest of his master's?"

"I did." His green eyes twinkle.

"You can't pay for my brother's school."

"I can, though, and I have."

"Why?" I ask, wonder and surprise etched in my voice.

"Because it makes your life easier. Because that's what I want to do."

"But Flynn . . ." I begin, only I'm not sure what I'm protesting. His generosity? "You can't."

He sets a hand on my thigh. "I had a feeling you'd be stubborn, so in case you're worried, this isn't just for your brother."

"What do you mean?"

"I wanted to make sure it didn't feel like a handout to you. And I didn't want to simply pay off his bill. So I set it up in a way you can't refuse."

I stare at him, waiting for him to say more.

"I set up a scholarship fund for . . ." he pauses, looks at the ceiling, pretends to count, then turns to me, "for all the current students at his divinity school. Everything is covered for all of them from now until graduation, including your brother."

My jaw comes unhinged. "Are you serious?"

"Completely." He dots a kiss onto my nose. "Let me ease your burdens, Sabrina. Including the ones here"—he stops to tap my breastbone—"where you think you can't accept this. This is for everyone, including your brother."

"You're too much."

"You're talking about my dick again now, right?" He winks.

I laugh and run my hands through his hair. "All of you. You're too much, too wonderful, too sexy, and too good in bed. And that means I'm not letting you go."

"Excellent. How about letting me go down on you?"

I shake my head. "It's my turn."

I get on my knees for him. He spreads his arms across the back of the couch, all of Gramercy Park and Manhattan and the world unfurled before him, all at his fingertips. He has so much, he gives so freely, and right now, he gets to take his reward.

Like a dirty Prince Charming. Like a man who deserves everything good his woman gives him.

Flynn

This is better than pineapple math. Better than free pizza. This is . . . my brain short-circuits as she draws me in deep.

I groan and curl my hands around her head, threading my fingers through her hair. I want to close my eyes, let my head fall back, and just revel in the feeling.

But I want to watch her more.

Sabrina's lush lips are wrapped around me, her hands moving over my length, along my thighs, her hair spilling on my skin.

This is . . .

Everything.

Blowjobs are as close to perfection as math and nature have given us. They are pure pleasure for a man and no work whatsoever. Honestly, there's never anything to complain about when it comes to oral sex.

But this is *more.*

Even though my brain is in a haze and my thoughts are all static and fuzz as she sucks me hard, her tongue flicking along me, this is an entirely new experience.

In some ways, it feels like the first time ever.

Like that brain-sizzling moment when a woman puts her mouth on you and awareness and utter bliss collide into you simultaneously, and you think *yes, fucking yes, blowjobs do reveal the secrets of the universe.*

But maybe *this* is the secret to the universe.

It's pleasure and lust, but it's also sex and love, and it's Sabrina treating me like I'm candy, like I'm hers, and like she wants me to feel so fucking good.

And I do.

God, I do.

My breath stutters as her warm mouth surrounds me. Pleasure crackles down my spine, climbs up my legs. It rolls around in my veins, and I gasp and I groan as I thrust up into her mouth, urging her to open more, take more.

"Angel," I rasp, and I feel her throat relax, and holy fuck, I can't stop thinking how extraordinary this feels. How extraordinary it *is* for all these things to reside in one person. This woman has my body, my mind, and my heart. Right now, she has my dick in her mouth, and hell, that's where I want to be.

I reach the finish line in mere minutes, coming in her throat as I say her name in a strangled cry.

She lets me fall from her lips and crawls up into my lap, kissing my cheek. She whispers in my ear, "I like the way you taste."

I shudder and plant a wet, deep kiss on her lips. "Say that again, and I'll come again."

"Good." She wears a naughty look. "I like when you come. I like making you feel good."

"You do more than make me feel good."

"What do I make you feel?" she asks coyly.

"You make me feel everything."

She snuggles against me. Blowjobs, dinner, sex, success, happiness—I'm not sure what I did to deserve her, but I don't intend to spend a single second taking her for granted. Ever.

Sabrina

The lights of the buildings twinkle across the Manhattan skyline, playing the part of the starlight that's so rarely seen in this city.

I rest my head against Flynn's shoulder and sigh contentedly. "I'm glad you were a stealth start-up at that party."

"I'm glad you were the only one who figured out my costume."

"I'm glad you twisted my arm and convinced me to escape to the library with you."

He scoffs. "Twisted your arm? Hardly."

I laugh too. "I know. I was willing to go anywhere with my masked duke." I sit up and meet his piercing gaze. "But it's you I love. I needed to meet you without knowing who you were to fall in love with you as you are."

"I know that," he says with a soft smile.

"With me, you always have an invitation to come as you are."

He presses a soft kiss to my lips. "Your wordplay sounds both loving and filthy."

"Sort of like you." I wiggle my eyebrows.

He slinks an arm around me, claims my mouth in a kiss, and takes me up on my invitation, no costumes needed, clothing optional, right there on the couch.

Later that night, we head to Gramercy Park.

He hands me the key, and I unlock the gate, entering the private park. I nearly skip. It's everything I imagined it to be—a gorgeous, verdant escape from Manhattan.

"It's like one of London's squares," I say, twirling around, taking it all in, the lush green leaves on the trees, the stone walkways, the benches. "At least I think so. I've never been."

"Do you want to go?"

"Do I want to go to London?"

He nods. "Yes. Do you?"

"Obviously."

"Then we'll go."

He takes my hand, and we walk through the park, and for the first time ever, maybe, just maybe, I begin to believe that fairy tales can come true, the kind where the commoner wins the heart of the prince.

And the prince wins the love of the commoner.

All because they make each other uncommonly happy. And that's what love should do.

EPILOGUE

Flynn

A few months later

I adjust my cap. Button the last button on my pin-striped shirt. Grab my glove.

All systems are go.

I head to the party at a mansion in the East Sixties. Music pounds from the ballroom, and I slide on my mask and head inside.

I make my way to the bar, ask for a glass of champagne, and then wait, scanning the room, hunting for a woman in white.

A few minutes later, she arrives, filling out the dress better than the actress herself did. Her hair is styled like the most famous blonde in movies, and the satin clings to her lush frame.

I ask for another glass, and when the bartender hands it to me, I head for the woman. *My* woman.

"You're no ordinary movie star," I say, a variation on the first words I ever said to her.

"And you're no ordinary center fielder," she says from behind her white mask.

I offer her the champagne.

We drink, and then I ask her to dance.

As I wrap a hand around her hip, she runs her fingers up my arms. "Nice arms. I've been admiring them all night."

"Have you?"

"And the uniform too. I love how it fits. Everywhere."

We move closer to each other, and I glide my hand around her waist, just like we promised we'd do at the costume shop a few months ago.

She loops her hands around my neck. "I've always had a thing for athletes."

"I've always had a thing for parties like this. You never know what might happen at a costume party. A dance, maybe more."

That's exactly what does happen. We dance, and then we *more* when we find a coat closet down the hall. Time is of the essence, so I kiss her deeply as my hands make their way under her skirt. She's fast too as she undoes my pants, and soon we're in the first position we ever found ourselves in.

She's against the wall. I'm inside her, and her legs are wrapped around my waist.

Tonight, we're Joe and Marilyn, skipping first, second, and third base, and sliding into home. When she comes, I'd say my costume is a grand slam.

Hers too.

We go to many more costume parties and masquerade balls. For Halloween, Sabrina designs a mad data scientist costume for me, complete with a lab coat with letters and numbers written on it. For herself, she crafts an internet cat meme, wearing a cat costume with cardboard mugs attached to the sleeves, which she can remove and knock off any surface.

We even find a few fancier fetes, and that's when we feel as if we're traveling in time. I don a waistcoat and top hat, and she wears a royal-blue gown. We dance with our Venetian masks on and then slip away to the library where we pretend we're Angel and Duke again.

* * *

Sometimes, Kevin takes the train into the city and joins us for dinner. One night over Thai food, he says, "Do you know why our last name is Granger?"

"She told me she just liked the name." Sabrina had said they changed their last name when their mom left.

He laughs, shaking his head.

Sabrina flushes pink as she points to her brother. "Don't believe him. He makes stuff up."

I sit back, waiting. "Oh, this is good. Now I have to know."

"Hermione," Kevin says with a grin.

I turn to Sabrina. "You named yourself for Hermione from Harry Potter?"

She shrugs happily. "I love Hermione. She's brilliant and clever, and she stood up for the people she loved. I defy anyone to come up with a better reason to pick a name."

I can't argue with her on that.

* * *

A month later, I take her to London as promised. We fly first class, and her eyes are stars when she lies all the way back in the seat on the plane. I like showering her with gifts and experiences, and she's learned not to be so stubborn in accepting them.

I show her all the sights—Big Ben, the London Eye, the National Gallery—but we find new ones as well, exploring the city in the way we like best.

That's what we do when we're home in New York too. We've tracked down bizarre street art in the Village, visited the Met and kissed in the Great Hall, and stopped by the underground gin joint in Chelsea.

Every day, we add to our list of favorite places in the city, and every night, she comes home with me because my home is her home now. The rollout of Haven has gone fantastically well, and Sabrina's job brings her the satisfaction of doing exactly the kind of work she loves.

Then at night, it's my job to bring her satisfaction, and that's exactly what I love doing too.

ANOTHER EPILOGUE

Flynn

A little later

It is a Sunday.

We have brunch with my sister, her husband, and my little niece. Dylan and Evie join us too, and Evie regales us with how much French toast she can eat at eight and a half months pregnant.

When we're done, we say our goodbyes and fan out across town, heading homeward. The sun shines brightly on this March day, so I suggest we walk through the park.

"Besides, we can let the lampposts guide us," I say, and Sabrina furrows her brow in a silent question.

"Did you know most of the lampposts have numbers on them to help you find where you're going?"

"I had no idea. But obviously, we need to verify this."

"Clearly. Since the park is one of our favorites places."

In the last several months, we've uncovered even more favorite places within it—the conservatory gardens, the literary walk with its statues of writers, and the Delacorte Musical Clock that sings a tune every thirty minutes.

We search for the lampposts, pointing out numbers to each other for the first few blocks as we head south.

She reaches for my hand. "Do you ever feel like we'll run out of things to do?"

I laugh and shake my head. "Nope. There's always something new to uncover."

She smiles and rests her head briefly against my shoulder before looking at me as we walk toward the Ramble. "I suppose that's true. We'll *always* have to keep looking for things we haven't seen."

I press a kiss to her forehead, keying in on something she said. "Interesting word you just used."

"What word?" she asks curiously. "Seen? Done?"

I shake my head. "A certain adverb, my grammar nerd."

She scrunches her brow. "Always?"

"Yes. Always," I say, looking ahead toward a bend in the path in the Ramble. I checked it out yesterday, and everything is the way I want it.

"*Always* is a nice word," she adds, giving me a look that says she knows I'm up to something.

I am definitely up to something.

When we pass the curve on the path, a freshly washed green bench with a polished and gleaming plaque greets us.

"But as I was saying, your worries about us finding something new are unfounded. That's something new to uncover, for instance." I point to the bench.

She peers at the plaque and anticipation winds tight

in my body. Hope fills my cells. When she gasps, that's my cue.

I bend to one knee and flip open a jewelry box. "What does it say?" I ask, though I already know.

Once upon a time, a duke met an angel and fell madly in love. He fell in love so deeply, so truly, he asked her to marry him. Marry me, Sabrina, and be mine always.

She spins around, tears sliding down her face over a smile more radiant than any I've ever seen. "Yes. I say yes."

I slide the ring on her finger, and the princess-cut diamond shines brighter than the sun. It better. It's huge.

Well, I wasn't going to buy her a tiny ring.

She deserves the best.

"It's perfect, because you're the perfect guy," she says, and kisses me as deeply and as passionately as she did that first night.

When she breaks the kiss, she takes my hand and guides me to the bench. "Let's go enjoy our bench."

We sit, and we kiss more, and we talk more, and she stares at her ring, and I tell her that it was either the bench or a knock-knock joke for the proposal, but the bench won out.

"I still want to hear the knock-knock joke."

"Are you sure?"

"I'm sure."

"Knock, knock."

"Who's there?"

"Marry."

"Marry who?"

"Marry me."

Sabrina

I laugh and wrap an arm around him. "My answer is still yes."

"Good because we have lots of favorite places to find. Always is a long, long time."

"I like always with you."

"You should. Want to know why?" my fiancé asks as a bird chirps overhead. He squeezes my finger and admires my ring.

I admire it too. When I look at it, I see hope, and a future, and love. This certainty was worth every risk. "Why?"

"Because *always* means we live happily ever after."

THE END

Dear Reader:

You may be curious about the NYC locations in this story. The hotel where Sabrina and Flynn first meet is inspired by the New York City mansions and clubs on the East side, and The Dollhouse is inspired by a number of underground speakeasies.

The abandoned subway stations are real, including the City Hall one, as is the Starry Night locksmith, the Elevator Museum, and the inscriptions on the benches in Central Park, including the ones from Tony and Karen, and Vic and Nancy. The streetlamps are also numbered to help you find your way. Gramercy Park requires a key.

Manhattan is also magical when you fall in love.

MOST IRRESISTIBLE GUY

A PREQUEL NOVELLA TO MOST VALUABLE PLAYBOY

A PREQUEL NOVELLA TO MOST VALUABLE PLAYBOY

Dear Readers: Please enjoy this short novella, MOST IRRESISTIBLE GUY. It's only available in paperback here as a bonus in this book.

About

When he wrapped his arms around me and pulled me close at my brother's wedding, my heart beat faster. When we danced into the night, my mind raced far ahead, entertaining all the possibilities I'd longed for. And later, when Cooper told me he'd won the starting quarterback job before he shared the news with anyone else, I started to believe we could be more.

But that didn't happen, and I didn't want to lose him as a friend, so I chose to focus on him solely as my buddy. That worked well enough for a while.

Until that night, in front of everyone, when he shocked my world to its core.

1

I can't stop staring at the best man.

As I walk down the aisle, strains of classical music rising in the church, my eyes are inexorably drawn to the man next to the groom.

That tux. That crisp white shirt. That bow tie.

Most of all, that smile. A grin I've never gotten over.

Clutching a bouquet of yellow tulips, I march. Hundreds of pairs of eyes are watching. Smiling. Tears welling.

Everyone loves a wedding.

My gaze is firmly fixed on the best man, the way the tux fits him, how it's snug against his toned, muscular frame, how his soulful brown eyes lock with mine.

Oh, God.

He's looking at me.

He's staring.

My heart skids in my chest, pounding painfully against my rib cage as his gaze lingers on me, like he's taking a stroll up and down my body as I approach the altar. With every step I take, tingles spread down my bare arms, and for several brief and torturous seconds, I let myself imagine I'm walking to him, and he's mine.

Mine to link arms with. To hold hands. To brush a kiss to his cheek.

This is a game I play now and then. I can't resist in this moment, even though I've learned how to live with this riot of emotions in my chest, like a flock of birds soaring to the sky all at once.

I learned to live with this wild sensation in my chest because I have to.

Cooper Armstrong isn't my man.

Instead, he's my best guy friend, and he's my brother's best friend, too.

He's someone I'm incredibly lucky to have in my life. He's supportive, and caring, and funny, and so damn easy on the eyes. When I reach the front of the church, I smile at him, then at my brother Trent, the groom. I take my place across from the best man. We turn as the wedding march begins and the bride glides down the aisle to marry my brother while I steal glances at his best friend.

When the vows are exchanged and the rings are slid on and when the groom kisses the bride, we all cheer. A wave of happiness rushes over me for my brother. He's marrying Holly, the love of his life. They walk back down the aisle as husband and wife, the crowd standing and clapping for the newlyweds.

Cooper and I follow, arm in arm.

He leans in close, his lips dangerously near my ear. A shiver runs through me, and I try to hide it so he won't know how he affects me, how he's always affected me. "Save a dance for me, will you, Violet?"

I give him a playful little smile, so he knows he's my friend, not the object of my desires. "I'll see if there's room for you on my dance card," I say, adding in a wink for good measure.

"Then I'll do my best to monopolize it."

He can have every single dance if he wants to, but I can't let him know that. I've been friends with him my whole life, and there's no way I'll jeopardize that for the dark-horse shot of something more.

For the record, I've crushed on Cooper for a long time.

Okay. A crazy ridiculously long time.

Fine, let's call a spade a spade. Decades. Nearly two decades. After all, he was my first ever crush way back when I was in second grade.

Yup, I'm *that* girl.

But, in my defense, he is adorable.

And sexy.

And fun.

And sweet.

And smart.

He's the right mix of a little bit cocksure attitude, a lot of charm, and a canyon of determination. Plus, he's a total gentleman.

It's impossible not to like him.

My crush that launched in second grade only intensified when we were teenagers. I might have enjoyed watching him work out on the football field in high school. I definitely liked the view when he took off his shirt. And sure, I've imagined what it would be like to kiss him, countless times.

But I've always kept my emotions in check. We're friends. Great friends. We've watched movies together, gone for runs along the water, broken bread at his mother's house. We've gone out with friends and sung karaoke together as a group—my brother and Holly, Cooper and me. For the record, I am most excellent at crooning "Sweet Child O' Mine," and Cooper kills it at anything Bon Jovi. We've also crushed it duet-style to Human League's "Don't You Want Me," and the irony of the title isn't lost on me.

We know how to have fun, and we've relied on each other over the years the way old friends—*good* friends—do.

Translation: I'm a big girl, and I've learned to live with this unrequited crush.

I've never even tried to *requite* it. He's too important to me to let words spill of how I feel. It's easier to be like this, like friends.

"Slice of cake?" I ask later that night as I grab a delicate china plate that's home to a mouth-wateringly fantastic-looking slice of wedding cake.

Cooper pats his belly. "I'm watching my figure."

I pat his stomach, too. Flat as a board. Tight as a drum. Delicious as candy. I mean, I *bet* it's as delicious as candy and as lickable, too. "You're right. If you have even one bite, you'll puff up, and you'll be sacked in the first game."

He rolls his eyes playfully. "Violet, don't be silly. I have to play to get sacked."

"You'll play. Sooner than you think." We sit down at the head table. My brother and his wife are circulating and chatting with other guests, so it's only the two of us right now. "Jeff Grant can't play forever."

Cooper scrubs a hand over his square jaw. "Some days, it feels that way. But I just have to keep waiting."

"You do, and it'll be worth it."

Jeff Grant is the starting quarterback for the local NFL team, the San Francisco Renegades. He's also one of the game's GOATs, as in greatest of all time. The veteran quarterback has three rings, impeccable statistics, an eye-goggling winning percentage, and a sterling reputation for coming back in crucial moments, including bringing the team from the brink and pulling out an astonishing fourth-quarter win in last year's Super Bowl after a fourteen-point deficit with ten minutes to play.

He is great. There is no debating it. As football fans, we're truly spoiled to have him helming the team.

But even so, I still want this guy next to me to be the one in the pocket, calling the shots, scanning the field, and marching the team down it, leading the Renegades to victory because I know that's what he can do.

"It seems hard to believe now, but Father Time will eventually catch up with Jeff. Just keep being patient," I reassure him.

Cooper shrugs. "Who knows when that'll happen." He flashes a smile, letting me know he can't let his bench-warming status bother him. He's learned to be cool about his backup status. Drafted two years ago in the first round, he's hardly seen any playing time because Jeff Grant is not only amazing, he's also durable. It's been frustrating for Cooper to watch Jeff take all the snaps, but he's learned to be patient, too.

"Soon," I say, as I take a bite of cake. "Your time will come sooner than you think."

"For now, I'm learning everything I can from the best." His eyes turn fiery, blazing with the kind of intensity I know he shows on the field. "And when I'm called up, I'll be more than ready."

"You will. Now, tell me what you're learning," I say, diving into the dessert for another forkful.

"You want to know what I'm learning from watching Jeff?" Cooper's lopsided grin is deliciously sexy and quirks up at the corner of his lips, almost as if he doesn't really believe that I want to know.

I tap his forearm. "Yes. I do. You know I love game talk."

"That's true. You have an endless appetite for football conversations. You could have been a sports talk host."

I shudder at the thought. "I detest sports talk shows."

He laughs. "Me, too."

I stare at him pointedly, drumming my fingers on the table. "Well? Are you going to tell me stuff? Or is it top secret?"

Laughing, he leans closer to me. Closer than I'd expect him to be. Anticipation weaves through me. "I'll tell you, but you can't tell a soul," he whispers, his breath ghosting over my skin, goosebumps rising in its wake.

Damn body.

I want to tell my libido to calm down. But when Cooper inches near me and turns up the flirting dial, I don't know how I can rein in the hot, tingly tremble that's threatening to run through my entire body, just from being near him.

I can smell his clean, woodsy scent. His aftershave. His minty breath. I want it all, but I can't have it so I practice my best I'm-cool-with-this skills, the ones I've needed my whole life. "Oh, is this your secret playbook?"

"I'm learning strategy, confidence, but also some amazing new plays." His eyes blaze as he talks, and the golden flecks in his brown eyes seem to shimmer with excitement.

This is his playground, and he loves it.

I do, too. I can't help myself. A rabid football fan, my love of the game is a part of me, and I can feel it in my bones. My passion comes from the strategy, the angles, the myriad ways the game can be played. I love trying to figure out what type of play a team will execute, how the defense will respond, and what risks the players are willing to take. Cooper and I talk about that as I nibble on the cake. As he dives into some of the plays, his eyes sparkle more, his expressions become more animated. I savor moments like this, to enjoy these conversations with my good friend.

He shakes his head, amused, when I ask about a particular play-action fake strategy.

"Did I get the question wrong?" I ask, curious why he's laughing.

"No. You had it right. All of it. It's impressive."

"What can I say? I'm a junkie. I'll probably be more of one when you're the starting quarterback. I'll be cheering the loudest."

"At every single home game?"

I nod. "Consider it done."

"Yeah?" He says it almost as if he doesn't quite believe I'd be there.

"Of course."

A slow smile spreads across his handsome face, lighting up his features. "I'd like that."

I nudge him with my elbow. "You'd like that because you'd be the starting quarterback."

"Yes. But I'd like it because I like it when you come to the games."

My heart sits up, looks around, wonders if he really said that. If it meant something more. "You do?" I ask, my voice feathery.

"I always have. I like playing for you, Vi. You're my favorite spectator. Even back in high school, I got a kick out of knowing you were in the bleachers."

My heart stutters, tripping a switch in me, the one that longs for him. I distract myself with another bite of cake. "Too bad you're too busy watching your figure, because this cake is delicious. You should consider giving in to temptation."

He quirks an eyebrow. "You think I should?"

There's something borderline flirty in his voice. Something I ought to ignore.

"You should." Using the fork, I point to the cake. "This is heaven."

"Damn. You're making it sound too appealing." He grabs the utensil, dives into the cake with it, and takes a bite. He groans as he chews.

The sound of it is carnal, masculine, and too damn sexy for my own good. I should not be turned on by the sound of him eating a bite of cake.

But yet, here it is. A pulse beats inside me.

He sets down the fork with gusto. "And now I'm going to dance off this cake." He takes my hand and pulls me up.

"I'm dancing it off, too?"

His gaze travels up my body once again, like it did at the ceremony. "You're perfect. But I still need you to shake it up, baby."

Baby.

Holy smokes, he just gave me an affectionate nickname. And he called me perfect. I'm not at all, but I adore his compliments.

I don't have time to soak them in since he guides me to the dance floor where we shake and shimmy through some fast numbers.

"Are you dancing off that one dangerous bite, Cooper?"

"Absolutely. Can't you see me get trimmer as we speak?"

A slow song begins, and I half expect we'll do that thing people do when they wander away from the dance floor.

But that's not what happens.

3

He slides in closer to me, setting his hands on my waist. "You weren't going to take off for the slow song, were you?"

My throat is dry. My pulse hammers. "No."

"Good," he says, his voice soft, and the gentle sound of it makes me freeze, my arms in mid-air.

I know I need to put my arms around his neck, but I haven't been this close to him since prom. Cooper Armstrong was my date at prom. He was a freshman in college, I was a senior in high school, and he came back to town for that weekend. I'd been planning on going with my boyfriend but the guy broke up with me shortly before the big dance. Cooper swooped in and saved the day. He said he didn't want my dress to go to waste. He wanted me to wear it and to have a good time. I wound up having the best time with him.

"You can put your arms around my neck," he says tenderly.

I blink. "Sorry. I was kind of out of it for a second."

"That's okay. I have that effect on women."

Right. *Women.* I need the reminder. Cooper is a hot, single, eligible bachelor. He dates. He plays the field. He doesn't know I have a long-standing crush on him. He doesn't know I have feelings that run much deeper than friendship. We've never been together, even though in moments like this, with his hands on my waist and my arms slinking around his neck, something starts to feel inevitable in the way we touch.

Like we were meant to come together on this dance floor.

Only I know that's my foolish heart talking. Or my eyes, since they're busy drinking in the up-close-and-personal sight of this most handsome man, his square jaw, his messy brown hair that the hairdresser in me wants to get my scissors on and cut, but the woman in me wants to get my hands in and run my fingers through.

Most of all, there's a part of me every now and then that wishes we could have this. These long chats that unfurl late into the night and lead to more.

That lead to dancing.

To his hands on my waist.

To my fingers tiptoeing dangerously close to the ends of his hair. "Cooper," I say, chiding him. "Your hair is getting long. We need to cut it again."

He arches an eyebrow, pretending to think. "Know any good hairdressers?"

As if I'm also contemplating, I stare at the ceiling as the soft strains of Ella Fitzgerald cocoon us. "I do, but I wonder if she can fit you in."

"I'll just go to a barber."

I gasp. "Horrors. What a terrible thing to say. You can't take this pretty hair to a barber."

"So you'll fit me in, then?"

Anytime, anywhere.

"I'll do my best to get you on the books, and I'll give you a very nice haircut."

He moves in closer. "You give the best haircuts."

It doesn't seem as if we're talking about haircuts.

It doesn't seem that way at all.

His lips skate tantalizingly close to my neck, as his mouth comes near my ear. "As if I'd let anyone else touch my hair."

This time, I don't shiver. I melt. I'm molten all over, and I can feel the effects of his words everywhere in my body.

He inches even closer, and I do, too, like it's the next step in the dance.

An inch here, an inch there, and we'd be indecent.

I wonder if it's apparent to anyone else that the bridesmaid is thinking about doing filthy things to the best man and wishing, wishing, wishing he would take her home.

Wishing, too, she knew what the best man was thinking in this moment.

We're quiet as we sway, the twinkling lights scattering across the dance floor.

Like this, it feels like fantasy could slide into reality. It feels like we're one slip of the tongue away.

It might be the way his right hand curls tighter around my waist. It might be the way he moves almost imperceptibly closer. It might even be the slightest rumble in his throat as the song nears its end.

Or it might all be in my imagination.

The music fades, and when a faster song begins, we break apart.

4

One year later

The chorus to Sam Smith's new single plays in my salon, faintly in the background, providing the soundtrack for my customers. With my high-heeled boots planted wide on the smooth tiled floor, I stand in front of Gigi, concentrating on snipping the last little uneven strands of her pretty blond bangs.

One last clip.

And there.

"You look gorgeous," I declare.

"Do I?" Her voice rises in excitement. She has a fifth date tomorrow night with a guy she thinks might be the one. He's a chef, a baseball fan, and he loves to send her good morning and good night text messages. She's told me everything about their budding romance during her half hour in the hot seat, since that's what people usually do with their stylists.

Just call me a priest, a therapist, a temporary best friend, as well as the wizard with scissors.

"You're going to knock that man to his knees." I spin her chair around so she can face the silver-lined mirror. Gigi smiles widely when she sees her reflection, fluffing her hair, running a hand over her smooth locks.

"You're a miracle worker."

I wave off the compliment. "Please. Look at the raw materials you gave me to work with. You're naturally beautiful."

"And now you've made me feel even prettier."

It's my turn to smile since I honestly love helping people feel beautiful about themselves. "I want a full report," I tell her as she leaves, then I spend the next few minutes chatting with the other stylists who work for me to see what they need at my salon in the heart of Sausalito, a little tourist town right across the Golden Gate Bridge from San Francisco.

I opened the shop two years ago, and I've expanded it in the last year. Heroes and Hairoines has taken a lot of my time, but it's been worth it since business is booming. But I haven't had time for much else in the past year, except the rare date here and there. A regular client set me up with her brother. Holly suggested I have coffee with a guy she works with. Both were nice men, but there were no sparks.

I have no complaints about how much time my business has demanded of me, and I don't mind working nearly every day past closing time.

As I walk past the sinks to the back of the shop, I check my phone to see when my next appointment is. Five minutes from now. Just enough time to make a cup of tea.

My phone dings, the alert for a news story. I swipe my thumb and stop in my tracks. My jaw comes unhinged when I see the headline on ESPN: "Grant To Retire." Anticipation rises sky-high in me as I click it open and read.

Three-time Super Bowl champion and Renegades starting quarterback Jeff Grant announced his retirement today.

"It's been an amazing run and I am lucky to have played for my hometown team and for such amazing fans. I know the team will be in good hands with the new starting quarterback, Cooper Armstrong."

I squeal out loud. Excitement and effervescence run through me. I've just drunk a glass of champagne, devoured a mouth-watering truffle, watched a friend win the lottery.

One of my stylists turns to me, asking, "Everything okay?"

I must look like I've been dipped in a paint can of glee. "Everything is amazing," I tell her.

My heart skips and I want to jump for joy. I can only imagine how incredibly happy Cooper is, and I can't wait to congratulate him myself—this is what he's worked for his whole life. This is what he's wanted more than anything.

I start to tap out a text to him, when the receptionist sets her hand on my arm. "Violet, your next appointment."

"Thanks, Sage."

I tuck my phone away, and honestly, I'm glad I didn't

have time to fire off a text. This calls for more than a text. I need to give him a phone call later.

I settle in at my booth and work on auburn highlights for Marissa, who tells me she's desperately trying to figure out why her husband is suffering from headaches. "They tend to get worse if he's in the kitchen, but they're fine when he's elsewhere in the house. Isn't that crazy?"

Today I'm playing the shrink.

"Not entirely. Is there anything in the kitchen that could be making him sick?" I ask as I wrap a section of her hair in tinfoil.

"My cooking," she mutters.

I laugh. "Maybe there's something going on with the stove. Perhaps something needs to be fixed with it."

And now I'm an electrician and a diagnostician.

She arches a brow. "You think that might be it?"

I smile at her in the mirror. "I think you look amazing with red highlights, and I have no idea why he's not feeling so great. But maybe check it out? Sometimes the answers to problems are under our noses and easier than we think."

An hour later, her hair is redder and she's tracked down a stove specialist, promising to update me in four weeks when she's back for her regular appointment.

I twist my index and middle fingers together. "My fingers are crossed," I say as I walk her to the door and hold it open.

I swear I'm seeing a mirage.

Cooper is at the door. His arms are raised in the air. His smile is as wide as the sea, and he strides to me, picks me up, and lifts me in the air.

5

"Did you hear the news?"

I nod as his strong arms hold me tight. "I did. I told you so!"

He smiles as wide as the sky. "This is the one time I don't mind hearing 'I told you so.'"

"Then I'll say it again. Told you so."

He sets me down and grips my shoulders for emphasis. "*Three years*, Vi. I've watched every single play from the sidelines with the exception of two games I started when Jeff sprained his ankle. Three. Whole. Years. And come September, I finally get my chance to start the season."

That champagne feeling when I read the news? It has nothing on the rocket ride I'm on now. It's not even *my* news. But it doesn't matter. I've rooted for Cooper my whole life. "I couldn't be happier for you. This is so amazing."

His hands curl tighter around me. "I wanted you to be one of the first people to know."

"You did?" This information sends a dangerous thrill through me.

"Hell yeah. You're one of the most important people in my life. I told my mom first, and I had to see you next. I knew you'd be excited."

"I'm glad you came here," I say, my voice a little softer, and even though I want to believe he's telling me because he harbors the same crazy, lifelong crush as I do, I know better. That wedding dance and the closeness I felt that night was a sliver in time. It hasn't been repeated, but our friendship has grown even stronger.

Now that my brother's married and busy with his wife, Cooper and I talk more. He's here every few weeks for his haircut, and when he comes by in the evenings, we usually grab dinner after. That's why he stopped by today. Because we're friends. Great friends.

I give his hair a quick once-over. "I don't think you have an appointment for a few days, but if you're going to be the starting quarterback, we need to give you a haircut."

He bats his eyes. "Think you can fit me in?"

"It just so happens I had a cancellation, so I can give you a quickie."

A laugh bursts from his mouth. "A quickie? Hell yeah."

I swat his arm as I realize my faux pas. "A quickie cut."

"Other quickies are fine with me, too," he says, a little flirty, a little dirty.

"Get over to the sinks," I say, trying my best to make light of the comment, so he won't notice the fierce blush radiating over my cheeks.

Quickie.

What was my brain thinking, letting that word spill out?

He parks himself in a chair at a sink, and I partake of one of my favorite things—shampooing his hair. He shuts his eyes and sighs contentedly as I scrub in the shampoo, lathering it up.

I take my time, making sure I don't miss a single strand, running my fingers through those lush locks, massaging his scalp.

I rinse his hair, my hands running through his hair one more time to get all the suds out.

Another soft sigh falls from his lips, and it makes my heart flutter.

If he were mine, I'd do this every few weeks, and then we'd kiss, and he'd bring me close, and we'd slink away for a little while.

I squeeze the brakes on the fantasy, shut off the water, and run a towel over his head. We head to my booth, and he sits in the black leather chair, where I cut his hair.

I have free rein to look at him, to study him, to touch the soft strands.

As I snip his locks, I pepper him with questions about how the news came down.

He tells me he heard from his agent, and tomorrow is his first press conference.

I rest my hand on his shoulder and meet his gaze in the mirror. "And you're going to look so handsome."

A grin crosses his lips. "Thank you."

I run my hands over his hair, enjoying this opportunity to touch him more than I should.

Maybe that makes me a pervert. It's only hair, really. But it's great hair. I relish the chance to make him look his finest, to take care of him in this small way I can.

I move closer, trimming the ends. His gaze drifts up in the mirror, his brown eyes locking with mine.

He says nothing. He simply stares at my reflection. I could be wrong, I could be reading something into nothing, but I swear there's heat in his eyes, maybe a little flicker of desire.

It makes my breath catch. My heart speeds up. My pulse hammers.

It's the same look I saw at the wedding. It's the look I see when our bodies move closer when we seem to connect in unexpected ways.

I stop snipping for a few seconds, trying to get my bearings. I want to know what's going on in his head.

But soon enough, it's time for him to go. As he leaves, I'm hit with the realization that I need to find a way to let go of this lifelong crush once and for all. I need to focus solely on the friendship, because that's the only thing that lasts.

6
_____

The start of the season

"Excuse me."

A burly, bearded Renegades fan tucks himself into his seat and lets us pass by his knees.

"Thank you so much," I say to him.

He nods and shouts, "Go Renegades!"

I pump a fist, and Holly and Trent behind me do the same thing.

The pre-game excitement hum is in the air, coursing throughout the stadium. The three of us make our way down the row and find our seats on the fifty-yard line next to Cooper's mom and her boyfriend, Dan. Cooper's mom gives me a big hug. She waves a foam finger and hollers, "Number Sixteen!"

A vendor tromps down the concrete steps, offering beer and pretzels. Another one from the next section over shouts out that he has sushi and wine.

That's San Francisco for you, and our beautiful new stadium has a little bit of everything, including gorgeous September weather.

No jackets required today.

I opt for a pretzel and Holly grabs beers for my brother and her.

Trent raises his cup. "Here's to pulling out a W."

I tap my pretzel against my brother's beer cup. "I'll nosh to that."

Cooper's mom joins in the toast with her blue foam finger. "Go Coop! You can do it."

The game hasn't even begun, and we're all a little overly enthusiastic today.

"Last week was only jitters," she adds, as she should know. She knows her son as well as anyone, and she's attended nearly every single game he's ever played.

"It was absolutely only jitters," I say, smoothing a hand over my Number Sixteen jersey. "He'll be great today. He's a star."

The announcer's voice booms throughout the stadium, like he's using two hundred megaphones and each word has ten syllables. "Welcome to the Renegades stadium for the first home game of the year."

"He's going to be amazing," Trent says, pumping a fist.

"He'll be great," Dan says, chiming in.

"Bring it, Coop," Holly shouts.

Okay fine, we're a tad more than overly enthused. We might be bordering on nervous. After all, last week's game bordered on abysmal, and Cooper played terribly. There's no way to sugarcoat his performance.

But it can't be easy replacing a legend.

Images of the players flash on the jumbotron as the

announcer shares the lineup. The visiting team is properly and soundly booed, and all the home team guys are cheered, including the last few guys announced.

Harlan Taylor, the star running back. Jones Beckett, the fantastic wide receiver. And at last, the guy I'm here for.

The announcer's voice thunders across the stadium like an echo from Zeus. "And your new starting quarterback in his first home game . . . Cooper Armstrong."

Everyone stands and cheers as the handsome new quarterback runs onto the field.

"That interception last week was a fluke," Trent says with a confident nod. "Today will be different."

"Today will be amazing."

* * *

I hold my breath. I don't think I will ever be able to let it out again. I'm making promises to the universe. Promises I have no right to make. I tell myself it's just a game. It's just football.

We're only behind by fourteen and he can do this, he can pull out a win. But as Cooper goes into the pocket at the end of the second quarter, scanning right, scanning left as Jones runs downfield, he overthrows.

My heart craters when the ball lands squarely in the open arms of the opponent.

The crowd groans collectively.

My heart breaks a little bit when the fans boo him.

"Bring back Grant."

"You suck."

"Go back to the bench, bench boy."

My jaw clenches, and I want to go personally reprimand every single naysayer in this stadium. "Mark my words," I'll tell them.

"Just you wait," I'll say.

But frustration wends through me, and I can also feel it from Trent, Holly, Cooper's mom, and Dan. We're all rooting for this guy so badly. We want him to succeed as fans, but mostly for him.

"Shake it off," says Trent, talking under his breath.

Cooper's mom waves that finger again. "You can do it."

When the third quarter begins and Cooper starts it with another interception, my heart sags once more. Even though he delivers two touchdowns after that, it's not enough and the Renegades finish with their second loss of the season.

Silence blankets the stadium as we leave, that clawing sense of potential doom hovering over us. I have to wonder what Cooper feels like. If he thinks he's letting everyone down, from the team to the coach to the fans.

I want to reassure him that he's not. That he's got this. And I know what to do. I know how to lift him up.

Later that night I send him a text message.

Violet: Why did the football go to the bank?

Cooper: I've been wondering that very thing.

Violet: To get his quarterback.

Cooper: :) Thank you. I needed that.

Violet: Hey, if you have any free time this week, can you meet me at the high school field?

He writes back, telling me he'll be there Thursday night.

7

We don't need stadium lights. There is enough starlight tonight in Petaluma, our hometown.

Nearly twenty years ago, I met Cooper in this town when I was in grade school. I was riding my purple banana seat bike, and he moved a block over from my house. This is the high school we both attended, and this field is where I watched so many of his games, cheering from the sidelines.

I was never a cheerleader. *Please.* I'm not that kind of girl. But I still went to his games, and I shouted and clapped.

Tonight, I'm here to cheer in a whole different way. I have everything we need—a football and some music. I wait at the fifty-yard line.

When Cooper shows up a few minutes later, striding across the grass, his thumbs tucked into the pockets of his jeans, a gray T-shirt hugging his firm frame, he shoots me a curious look. "Are you my new coach?"

I toss the ball back and forth in my hands. "Nope. I want to play for fun."

He raises an eyebrow. "Are you holding out on me, Vi? Are you really a ringer for Brady?"

I flash him a big smile. "There's only one way to find out."

I turn on the playlist on my phone, cueing up Guns N' Roses' "Welcome to the Jungle."

"How apt," he deadpans.

"It is a jungle out there." I launch the ball up and down, then tip my forehead toward the goalposts at the end of the field. "Come on! Go deep."

"You're the quarterback now?"

I shimmy my hips back and forth. "Maybe I am. Thirty-six. Zone. Lion. Sail. Ten." I rattle off one of the plays he gave me at the wedding.

His eyes widen. "You remember the playbook?"

"I told you I love strategy. Now get your butt down the field and catch this ball."

Saluting me, he takes off, running a post route, as I launch the ball toward him. I don't have a cannon for an arm. That's why I picked a skinny post route. But I do manage the fifteen yards just fine, and he catches it beautifully.

Of course.

"Now if only I could've done that last Sunday," he mutters.

"You can," I say with enough confidence for both of us. "Now throw it to me."

He palms the ball, considering the options, it seems. He raises his face, meets my gaze, and calls out a play. It's an easy one, and I remember it from our talk. A simple, short route. I run a few yards as he lobs an easy spiral in my direction.

Even though I know he's not putting all of his strength

into it, he can't help but throw hard. I haul it in, but I can still feel the punch that he packs as I grab it, the ball smacking me in the chest.

A cough bursts from my throat.

"Are you okay?" Cooper trots towards me.

I hold out my hand like a stop sign. "I'm fine. I can handle catching a football."

"And you caught it well. Too bad I can't get it to the receiver when I need to."

My eyes narrow and I march the final feet to him, stabbing him in the chest with my finger. "No."

"No, what?"

"No feeling bad for yourself," I say firmly and crisply, shoving the football at him.

"I'm not feeling bad for myself."

"You are and I'll have none of it."

He heaves a sigh. "Fine, but you would, too. Have you heard the crap they're saying about me on sports radio?"

I shake my head. "I don't listen to sports radio. And you shouldn't, either."

"Have you read what they say about me on the Internet?"

Another shake. "Stop googling yourself."

He raises his hands in surrender.

"I mean it. Get your head out of the Internet and focus on the game. That's all you have to do. Just remember that." I tap his temple. "This is yours. This belongs to you. Don't let them in here."

A slow smile spreads across his face and he nods, taking it in. "You're right. This is mine."

"Your mind. Your head. Your best weapon on the field."

"Mine. All mine," he repeats like he needs to remind himself, then he shouts another play.

I follow his directions easily, taking the spot of his receiver, and we play like that for the next thirty minutes. Running easily, tossing balls, barking directions and audibles, and having a blast running into the end zone, arms raised, scoring touchdowns, pretending to kick extra points.

Until finally we flop down on the cool grass in the middle of the field and stare at the stars. I turn to him, and I'm delighted to see not only relief on his face, but happiness and confidence.

He looks my way and our eyes connect, his brown eyes holding mine longer than I expect.

"Hey you," he whispers.

"Hey you, too." Tingles sweep over my skin.

"Thank you."

"It was nothing," I say, though I know that's not true.

I wait for him to look away, but he doesn't break the hold.

And my brain reassembles the scene. My mind says this is the moment in the script when they kiss. When the hero touches her shoulder, runs a finger along a strand of hair, moves in close.

But the better part of me, the stronger part, the piece of me I've kept in check since the wedding, rises to the surface. Reminding me. I'm here for the friendship. That's what's steady. That's what lasts. That's what I'll protect in the same way Cooper's offensive line protects him. I will guard our friendship fiercely because it means the world to me.

This is not the moment when friends turn into lovers.

Instead, this is the time when he needs to know I'll be there for him always.

He taps my shoulder. The look in his eyes is soft and earnest. "It was everything."

My heart somersaults. My throat goes dry.

"I'm glad you had me come here tonight," he adds.

"Me, too," I say, and it's wholly true, somersaults and cartwheels aside.

I let go of that swoopy, crazy feeling in my chest. I say goodbye to all the tingles and shivers. This is where I want to be right now. His friend.

I punch his shoulder. "Go get 'em, Tiger."

He does.

He turns the season around the next week, and the next and the next, putting the Renegades in playoff position by early December, and making the city fall in love with the new quarterback again—handsome, talented, good, and *winning*.

He's the most valuable guy on the team, and he's become the toast of the town.

When December coasts into San Francisco, it's time for the annual players' charity auction.

That means he needs me to work my magic.

8

Cooper's hair is sticking up. He has some kind of crazy bed head look going on tonight. But that's part of his appeal.

So is his tailored charcoal suit, which makes him look completely edible.

Not for me, of course.

I'm over all those crazy crushing feelings.

My goal tonight is simple. Make the guys look good before the auction to raise money for the children's hospital. "We need to domesticate your lovely locks, Cooper. I think this gel will do."

I hold up a tube of hair gel, my silver bracelets jangling on my wrists, as I prepare to put the finishing touches on the stars of the team.

"What is that goop?" he asks suspiciously.

"Why this? It's called Goop for Guys. It's perfect for you."

We joke some more, along with the other guys here in the suite. They're all wearing three-piece suits, and damn, there's something so yummy about a good-looking man wearing a vest with a suit.

Something that gets my blood heated to hot.

But I'm not that girl anymore. I'm not longing for him like I have in the past. I can simply appreciate him as a man, while enjoying him as my buddy.

As I work on his hair, I eye his attire. "I like this. You rarely see anyone wearing a vest around here."

"Is that your way of telling me you're a vest woman?" he asks in a flirty voice that makes me want to flirt back with him.

Just for fun.

Not for anything more.

I laugh and whisper, "I'm an everything woman."

He blinks, like he's surprised I said that.

Hell, maybe I am, too.

But even though there's some kind of energy and excitement in this room tonight, I know that's all it is. Maybe a year ago, I would've wondered if our friendship would catch on fire and make us both melt from the heat.

Tonight, though? I know we're solid, and we'll finish the evening as we started it.

I run my gel-covered hands through his hair, taming it for the camera since the auction is being carried live on local TV. Surveying my handiwork, I issue my pronouncement.

"You are one hot quarterback."

His lips part. He takes his time answering. "I am?"

I flash him a coy smile and pat his shoulder. "Of course you are."

If I were in the audience, I'd bid on him. Not that I'm a bidding girl, and I don't have that kind of money to play with, but he looks like a prize.

They all do.

I spin around, regarding the guys. Harlan, the running back; Jones, the receiver; and Rick, the kicker. "You boys are all so pretty."

Rick crosses his legs. "You want to bid on me tonight, Vi?"

I decide to have fun with them since I'm in that kind of mood. "It's all I can think about." Rooting around in my purse, I find my wallet and grab a few bills. "Will twenty dollars be enough for you?"

As the guys tease about whether that's too much to pay for Rick, Cooper tenses and scowls, almost as if he dislikes the idea of me bidding on Rick.

I point to Harlan. "How much for you?"

Another round of joking ensues, as well as more grumbles from Cooper.

I glance back at my friend. "Coop, are you as cheap as the others? Should I try for you?"

He scoffs. "I'm a premium kinda guy," he says, confidently. Then, with those brown eyes pinned on mine, he adds, "But if you wanted to bid on me, I'd foot the bill for it."

His tone is intense and serious. Like he means it, and I can't help but wonder if he's saying I should bid on him for some reason. I don't know why he would want that. Everyone will be bidding on him—he's the main attraction.

Soon, the auction is about to start, and Jillian, the team publicist, leads the guys out of the room.

I call out to Cooper, and he turns around. I walk over to him in my high-heeled boots that don't make me as tall as him, but do shoot me a little bit closer.

I raise my hand and smooth out a strand of his hair

that's out of place. He's been part of this auction for the last three years, but this is the first time he's going out there as the team's starting quarterback. "You've killed every year as the backup. You'll kill it even harder as the starter, and you've been playing great the last three months."

He knocks on the wall. "Knock on wood. We need to keep playing great. And I know you're part of why I'm playing so well."

"Am I?"

"That night on the high school field was everything I needed to turn it around."

I smile. "I'm glad I could help."

"Vi, you did more than help. That was everything I needed to hear."

I beam, my heart soaring with contentment. "All right, tiger. Get out there." I straighten his hair one more time, then I adjust his tie, even though it's perfect.

He meets my eyes, his voice going a bit husky. "Does my tie look good?"

My stomach swoops. But I remind myself that it's a vestigial response. It's borne from the past, and I don't need to be anchored to those feelings. The ones I'm getting over. "Everything looks good. Now get out on stage. I'll be in the audience watching every minute, and I can't wait."

He turns to head down the hall then stops at the sound of the owner's sister.

He groans. "It's Maxine."

And she's singing "It's Raining Men."

9

Ten minutes later the auction is in full swing.

The host, local TV reporter Sierra Franklin, is running the bidding and extolling the virtues of Jones. As she waxes on about his hands, I find Cooper backstage.

He paces, tension written all over his face.

I ask what's wrong, but he simply jokes about having Holly's friends bid on him when it's his turn. The comment nags in my brain, makes me wonder if something went down in the hall.

I touch his elbow. "Is everything okay? Did something happen with Maxine? You mentioned her right before you left the suite, and now you don't quite seem like yourself."

Before he can answer, Sierra's voice echoes from the on-stage mic. "And now we're getting ready to bring our starting quarterback on the stage."

Cooper whispers quietly. "I wouldn't use the term *okay* to describe my interaction with her."

The tension winds tighter, and I wrap my hand around him, feeling protective of him. "What happened?"

Through tight lips, he says, "Let's just say I would rather ride the bench again than have her win me."

With that, he strides onto the stage, and I can hear everyone in the ballroom cheering and clapping for their chance to bid on the star athlete. While a part of me is thrilled the crowd is excited to see him, his comments worry me, and that part of me takes over. I scurry through the hotel and make my way to the ballroom, scrambling to watch his blind side.

The ballroom is packed, and I wedge my way through crowds of cheering women and men, laughing and clapping as Sierra interacts with Cooper on stage.

He gives her a peck on the cheek, and she clasps her hand to her face, saying, "I'll never wash this cheek again."

She gestures to Cooper and sings his praises before the audience. "And now, ladies and gentlemen, for the pièce de résistance, this year's starting quarterback, at long last, and the winner of the Most Valuable Playboy auction for the last three years in a row. After all, who wouldn't want to take this handsome and talented man out for a night on the town? Everyone loves the quarterback."

Truer words were never spoken.

Cooper smiles for the crowd, seemingly shucking off his backstage concerns, as he takes off his jacket and shows off how absolutely decadently delicious he looks in his pants, shirt, and vest.

Yes, I am a vest woman indeed.

He scans the crowd and finds me easily. I mouth, *Vests are hot.*

When he smiles, it feels like a private grin just for me.

Even though I know it's a friendship grin, and I'm completely cool with it being just that.

Sierra sings his praises, from his stats to his skills—six-foot-four inches, light brown eyes and dark brown hair, great cheekbones, talented in the kitchen, and a rock star at karaoke.

Yes, yes, yes.

I know all that cold.

Cooper launches into a few lines from his favorite Bon Jovi tune, and all seems well. I'm not so sure what he was worried about with Maxine, but I do know she's a little flirty with the players, and her brother, the team's owner, lets her get away with basically anything.

But she's nowhere in sight, so perhaps it's much ado about nothing.

When the bidding begins and my brother and Holly offer measly bids for fun, I figure there's truly nothing to worry about.

Until a flash of red catches the corner of my eye.

Maxine is here. She thrusts a jeweled hand high, and when her voice rises above the crowd, upping the bid from a paltry fifty dollars to a startling three thousand, I understand why Cooper was concerned.

She wants him.

Her hands are parked on her hips.

Her eyes are guns, aiming for him.

Chills skate down my spine as she stares at the quarterback, licking her lips.

Holy smokes. The owner's sister wants to take Cooper home tonight, and that can't sit well with the guy who's trying to prove his worth to the team.

"That's quite a large jump," Sierra says.

"And that handsome fellow is worth every penny," Maxine replies, her voice dripping with desire.

"Three thousand," Sierra repeats. "Do we have thirty-one hundred?"

A few others in the crowd jump in with higher bids.

But Maxine raises her price every time, staring at Cooper like she wants to eat him for breakfast, lunch, dinner, and a midnight snack.

She keeps outbidding everyone, determination in her tone.

Sheer certainty she'll win him.

And in that moment, the stark realization hits me.

I don't want her to get her hands on him. I know Cooper is no saint. I'm not trying to keep him pure for me because this isn't about me. This is about Cooper. I can read him. I can see something in his face. It borders on fear. A whole new kind of worry.

This is the owner's sister making a play for him. This is his first year as the starting quarterback, and all I can think is Cooper doesn't want to ruin his big chance by having to fend off an out-of-nowhere bid from a woman who wants to sink her sharp teeth into him.

My friend. My guy. *Mine.*

Maxine stares at him, slashing an arm through the air and declaring five thousand dollars, eliminating pretty much anyone else.

Sierra's eyes light up. "Going once?" she asks, scanning the crowd, waiting for one last bid.

My brain whirs.

My mind races.

When I see Maxine wink at Cooper, I burn.

She thinks Cooper wants her.

I clench my fists, flashing back to what Cooper said to me about footing the bill.

I can't let Maxine win him. I can't let his entire season go to hell over something he's not expecting.

She's gunning for the quarterback's blind side, and that does not fly with me.

I'm his left tackle. It's my job to protect him. I won't let him get sacked.

I make eye contact with him, tapping my nose, a signal.

"Going twice," Sierra says, her voice trailing off.

Cooper's eyes light up, and he brushes his finger on the side of his nose.

We are the only ones speaking each other's language. He wants me to do this.

My arm shoots high in the air. Like a determined woman who won't let anything take her guy down, I shout, "Ten thousand dollars!"

Sierra smiles crazily. "Do we have ten thousand one hundred?"

No one else speaks. No one says a word. I'm not sure if Maxine is shocked into silence or if everyone is.

But I think I am, too, especially when Cooper sweeps me up on the stage, and before I know it, he kisses me in front of the whole crowd.

Cooper and Violet's story continues in MOST VALU-ABLE PLAYBOY, available everywhere.

MOST VALUABLE PLAYBOY, a sexy multi-week USA Today Bestselling sports romance!

THE V CARD, a USA Today Bestselling sinfully sexy romantic comedy!

The New York Times and USA Today Bestselling Seductive Nights series including *Night After Night*, *After This Night*, and *One More Night*

And the two standalone romance novels in the Joy Delivered Duet, *Nights With Him* and Forbidden Nights, both New York Times and USA Today Bestsellers!

Sweet Sinful Nights, Sinful Desire, Sinful Longing and Sinful Love, the complete New York Times Bestselling high-heat romantic suspense series that spins off from Seductive Nights!

Playing With Her Heart, a USA Today bestseller, and a sexy Seductive Nights spin-off standalone! (Davis and Jill's romance)

21 Stolen Kisses, the USA Today Bestselling forbidden new adult romance!

Caught Up In Us, a New York Times and USA Today Bestseller! (Kat and Bryan's romance!)

Pretending He's Mine, a Barnes & Noble and iBooks Bestseller! (Reeve & Sutton's romance)

Trophy Husband, a New York Times and USA Today Bestseller! (Chris & McKenna's romance)

Far Too Tempting, the USA Today Bestselling standalone romance! (Matthew and Jane's romance)

Stars in Their Eyes, an iBooks bestseller! (William and Jess' romance)

My USA Today bestselling No Regrets series that includes

The Thrill of It (Meet Harley and Trey)

and its sequel

Every Second With You

My New York Times and USA Today Bestselling Fighting Fire series that includes

Burn For Me (Smith and Jamie's romance!)

Melt for Him (Megan and Becker's romance!)

and *Consumed by You* (Travis and Cara's romance!)

The Sapphire Affair series...

The Sapphire Affair

The Sapphire Heist

Out of Bounds

A New York Times Bestselling sexy sports romance

The Only One

A second chance love story!

Stud Finder

A sexy, flirty romance!

CONTACT

I love hearing from readers! You can find me on Twitter at LaurenBlakely3, Instagram at LaurenBlakelyBooks, Facebook at LaurenBlakelyBooks, or online at LaurenBlakely.com. You can also email me at laurenblakelybooks@gmail.com

ALSO BY LAUREN BLAKELY

FULL PACKAGE, the #1 New York Times Bestselling romantic comedy!

BIG ROCK, the hit New York Times Bestselling standalone romantic comedy!

MISTER O, also a New York Times Bestselling standalone romantic comedy!

WELL HUNG, a New York Times Bestselling standalone romantic comedy!

JOY RIDE, a USA Today Bestselling standalone romantic comedy!

HARD WOOD, a USA Today Bestselling standalone romantic comedy!

THE SEXY ONE, a New York Times Bestselling bestselling standalone romance!

THE HOT ONE, a USA Today Bestselling bestselling standalone romance!

THE KNOCKED UP PLAN, a multi-week USA Today and Amazon Charts Bestselling bestselling standalone romance!

MOST VALUABLE PLAYBOY, a sexy multi-week USA Today Bestselling sports romance!

THE V CARD, a USA Today Bestselling sinfully sexy romantic comedy!

The New York Times and USA Today Bestselling Seductive Nights series including *Night After Night*, *After This Night*, and *One More Night*

And the two standalone romance novels in the Joy Delivered Duet, *Nights With Him* and Forbidden Nights, both New York Times and USA Today Bestsellers!

Sweet Sinful Nights, Sinful Desire, Sinful Longing and Sinful Love, the complete New York Times Bestselling high-heat romantic suspense series that spins off from Seductive Nights!

Playing With Her Heart, a USA Today bestseller, and a sexy Seductive Nights spin-off standalone! (Davis and Jill's romance)

21 Stolen Kisses, the USA Today Bestselling forbidden new adult romance!

Caught Up In Us, a New York Times and USA Today Bestseller! (Kat and Bryan's romance!)

Pretending He's Mine, a Barnes & Noble and iBooks Bestseller! (Reeve & Sutton's romance)

Trophy Husband, a New York Times and USA Today Bestseller! (Chris & McKenna's romance)

Far Too Tempting, the USA Today Bestselling standalone romance! (Matthew and Jane's romance)

Stars in Their Eyes, an iBooks bestseller! (William and Jess' romance)

My USA Today bestselling No Regrets series that includes

The Thrill of It (Meet Harley and Trey)

and its sequel

Every Second With You

My New York Times and USA Today Bestselling Fighting Fire series that includes

Burn For Me (Smith and Jamie's romance!)

Melt for Him (Megan and Becker's romance!)

and *Consumed by You* (Travis and Cara's romance!)

The Sapphire Affair series...

The Sapphire Affair

The Sapphire Heist

Out of Bounds

A New York Times Bestselling sexy sports romance

The Only One

A second chance love story!

Stud Finder

A sexy, flirty romance!

CONTACT

I love hearing from readers! You can find me on Twitter at LaurenBlakely3, Instagram at LaurenBlakelyBooks, Facebook at LaurenBlakelyBooks, or online at LaurenBlakely.com. You can also email me at laurenblakelybooks@gmail.com

Made in the USA
Middletown, DE
11 November 2018